TWO-WAY
MURDER

TWO-WAY MURDER

E. C. R. LORAC

With an Introduction by
Martin Edwards

Poisoned Pen
PRESS

Introduction © 2021, 2022 by Martin Edwards
Two-Way Murder © 2021, 2022 by The Estate of Edith Caroline Rivett
Cover and internal design © 2022 by Sourcebooks
Front cover image © Mary Evans Picture Library

Published by Poisoned Pen Press, in imprint of Sourcebooks,
in association with the British Library
P.O. Box 4410, Naperville, Illinois 60567-4410
(630) 961-3900
sourcebooks.com

This is the first edition of *Two-Way Murder* to be published in book
and ebook form. The publisher would like to express its gratitude to
James M. Pickard for sharing his copy of the author's typescript with
Martin Edwards and the British Library Publishing team. Without his
generosity, this accomplishment would not have been possible.

Library of Congress Cataloging-in-Publication Data

Names: Lorac, E. C. R., author. | Edwards, Martin, writer
   of introduction.
Title: Two-way murder / E.C.R. Lorac ; with an introduction by Martin
   Edwards.
Description: First edition. | Naperville, Illinois : Poisoned Pen Press,
   2022. | Series: British Library crime classics
Identifiers: LCCN 2021023660 (print) | LCCN 2021023661
   (ebook) | (trade paperback) | (epub)
Subjects: GSAFD: Mystery fiction. | LCGFT: Detective and mystery fiction.
Classification: LCC PR6035.I9 T96 2022 (print) | LCC PR6035.I9 (ebook) |
   DDC 823/.912--dc23
LC record available at https://lccn.loc.gov/2021023660
LC ebook record available at https://lccn.loc.gov/2021023661

Printed and bound in the United States of America.
KP 10 9 8 7 6 5 4 3 2 1

INTRODUCTION

THE APPEARANCE OF *TWO-WAY MURDER* AS A BRITISH
Library Crime Classic represents a pleasing landmark in vintage detective fiction publishing. A novel by a successful
female author is finally seeing the light of day after being "lost"
for more than sixty years. This is the first novel in the Crime
Classics series that has *never* appeared in print before, and its
belated publication makes a fascinating contribution to crime
fiction heritage. The rediscovery of this story will undoubt-
edly give a good deal of pleasure to the legion of readers
who have enjoyed the work of E. C. R. Lorac—the principal
pen name of Edith Caroline Rivett (1894–1958)—since the
British Library revived *Bats in the Belfry* a few years ago.

The mysteries of the whodunit puzzle in *Two-Way Murder*
are matched by those surrounding the history of the typescript and its failure, until now, to achieve publication. I've
undertaken some detective work of my own, although I feel
sure that further clues remain to be discovered.

I first became aware of the existence of the unpublished
typescript of *Two-Way Murder* more than a decade ago,

through James M. Pickard, a leading dealer in rare books and also a discerning collector. James has a particular specialism and expertise in Golden Age fiction, and many of the most sought-after and valuable vintage first editions have, over the past twenty years, passed through his hands. He acquired a number of rare Lorac manuscripts, including this one, at a country auction. It must have seemed like a treasure trove, although at that time only a limited number of crime fans were aware of the merits of Lorac's writing, because her books had been out of print for decades.

I've been interested in Lorac for many years, thanks to the influence of my parents, who enthused about her Lunesdale mysteries in particular. I'd even given a hat-tip to one of her most memorable plots in a novel of my own, *The Serpent Pool*. I was therefore fascinated to learn from James about a hitherto unknown Lorac novel.

This prompted me to write a post about *Two-Way Murder* on my blog, "Do You Write under Your Own Name?" as long ago as September 2009, expressing the hope that the manuscript might one day be made more widely available. At that point there seemed no prospect of my ever playing a part in making that happen. Some years later, however, having become consultant to the Crime Classics series, I discussed my enthusiasm for Lorac with the then series editor Rob Davies. To my delight, the British Library ultimately agreed to publish her, and the new editions of Lorac's books, including one produced under her alternative pen name, Carol Carnac, have reinforced her reputation as an author of well-made traditional detective stories with nicely evoked settings.

Two-Way Murder was clearly worth investigating. My main reservation was that, if a book has never been published, it's usually for a good reason; perhaps it was written towards the end of the author's life, at a time of waning powers, and the publisher rejected it.

The British Library did not have a copy of the manuscript. As one of the UK's legal deposit libraries, it is entitled to receive all published books—but *Two-Way Murder* had never been in print and, so far as is known, there is only one copy of the typescript. However, thanks to the generous cooperation of James M. Pickard, it became possible for both the British Library and myself to read the book.

When I studied *Two-Way Murder*, it seemed clear that its disappearance from sight was not the result of feeble storytelling at the tail end of the author's career. On the contrary, Lorac seems here to have been making an attempt to break fresh ground. The writing is crisp, despite the fact that editing must have been minimal. The author's name on the cover sheet is "Mary Le Bourne"—evidently a pun on "Marylebone"—and the police detectives in the story are not the investigators familiar from the Lorac and Carnac series. The setting on the south coast of England is also something of a departure from the backgrounds to most of her post-war novels. Was she trying to write a different type of detective story? Might she have had in mind a distinct series featuring Waring, the likeable police officer who solves the puzzle? The answer to both questions may well be yes.

So why was the book never published? We can only speculate, but the first point to make is that the book was written shortly before Lorac died. Internal evidence suggests that the events of the story take place in the January of either 1956 or 1957. She died in 1958 after a short period of ill health brought an end to a previously active life. She left one novel substantially written but incomplete; in the year of her death, no fewer than three new books of hers were published. Two more followed into print in 1959. It seems likely that this book was finished after those novels were sent in.

One possibility is that she had not submitted *Two-Way Murder* to her usual publisher at the time of her death, and that in effect it simply fell through the cracks. Or perhaps she wanted to try a different publisher, carving a fresh identity as Mary Le Bourne and launching a new series with a fresh background and likeable new detective.

One of the manuscripts that James M. Pickard handled a decade or so ago was Lorac's autobiography, which remains unpublished. It is just conceivable that this answers some of the questions about this book, as well as casting further light on her life generally. So far, however, I haven't been able to trace the present whereabouts of the autobiography; apparently it has passed through several hands over the years. I hope that one day it too will turn up, enabling us to gain a fuller understanding of an interesting and talented woman.

The typescript of *Two-Way Murder* bears several amendments in Lorac's hand, but there remain a few infelicities that would probably have been picked up during a thorough professional edit—examples include occasional repetitions of words and phrases. The British Library decided that it would be appropriate to undertake a limited amount of editing in-house, and, accordingly, the text presented here is the publisher's edited version.

What of the story itself? It opens on a dark and misty winter night, with the central characters eagerly looking forward to a ball that is a highlight of the local social calendar. Two men are making their way to the ball by car. Nicholas Brent, an ex-naval commander who now runs an inn in the neighbourhood, has offered a lift to a barrister called Ian Macbane, who comes from out of town but has local family connections.

Their conversation turns to Dilys Maine, a beautiful young woman admired by both of them, and also to the strange disappearance of a local girl, Rosemary Reeve.

Nick Brent has arranged to drive Dilys home, but on the way back after the ball, he brakes to avoid hitting a corpse that is in the middle of the road. When he goes to a nearby house to call the police, he is knocked out by a man he presumes to be Michael Reeve, brother of the girl who went missing.

These events set in train a police investigation which is hampered by the reluctance of witnesses to tell the truth. Who is the deceased, and what could have been the motive for killing him? These are the central puzzles, but there are a number of subsidiary mysteries. Lorac shifts the perspective from which the story is told time and again, keeping the reader off balance as the plot thickens like coastal fog. This adroit use of viewpoint is—as with several of Agatha Christie's finest mysteries—crucial to distracting the reader's attention from the identity of the culprit.

Although this novel was written more than a decade after the end of the Second World War, and differs from the author's other fiction in some respects, nevertheless it bears a much closer resemblance in terms of style to the Golden Age detective writing which Lorac first embraced in the early 1930s than to the work of younger authors such as Julian Symons, Margot Bennett, and Shelley Smith, who focused increasingly on homicidal psychology in the novels they produced at around the time this book was written.

In short, *Two-Way Murder* is a good, old-fashioned whodunit which displays many of the virtues which have won Lorac so many new admirers in the twenty-first century. Its journey into print has been even longer and more winding than the roads which play a part in the storyline, but it's thrilling to see it in print at last. And I like to think that the author herself would be gratified that her final completed book has not been lost forever.

Martin Edwards
www.martinedwardsbooks.com

Chapter I

I

"Jolly decent of you to give me a lift, Nick. It's going to be a dirty evening and I'm none too sure of my road in the dark."

"Only too glad to have you, old boy," replied Nicholas Brent, as he switched on his headlights. "I like to have someone to talk to while I'm driving. This is only a hill mist, not a real fog. You'll find it'll be perfectly clear when we run down into Fordings. Let's think—were you at the Hunt Ball last year, too?"

"No. It's two years since I was at the ball, although I stayed down here a bit last summer. I'm no end bucked I made it tonight—it was touch-and-go. I always say the Hollydown Hunt Ball is the best of its kind I know, and by Jove, you've got some lovelies in the neighbourhood."

"We're almost famous for it—prettiest girls in the south of England," chuckled Nicholas Brent. "The Navy knows that. Fordings is the most popular town on the coast when the fleet pays courtesy calls. Sorry the car's bumping a bit. They've just repaired this bit of road and it could have done with some more rolling."

"Seems O.K. to me," said Ian Macbane cheerfully. Ian was feeling in fine fettle and it would have taken more than a few bumps to disturb him. He was thirty years old, a bachelor, doing nicely in his profession—the law—and he was a keen dancer.

"I think the roads round here are pretty good," he responded cheerfully. "It's what you might call off the beaten track, very literally. We're on the Greenham Road, aren't we?—isn't that the pub—the Rose & Crown? Just before we cross the little bridge?"

"We're just going to cross the bridge—or culvert," agreed Brent, "but the mist's got you muddled. We're on the road to the south of the Greenham one—they're more or less parallel, you remember. That wasn't the Rose & Crown we passed, it was Michael Reeve's place—Netherdown—and here's the bridge—hold on, it's a switchback effect. That line of new fencing beyond is the boundary of Reeve's land."

Macbane leant forward and wiped the blurred windscreen. "I remember now," he said. "It's a good thing I didn't take old Tim's offer and drive his Austin 7, I'd have got lost for a cert."

"Ditched, perhaps—the mist's tricky," said Brent. "You couldn't have lost yourself, any of these roads takes you to Fordings eventually. This is the Hollydown turn. A pity about the old house going out of the family: it's a lovely property."

"Gad, yes: wonderful old house," said Ian. "They tell me it's been sold for a loony bin: is that true?"

"Watch out on your phrasing, laddy, or you'll be in trouble. Hollydown Manor is now a Hospital for Maladjusted Juveniles—young criminal toughs, I call them, off the record, but the authorities call the place a hospital, and it certainly sounds better."

"It was bad luck on Michael Reeve, having to sell Hollydown," said Ian, and Nicholas Brent replied:

"In a sense, yes, but he must have been thankful to find a buyer. A house that size is a millstone round your neck these days, and the old man had lived on capital for years. There wasn't much left, and they had to sell the estate to meet death duties. Michael kept one of the best bits for himself—twenty acres on either side of the river, and the old cottage with it—the place we passed just now."

"How's he shaping?" asked Ian.

"Doing nicely, I'm told—pedigree cattle. Very able chap, Michael: best of the bunch."

"They were a rum lot, weren't they?" asked Ian, and Nick grunted.

"Maybe; these old families go downhill, like their houses. There've been Reeves at Hollydown since Domesday, I believe."

"Did they ever hear anything more about the sister—the girl who disappeared?" asked Ian.

"Nix. Not the least thing. Rotten story," said Nick gruffly. "Broke the old man up. I always believed she bolted deliberately. If it'd been foul play the police would have spotted something. I'm a great believer in the efficiency of our police system."

Ian Macbane nodded. "Miserable story, the girl just disappearing like that," he said. But because he was young and light-hearted and out to enjoy a merry evening, Macbane changed the subject and turned to his companion with a question: "How's your pub going?"

"Pretty fair," said Nick cheerfully. "I've paid out more than

I've paid in to date, but the place is really ship-shape now, and next season I ought to make a packet. I can take twenty guests now I've got the annexe built."

"It's a grand spot," said Ian. "It was a brainwave of yours to buy up the old Mermaid and convert it."

Nicholas Brent, aged thirty-two, a one-time Naval Commando, had used his wartime gratuity to good effect. He had bought an ancient, almost derelict inn—the Mermaid—built centuries ago on a ledge of the chalk banks where the small River Cookbourne ran out into the English Channel. Nick had spotted the place during his commando training (he had once commanded a raiding party who "captured it" from the sea), and from that day he had marked it down as his own. The owner and licensee was an old man, and he had agreed to negotiate with Nick before the war was over. For the first year or so, Nick Brent had more or less camped out in his derelict property, painting and patching with his own hands, running the small bar, dispensing such hospitality as conditions permitted, and making friends among the tourists and holidaymakers whom he hoped would come again when "his ship was in commission." Now, ten years later, he was sitting pretty—or so the neighbourhood said—owner of one of the most attractive and original small hotels on the south coast; owner of a good motorboat and a good car—the car in which he was driving Ian Macbane to the Hunt Ball at Fordings.

"Seems to me you want a wife," said Macbane. "I know you're pretty hot at all the organising, but a woman's needed for the finishing touches in a show like yours."

Nick chuckled. "I like to hear you sounding authoritative. Not that I disagree, but things have been pretty tough while I was building up, and I might have gone bust any time—very much touch-and-go at times. I couldn't have afforded a wife."

"And now you can?"

"Now I can. What's all this leading up to?"

"Nothing," said Ian hastily, "but when I heard you were going to the Hunt Ball, I assumed you'd lived through the hermit-crab stage which possessed you for a bit and that you were out to enjoy life again."

Nick chuckled. "Very cogently put; well, I admit nothing, nor I deny nothing—as Beatrice said to Benedict in *Much Ado*—and a man's got to marry sometime, or dry up into an eccentric. So, as you may have noticed, I offered you a lift into Fordings, but I made no offers about the return journey."

Ian laughed. "O.K., Nick. Fair enough, and I wish you all the luck in the world. Incidentally, I wonder if any of the girls I danced with before will be around tonight."

"Almost certainly, though some of them may have got hitched up in the interval—I've had more than one honeymoon couple at the Mermaid, God bless 'em! Who are you thinking of?"

"Well, there was a fair girl named Gillian Parsons, a marvellous dancer, and she had a younger sister, Mercy, was it?"

"Bless you, yes. They're both married: Gillian married Robert Brownham, and they're out in Malaya; Mercy married Tom Fowler of Greenham, and they'll probably both be at the ball. Anyone else?"

"What about Dilys Maine?" asked Ian. "I believe the ball I came to two years ago was her first ball: she was only eighteen, but she was, well, breathtaking. I've never seen a lovelier kid."

Brent heard the subtle difference in the sound of Ian Macbane's voice when he spoke of Dilys, and drew his own conclusions: Ian wasn't the only chap who spoke of Dilys with a catch in his voice.

"Yes, Dilys Maine," rejoined Brent. "She isn't

married—yet—and she may be coming this evening. It depends on that curmudgeonly old father: he's one of these puritanical Nonconformists who hates anybody to have a good time. He's dead against the Hunt Ball because there's a bar: he's a rabid T.T."

"Cripes!" groaned Macbane. "You think he'll prevent her coming?"

"I don't know. I believe—and hope—he had to go over to Southampton on business tonight. If so—well, we shall see."

"She was lovely," said Ian softly and Nick retorted,

"You don't think you're the only person who's noticed that? Anyway, for your information, if Dilys Maine does manage to make it, I've promised to drive her home: she'll probably have to emulate Cinderella and vanish by midnight. I just thought I'd tell you."

"I see," said Ian, and his voice sounded deflated, but Nick Brent chuckled.

"See here, laddy: if you only honour the neighbourhood with your presence once in two years, you can't expect to sail in and be a winner against chaps who've been studying the course in fair weather and foul every day of their lives."

"All right, all right," said Ian hastily, "but it's not true I haven't been down here for two years. I have. Still, I don't want to argue... Glory, there's Fordings. It always comes as a shock to see it suddenly like that."

The car had topped the last rise of Bramber Head, the great chalk ridge which jutted out into the Channel; below, the ground dropped steeply to the wide basin of Fairbourne Bay, and the lights of Fordings were stretched out like jewelled necklaces, crossing and intertwining, with coloured lights along the seafront and a blur of chromatic brilliance over the cinema on the pier.

"I always enjoy coming on it suddenly like that, especially at night," said Ian, as the car began the run down, swooping round the bends of the curving road which was cut into the steep slopes of the chalk.

"It's not that I like Fordings as a place: all said and done, it's just one of those prosperous genteel resorts which attract lashings of trippers in the summer," went on Ian, "but it looks marvellous when you see it over the top of Bramber Head like that."

"Yes, I know what you mean, all right," said Brent. "It's the contrast between the darkness and solitude of the downs and the glitter and liveliness of what we call civilisation, God help us. I loathe the town myself—it's a lousy place. I like room to move and air to breathe and fishermen and countryfolk for my neighbours—but one man's meat is another man's poison. I'm a bit surprised you choose to stay out at Stenfield, though: wouldn't one of the Fordings hotels have suited you better? You'll be dancing into the small hours, I take it."

"I hope so. It's quite true that a hotel in Fordings would have been more convenient for tonight, but my aunt and uncle would have been bitterly hurt if I hadn't stayed with them at Stenfield. They're a bit lonely, and I don't often get down to see them."

"Yes, there's that," agreed Brent. "I often think they must feel a bit cut off, especially now the old man doesn't drive any longer, but I suppose they're fond of the place."

"They love it, and they don't really mind being isolated," said Ian. "Oh, good, I'm glad you're going along by the sea. The backstreets of this town are dreary beyond words."

"I like this bit, at night anyway," rejoined Brent. "One is so conscious of the sea just below there, and this flummery of lights is gay without being raffish—rather like a regatta. It's got the taste of the sea about it, somehow."

II

The Prince's Hall at Fordings had seen many ups and downs in its century and a half of existence. Built for use both as concert hall and ballroom in Hanoverian days, it had the beauty of its Regency period, plus a slight flamboyance in decoration added by ducal patrons who had believed that joy should be unconfined. Victorian days had sobered it, and the hall had been used for the rendering of oratorios and for political meetings of deep import. The Edwardian era re-established it as a place of gaiety, but in the First World War it had been lent to the Red Cross. The twenties and thirties altered all that: even in the slump of the early thirties, visitors to Fordings had patronised the Dansant, and the dignified building had a hectic period of prosperity as a *palais de danse*. From 1939 to 1950 it was in turn recruiting centre, civil defence post, and—alas—"food office," to use the jargon of rationing days. But once the hall was de-requisitioned, the Fordings Council had recognised its value in a seaside resort of ever-growing popularity: following the advice of Lord Timberlake (the town's largest landowner) the Council had restored the battered decorations, repainted the frescoes, rewired it with the most modern of lighting and relaid the great floor. Now, whatever else Fordings lacked in the way of modern amenities, it had the most beautiful ballroom on the south coast, and every appurtenance for catering and cloakroom accommodation.

A Hunt Ball is always a picturesque occasion, and the Fordings Ball had a lot to commend it to many varieties and conditions of people: the Hunt had supporters among all ranks of society, from the noble Master to the small farmers who still managed to turn out on ageing mounts, and the crowded floor showed a real cross-section of country society, gliding, sidestepping, swirling, and pacing under the changing lights.

When Nick Brent went to make his bow to Lady Timberlake (for Nick knew everybody), that gracious lady smiled on him in complete approbation.

"It's lovely to see you, Commander—we don't see enough of you. I'm told you've made the Mermaid into the most charming place; all my friends love it. And isn't it a delight to see all these young things enjoying themselves—and looking so perfectly beautiful!"

"They do indeed," said Nick, "and one of the things that I like is that you can't tell the farmers' daughters from the county, or the typists from the millionaires. They all look equally exquisite."

"That's quite true," agreed Her Ladyship, "and I'm like you, quite delighted about it. The taste of these girls today is marvellous, and whether it's costume jewellery or pearls and diamonds just doesn't matter a bit. Who was that lovely child you were dancing with just now—the fair girl?"

"Dilys Maine. Her father owns the mill at Foxlea—a somewhat cantankerous character. Between you and me, Dilys is stealing her night out while her father is away."

"I'm delighted she's managed to come. There's something very moving about the child, Commander. The sight of her reminds me of the narcissus in the Alps, blooming on the verge of the snow."

It wasn't only Lady Timberlake who was moved by Dilys Maine's fair, slender beauty—though Her Ladyship used a prettier metaphor to express herself than some of the young men did. Nicholas Brent—who wasn't given to flights of fancy—was reminded of the petals of apple blossom floating in the sunshine, and Ian Macbane found a long-forgotten line of Tennyson running in his mind—"petals from blown roses on the grass." Veronica Addington (a dark beauty who had her own following) said simply: "Dilys looks a peach, she's got everything," and her brother Charles just said, "Cripes…"

Lord Timberlake, resplendent in his Master's coat, turned to Geoffrey Elderton (the owner of Blackthorn Place), and said: "That child puts everyone else in the shade, even young Judith Merrill can't compete. Looks to me as though Nick Brent's making the running."

"Isn't he a bit old for her?" queried Elderton.

"Old? Fiddlesticks!" exclaimed the silver-haired peer. "Nick's not much over thirty and he's a man of substance. He's done marvels with that old inn of his, and there it is—a beautiful home for any girl to step into. Between you and me, I'd like to see her married, Geoff. That father of hers is a cantankerous old cuss, and I'm told he's getting awkward—very awkward. You can see from the girl's face life isn't too easy."

Elderton laughed: "She's had an effect on you, sir—by Jove, she has. But I don't think Brent's going to have it all his own way—and I don't see why he should. Ian Macbane's come down from London just in the hope of dancing with Dilys, and young Michael Reeve is said to be in the running—oh, and half a dozen others at least."

"I'm sorry for Michael," said Timberlake in a lower voice. "He's having a tough time, I know that, but I should hate to see that child marry a Reeve. There's something wrong there, Geoff: that family's unpredictable."

"You're thinking of the girl who disappeared, sir?"

"Rosemary—poor child, poor child. I suppose we shall

never know the truth about that story. The police believe it was suicide. It seems true that at certain states of the tide on this coast a body may be carried out to sea and never washed up at all. Brent says he knows that's true, and he knows the coast as well as any of the fishermen or old coastguards. But it wasn't only Rosemary: there was Norman Reeve, her brother. A real bad hat, I believe. Reeve me no Reeves, Geoff. Who's that young lovely dancing with Addington over there? Gad, that's a pretty frock—reminds me of champagne, bubbles of faint gold…"

"That's Tom Verity's daughter, Jennifer—pretty as a picture, isn't she? I think this is where I plunge in again, sir. I'm due for a duty 'old-fashioned' with the Honourable Mrs. T."

"Rather you than me, but she's a marvel, on my soul she is. She was riding to hounds before I had my first pony—and that's longer ago than I like to remember. I don't think she's missed a single Hunt Ball this century."

"Gad…" said Elderton. "She deserves a medal—and I reckon I do, too."

III

"Enjoying it, Dilys?" asked Nick Brent. They had just danced a waltz to "The Blue Danube," and Nick had almost marvelled at the girl's exquisite movement and poise: she had seemed to float, as effortless and constant as his shadow, a projection of his own sense of rhythm and music.

"It's heaven," she replied. "I really do love dancing, you know, there's nothing which gives me so much thrill. It isn't the excitement—though this *is* exciting—nor the lovely hall and gorgeous frocks, not even all the friendly, happy people, it's the delight of dancing for itself."

"I know, my dear," he rejoined, and she added quickly,

"You're a perfect partner. I can't tell you how much I'm loving this—and it's terribly kind of you to say you'll drive me home. I feel mean about it, I shall be spoiling your evening."

"You'll be doing the exact opposite," said Brent. His voice was very quiet, and he bent his head to murmur into her ear. "Eleven forty-five outside the west door: I'll be there, waiting."

"Thank you very much," she replied. "You see, I've got to beat Alice back. She's had the day off and I told her not to come back till midnight—the last train gets into Fordings at 12.0, and then she's got to get a taxi. If I leave here at 11.45, I can be in bed before Alice gets home." She laughed softly. "It's awful of me, isn't it? But I did want to come so much, and as the ball was never even mentioned at home, I didn't have to tell any fibs—not one."

"It's not awful at all—except that you can't stay until the end," said Brent. "But as I can drive you home, far be it from me to complain about that."

They stood still together for a moment when the waltz was over and Dilys looked up at him with serious questioning eyes, the faintest pucker of worry showing on her level brows, but she only said again: "Thank you very much. You're much too kind to me."

Ian Macbane was Dilys Maine's next partner: he was a very good dancer, and she found herself slipping into his new steps with the ease which made dancing a delight to her. Ian managed to extract a promise from her that she would meet him the next day (Sunday) and walk over to High Down for tea. "And if it rains, I'll raise a car somehow, so don't call it off," he pleaded.

"I shan't do that—and don't bother about the car, I don't mind rain," she laughed back. "I'm much tougher than I look… Why, there's Michael Reeve. I thought he said he couldn't come," she exclaimed, as dark-eyed Michael came forward to greet her.

"Hullo, Michael, how did you manage it?" she asked, and Ian heard him say:

"That heifer calved early, and I managed to clean up and get the old bus started…"

"Hullo, Ian! Nice to see you," called a voice beside him, and he turned to see Jennifer Verity, screwing up her pretty nose.

"I've known Michael all my life," she said, "but he really is a tough. Dancing with him's like being caught in a tornado. I'm not really robust enough for that sort of thing: I wonder how Dilys will cope. I'm longing for ours, Ian—don't forget, the first extra, and you can show me that lovely variation you just taught Dilys."

"Love to—I'm counting the minutes," laughed Ian, but as he turned away to look for his next partner, his eyes followed Dilys and Michael—the very fair head, sleek and shining, the very dark head with stubborn hair which nothing could keep smooth.

"Tough…he looks a fair-sized mess to me," thought the urbane young barrister.

Chapter II

I

"I LOVE BEING DRIVEN AT NIGHT," SAID DILYS. SHE WAS leaning forward a little, sitting beside Nicholas Brent in his big comfortable car, gazing out at the white swathe cut by the headlights as they drove up the bends of the hill above Fordings. "It's like a secret world, all your own, as though nothing exists beyond your own lights." She laughed a little and added quickly, "I expect that sounds childish to you, but you see I don't often go out in a car like this one: I trundle round sometimes in Tim's old Austin 7—but this is different."

"It doesn't sound childish at all, it sounds very charming," said Nick, "and if you like being driven, well, you must know that I like driving you, and if ever you'd like to come out, both the car and myself are very much at your service."

"You're much too kind to me," she said quickly, "and I wasn't trying to hint that I'd like another drive: this one— well, it's sort of special. It all happened so marvellously, I never thought I should be able to come. It was just that my father was going to be away and then Alice said she'd go up to London and it was as though the chance had been made for me—and then you saying you would drive me back made it quite perfect."

"I'm only too happy to have a finger in the perfection pie," laughed Nick, "but do please remember that I meant what I said about driving you—any time you like. I so seldom see you, Dilys: can't we meet a little oftener?"

"I should like to, but it's all a bit difficult," she said. "You know what my father's like."

"Yes, I do know; but you can't let your life be conditioned by a difficult father; you've got to have a life of your own."

"I know. I often think about it," she said, "but I can't help feeling sorry for Daddy. People think he's just hard and selfish—and mean. But he isn't really; he can be awfully kind, and after all, since Mother died, I'm all he's got. Somehow he quarrels with people." She laughed a little ruefully. "I ought to feel awfully ashamed of myself: it's because Daddy so seldom talks to people in an ordinary friendly way that I risked coming to the Hunt Ball. Nobody will tell him about me having been there—they never gossip to him because they're too afraid of him. And I did love it so much… Oh, look—the mist's going to get thick again."

"It's nothing," said Brent. "Don't go getting frightened that we shall be held up by the mist, because we shan't. I drove Ian Macbane out this evening, by the lower road—the one we're on now—and the mist didn't slow us down at all. It's far more likely that your Alice will be held up—the taxi men take the main road and it's often a bit thick over the top, on Bramble Downs."

"I'll just sit back and enjoy it," she laughed. "I like sitting very quiet while I'm being driven—and your driving is super."

Once over the crest of the Head, the car seemed to leap forward along the narrow road, and Brent fell in with the girl's mood and drove in silence. It was when they were less than half a mile from the top road (which ran north and south at right angles to that which they were on) that Dilys was surprised by the car jerking as Brent braked suddenly and they decelerated to walking pace.

"What is it?" she asked. "I was half asleep... Oh, whatever is that?"

In the path of the headlamps, which made the road shine white, Dilys could see a dark patch in the road, something humped and odd, about twenty yards ahead of them.

"I don't know, my dear. I'll get out and see," said Brent. "Sit still for a minute."

He got out and walked ahead and Dilys leant forward with her heart beating: she knew what it was that lay sprawled on the road ahead, but she didn't want to believe it. Right ahead, in the beam of the headlights, she saw Brent bend down over the blurred heap. He went down on one knee, put out a hand—but moved nothing. In a minute he stood up, walked back to the car and opened the door beside her.

"I'm sorry, Dilys dear—terribly sorry. It looks as though the chap's been run down by a driver who didn't stop."

Dilys gave a little cry of horror, and Brent went on: "I shall have to notify the police. Now listen carefully: I don't want you to be involved in this. If the police know that you were in my car, you'll be called as a witness—and I know that will mean all manner of bother for you. I can't drive on—for obvious reasons—and I oughtn't to move the casualty before the police arrive: but you're less than a mile from home if you take the field path. Can you walk home by yourself—and leave me to deal with this?"

"Of course I can—but wouldn't it be wrong—and unfair to you?"

"There's nothing wrong about it: you don't know the first thing about this accident, Dilys, and there's no reason why you should be involved in it. But if you're game to walk home, you'd better go at once—the sooner the better—and I'll do everything I can to keep you out of it. Nobody saw you get in my car—it ought to be all right."

She slid out of the car and stood beside him: "You're being terribly good to me—"

He broke in on her words: "My sweet, I'd do anything for you—and you must know that—but if you're going to get home before Alice does, you've got to hurry. Quick now— what about your shoes?"

"It's all right, I've got overshoes. If you're sure I can't do anything, I'll run. I know the field path by heart."

"Bless you, Dilys—off you go—and not a word to anybody! I'll do my best, you know that—take care of yourself."

She picked up her silken skirts and bunched the shining stuff over her arm, and Nicholas Brent walked back with her to a field gate and opened it for her. "The ground's quite dry, so it oughtn't to be difficult and it's not too dark. Sure you're not frightened?"

"Not a bit. I'm used to the dark—and thank you again."

"Bless you! Take care of yourself, my sweet, and get home as fast as you can."

II

Nicholas Brent stood by the gate for a moment until Dilys disappeared into the faint mist; then he closed the gate and walked back to the car. As he had said, he could not drive on:

a man's body lay sprawled across the narrow road, and there wasn't enough room left to get the big car past the body. Neither was it possible to turn—the road was too narrow and the gate through which Dilys had gone was only a small wicket gate giving access to the right of way across the fields. If he backed, he would have to back for nearly a mile before he could turn, and in the uncertain mist with ditches on either side of the narrow road, Brent didn't fancy the manoeuvre. But a quarter of a mile back was a path which led to Michael Reeve's house, and Reeve had a telephone. Brent got into the car, drew it in close to the side, switched off the headlights and left the sidelights on, locked the car, and then hurried back along the road, jog-trotting. He turned at the path and ran on towards the house: there were no lights showing there, but he didn't expect there to be—not after midnight. He went to the front door of the small ancient house, seized the knocker and banged. There was no answer and he banged again—and then swore aloud. Giving evidence to the police afterwards, he said: "What the hell was I to do? It was three miles to the nearest house with a telephone: if I tried to back the car I should probably have ditched it because my parking light wasn't working. I knew I'd got to report to the police, so I did what seemed most sensible."

What he did was to walk round the house to see if he could get inside and reach the telephone. Brent knew that very few old farmhouses—especially small ones in a remote area like this—had every window properly secured, and he was right. Investigation showed him an old pantry window which gave to a very little persuasion from his pocketknife. All the while he stood there fiddling, a dog in the yard barked like a mad thing, and Brent was thankful it was safely chained: if its barking attracted notice, so much the better, but there was no one within miles to hear it.

He clambered in through the window, using the torch he had remembered to bring from the car, let himself down onto the floor without smashing anything on the pantry shelves and went through to the kitchen. It was warm and dark in there, with the faintest glimmer of red among the ashes in the range and a kettle still singing on the crane above the embers. Brent had once been to see Michael Reeve and he knew the telephone was in the small room Reeve used as an office, in the front of the house. Brent found it without difficulty and gave a huge sigh of relief. He lifted the receiver and seemed to wait an interminable time before Exchange answered:

"Give me Brambledene police station, quickly," he snapped. "It's an emergency call—traffic accident. Jump to it."

A few seconds later he was through to a sleepy police constable. "Brent of the Mermaid Inn speaking: there's a dead man lying in the middle of the Fordings–Hollydown Road halfway between Michael Reeve's farmhouse and the Cookbourne–Bramwell pointer. The man's been run down so far as I can judge. I was driving back from Fordings by the lower road and I saw the casualty some yards ahead. I couldn't pass and I couldn't back, so I came to Reeve's place to telephone. There's no one in the house, so I got in through a window. You'll have to come out to see it—and bring a mortuary van. The chap's been dead some time—probably for a couple of hours or so."

The constable was slow-witted and sleepy: he could not follow Brent's quick incisive speech and he asked question after question until Brent, exasperated, almost shouted at him: "I've told you there's a dead man on the road; I've told you just where he is and I've told you who I am and where I am. Get moving and send someone out here: my car's in the road only a few yards from the casualty and you can't expect me to wait all night."

After a few more enquiries from the constable, Brent hung up the receiver and suddenly heard a sound in the front of the house and had time to realise his own anomalous position—that of a housebreaker in another man's house. Moving too quickly, he knocked down the torch which he had laid beside the telephone; it fell to the ground with a crash and the light went out, leaving the room in darkness. Almost simultaneously the door of the room opened and a furious voice shouted, "What the hell do you think you're doing?"

"Oh Lord, he's drunk," flashed through Brent's mind as he recognised Michael Reeve's voice, but even as he shouted: "It's Nicholas Brent, Reeve. It's all right—" and that was as far as he got.

He realised later that he had been standing in front of the window, in silhouette against the grey night, and the other man came at him like a charging elephant. There was no time for explanation or argument, for both men went down with a crash together. The telephone banged to the floor as a table went over; then as the two big men struggled in a wild melee, chairs got mixed up with their heaving limbs, there was the smash of china and thud of books and Brent realised that Reeves was on top of him, with a hand at his throat; then there was another crash and something hit Brent's head. In a whirl of stars and a sense of choking helplessness, Brent slipped into blackness and oblivion.

III

Ian Macbane had meant to see the Hunt Ball through—the dancing continued until two o'clock—but after Dilys Maine left the zest seemed to have gone out of the party. It was

Tom Hudson—a farmer in the Brambledene district—who offered Ian a lift.

"If it's any good to you I'm driving back your way, but I'm beating it early—before one o'clock. I've got to be up to load some stock into a cattle van at six, and if I don't get back I shall oversleep."

"Thanks a lot, Tom. That will suit me fine," agreed Ian. "I'll make a few excuses and be there when you're ready."

"O.K., laddy. One thing, we shan't be missed—there aren't enough girls to go round, can't think where they've all got to."

It was about an hour after Nicholas Brent had set out with Dilys that Hudson and Macbane got off and it was quite evident that the farmer wasn't going to loiter. His big old car was a bit noisy, but it roared up the bends of Bramber Head at a surprising speed.

"You came with Brent, didn't you?" asked Hudson. "Which road did he take?"

"The one they call the low road, past Michael Reeve's place."

"Oh, it's open again, is it? They were doing some work down by the bridge last week: good-oh, we'll go back the same way: you can get moving on the low road—none of those damned lorries and plane carriers you sometimes meet on the upper road."

Hudson certainly "got moving" and Ian Macbane had opportunity to reflect that there was a lot of difference between riding in a new car and an old one—Brent had apologised for the bumps which Macbane had hardly noticed; Hudson didn't apologise at all, but Ian Macbane fairly bounced in the broken springs of his bucket seat as the old Norroy hurtled at 70 m.p.h. along the narrow switchback road. It was Tom Hudson who said suddenly:

"That's funny, there's a car parked by the roadside ahead. I wonder if it's a breakdown—can't be a necking party at this hour—or can it?"

He slowed down and sounded his horn, because he was uncertain about the car in front of him on the narrow road, and Ian exclaimed:

"Why, that's Brent's car—XYY 2222. What the dickens..."

Hudson drove slowly past the parked car saying, "Yes, it's Brent's, but he's not in it... Good God, what's happened?"

He pulled up with a jerk as he saw the body lying in the road ahead and he and Macbane jumped out, the latter saying,

"Looks as though Nick's run some poor blighter down and gone to get help."

"—unless that's Nick's body...no, it's not..."

In the glare of the Norroy's headlights the two men bent over the casualty: the man was lying facedown in the road, and Hudson said:

"I don't know who the poor devil is but he's been dead for hours—or that's my guess. And where the hell is Brent?"

"Could he have walked back to telephone somewhere?" suggested Macbane. "What's the nearest place with a telephone?"

"Reeve's. We passed it a moment ago. Let's walk back to Nick's car and see if we can make out what happened."

They went back along the road and Hudson said,

"I'd better back my own car, it's blocking the road and if I go back our lights may help to show the wheel tracks."

A moment later Hudson, after bending over the road in front of Brent's car, said: "Well, that's plain enough. Nick didn't run the chap down: you can see where he braked; then he backed his car off the road and presumably he's gone to phone the police. I suppose he saw the poor devil, just as we did, went and had a look, realised he couldn't drive on unless he moved the body—and the cops get mad at you if you shift anything—and so he walked back—he couldn't have turned his car here, and it'd have been the hell of a long reverse before he could have turned it."

"Where's the nearest phone if he walked on instead of walking back?" asked Macbane.

"Oh—coup'la' miles—unless he walked across the fields, and I don't think he'd have done that. There's a side path to Reeve's house only a little way back—it cuts off the big bend round the marsh field. I bet Brent went back to Reeve's— matter of common sense. Wait a jiff though: wasn't Reeve at the ball?"

"He certainly was—draped round the bar when I saw him."

Hudson gave a long whistle. "You're right...but was he still there when we left?"

"I haven't the vaguest. I only saw him early on. Why?"

Hudson rubbed his fair head in perplexity. "If Reeve was still out, his house would have been locked up—he lives alone. Here's a mess, laddy. What does A do now?"

"You mean if Brent went to Reeve's house to telephone he wouldn't have been able to get in?—he'd have had to walk further back."

"Where he walked, G.O.K.—but we didn't pass him on the road, and if he took to the field paths, he may be anywhere. Hullo, what's this?"

Above the dip where the corpse lay, the road rose steeply to the T-junction on the ridge of the down, and it was up there that Hudson saw the lights of an approaching car.

"What's going to happen next?—if the bloke turns down this hill it'll be fun and games for him. Glory, he's turning— it's a police car. Nick must have telephoned as I said... What hopes for a night's rest—the cops'll keep us arguing for hours if I know their form."

IV

The police car pulled up on the steep descent, leaving its headlights on, so that the body in the road was illumined by the glare from both cars, and two uniformed men walked towards Hudson and Macbane. The foremost said: "Sorry we couldn't get here earlier, sir. We were called out to an accident on the Sandham Road. Commander Brent, isn't it?"

"No, it isn't, Inspector—although that's Brent's car. I'm Hudson of Greenbanks and this is Mr. Macbane, who's only a visitor to these parts. I was driving Macbane back to Stenfield and I pulled up when I saw the body in the road and Nick Brent's car alongside. We know nothing about it, either of us, but since you're here, I take it that Brent phoned you."

"That's correct, sir. He phoned the station at Brambledene, and that's the best part of an hour ago—we've had our hands full tonight."

"Not that it makes much difference to the poor devil on the road there," said Hudson. "He's been dead for hours. Well, as you may suppose, I want to get home, so make it as snappy as you can, Inspector."

"We've got our job to do, sir, and before I do anything else, can you tell me how far off Mr. Reeve's farm is?—Commander Brent said he phoned from there."

"Quarter to half a mile back, according to whether you take the shortcut," replied Hudson, "and if it's an hour since Brent phoned, where the devil is he now? I can't see him making a night of it with Mike Reeve."

"That remains to be seen, sir," rejoined the police officer. "If you'll stay here, I'll go and examine the casualty."

The two policemen went back to the body and Tom Hudson said: "May as well go and sit in the car, old chap. It'll be a bit warmer—this wind's damned nippy. The Lord knows how long they'll keep us sticking here. They'll want to get a police surgeon out, and I gather from what he said they've been having fun and games somewhere else tonight. It's damned odd about Brent, though, leaving his car standing there. What can he be up to?"

"The Lord knows, I don't," said Macbane. "I suppose he stayed at Reeve's—having a drink to warm him up."

"I can't see him doing that," said Hudson, and Macbane exclaimed suddenly:

"I've got one bit of evidence, now I come to think of it. That chap must have been run down sometime between the time Brent and I drove along here on our way to Fordings and the time Brent came back—or at any rate the time you and I came back."

"Yes…that'll give them an outside time limit," agreed Hudson. "What time did you pass here, on the outward journey?"

"About 8.30. Brent picked me up at Tim Grant's at 8.15."

Hudson bent to look at his wristwatch—the lights of the police car shone on them. "Half past one—five hours: quite a time. I reckon the chap's been dead most of it. He's stiffening. Do you know what time Brent left Fordings?"

"No, but it must have been about an hour before we did, judging by the time he telephoned."

"It's the devil of an odd business," said Hudson. "There's something I don't like about it. Brent would have come back here after he phoned, to wait for the police, it's the obvious thing to do. I wonder if those cops would agree to us going back to look for him. Seems to me anything may have happened."

"Damn all, you're not imagining Brent will have had a fit," put in Macbane. "He's a tough, if ever there was one."

"Maybe that poor devil on the road there was a tough, but he got his all right," retorted Hudson. "We're taking it for granted he's a traffic casualty, but we don't know."

"You can see the tyre marks on his raincoat," said Macbane, and Hudson replied gently:

"I grant you that—but it doesn't prove everything. I'm going to tell the Inspector bloke I'm going to look for Brent."

He got out of the car and walked forward to the dip in the road, where the two dark-clad policemen bent over the casualty, and Ian Macbane realised how macabre the whole scene looked in the glare of the crossed lights. "They might be a gang of body snatchers," he thought. Because sitting still suddenly seemed intolerable, Ian got out of the car and it was he who first saw Nicholas Brent coming up from the direction of Michael Reeve's. Brent was walking as a drunken man walks, swaying and uncertain, and there was blood still running down his face and blood on his torn collar and white scarf.

"By God!" he said thickly. "I'll see he pays for this…" and as Macbane put out a hand to steady him, Brent slumped down onto the running board of the car.

"Who?" demanded Macbane.

"Mike Reeve, devil take him," retorted Brent.

Chapter III

I

IT WAS SOME TIME BEFORE NICHOLAS BRENT WAS ABLE to tell a coherent tale: while he was sitting on the running board of the car, pouring out anathemas, the assistant police surgeon arrived. After a brief glance at the dead man, Dr. White put some strapping on Brent's wounded head and gave him a draught, muttering, "He ought to be in bed, no way to treat concussion, asking a man questions after he'd been knocked out…" White was an elderly man, and he had been working longer than an elderly man should and he hadn't enough energy left to argue with a zealous police inspector and an irascible patient.

"Might as well tell them what happened and get it over," said Brent. "It's the hell of a silly story." While Brent told his story, White went back for a more detailed examination of the casualty and Brent said:

"I was driving home from the Hunt Ball—I chose this road because there's generally less mist about down here.

I saw the chap's body lying in the road, pulled up—more or less where my car is now—got out and went to have a look. He was obviously dead and I knew I'd got to notify the police; I also know the police make a fuss if a motorist moves a body—so I couldn't drive on, because there wasn't room to get past unless I heaved the poor devil out of the road. I decided to walk back to Reeve's place because that was the nearest phone. Well, as I told you, the house was empty—or at any rate no one answered when I knocked—and I got in through the pantry window." Brent eyed the Inspector truculently: "Housebreaking, eh? But I was on the horns of a dilemma—remember that. It was my duty to report that I'd found a corpse on the road and report it without delay. I gave that precedence. I rang the station and just as I hung up I realised someone had come in, at the front door I think it was. Then I knocked my torch over; there's no electricity in that house and I hadn't bothered to find a lamp. So it was as dark as Hades and I heard a chap bawl 'What the hell…' It was Reeve, or I thought it was Reeve, and I shouted back, 'It's all right, it's me, Nick Brent'—but it wasn't all right. The chap came at me hammer and tongs like a lunatic and next thing we'd tripped up and were having a free-for-all on the floor. Then a bookcase or something came crashing down and hit me on the head and I was knocked out—blotto. How long for I don't know, but when I came to it took me quite a bit of time to sort out what the devil had happened and where the hell I was. When I remembered, I came back here—and that's the lot. Quite enough, too."

"What you might call a chapter of accidents, sir," said the Inspector sympathetically. "Now when you came to, was Mr. Reeve in evidence, or was there anybody in the house?"

"The devil alone knows, certainly I don't," retorted Brent.

"I was lying on the floor in the dark with a ton or so of furniture on my chest, or so it seemed to me. I had the deuce of a time getting clear of it and I made noise enough to wake the dead. If there was anybody in the house they took no notice." He paused a moment and then added: "I said I recognised Reeve's voice when somebody first bawled at me. Maybe I was wrong. Fact is I'm a bit fuddled and my head aches like the devil. Come to think of it, why should Reeve have behaved like a lunatic?—unless he was drunk."

Dr. White came back from his inspection of the dead man and put his oar in firmly. "Look here, Inspector, I don't want to cramp your style, you've got your job to do, I know that, but you shouldn't keep Commander Brent talking here. It's infernally cold and he's in no state to answer questions by the roadside. I've seen all that's necessary of the casualty—he's been dead between five and six hours as near as I can make it—fractured skull and multiple injuries. Get the body out of the road and I'll drive Brent home: he's not fit to drive himself. You can ask him any more questions that arise in the morning."

"Very good, Doctor. If you'll drive the Commander home, his car can stay here—I'll see it comes to no harm."

"You can see from his wheel tracks that Brent didn't run the chap down," put in Hudson, and Ian Macbane added:

"There's one other thing you ought to know, Inspector. Brent drove me to the Hunt Ball in his own car: we came by this road and we must have passed this spot at half past eight. There wasn't any corpse in the road then."

"No, by Gad, there wasn't," said Brent. "That's quite a point...seems the hell of a long time ago..."

"Now look here, you come and get in my car and I'll take you home," said White. "If you stay here any longer you'll have pneumonia as well as concussion and then the Inspector may lose his star witness, and you're not fit to drive yourself. No arguing, now."

He held out his arm to Brent and the latter went with him, while the Inspector gave orders for the casualty to be lifted to the roadside. The ambulance men had arrived and did the lifting.

A moment later, Inspector Turner came back to Macbane and Hudson. "I know you both want to get home and I don't blame you," he said, "but before you go, will you see if you can identify the casualty?"

The dead man was lying on his back now, and the headlights lit up his injured face with horrifying clarity.

Macbane took one glance and then turned away. "I've no idea who he is—never seen him before," he said, "but it's hardly to be expected I should—I don't often stay down here."

Tom Hudson stood and stared down at the marred face with deliberate interest. "I may be wrong, Inspector, but I believe this chap is one of the Reeves—Michael Reeve's older brother. I can't swear to it, but that's my impression."

"Thank you, sir. Constable Foot agrees with you."

"Norman Reeve, that's who this one is—or was," said the constable. "Did a bolt it was said…but they're a rum family."

"You'd better get Mike Reeve to come along and have a look at him," said Hudson. "If he's home, that is. He was still at the ball when we left, wasn't he, Macbane?"

"No idea," said Ian. "I hadn't seen him for an hour or so." He glanced at Inspector Turner's face and then added: "I have a feeling that Brent had got a spot mixed when he said it was Mike Reeves who went for him. It sounds quite mad."

"Very odd, sir," replied Turner noncommittally. "Now I

needn't keep you any longer. You'll be notified of the inquest in due course."

Hudson and Macbane got into the former's car and Hudson said as they got moving: "It looks a mess to me. I'm pretty certain that chap is Norman Reeve. The only good point about it is that it's quite clear that it wasn't Brent's car that did the damage. I've always had a horror of getting mixed up in a road accident and not being able to prove that I didn't run over some poor devil myself."

Macbane nodded. "There's that," he replied, but he made no comment on the point which had been uppermost in his mind ever since he had seen Brent's car by the roadside. Nick had said he was going to drive Dilys Maine home. Macbane did not know for certain that Nick had done so, but as he and Dilys had both vanished from the Hunt Ball about the same time, Macbane felt pretty certain that Dilys had left in Nick Brent's car.

"I suppose he told her to beat it—or else walked home with her," hazarded Macbane to himself. "Nick wouldn't have wanted Dilys to be a witness at the inquest—that'd have blown the gaff and no mistake. The Inspector didn't ask Nick if he were alone in the car, so possibly the point won't arise. But if it does, what does Nick do? Swear he was alone? He'll be taking a risk… Still, it's not my business: I don't know—fortunately for me."

II

After Dr. White's car and Hudson's had moved off, Inspector Turner sent off the ambulance and then set to work to study the car tracks, going conscientiously back and forth in the glare of the headlights.

"They're right about Brent's car tracks, Foot," he said to the constable, after he had examined the road behind Brent's big Wild Heron. "Brent was driving well on his own side of the road and the verge is soft enough to show where he first braked—here, it's as clear as daylight. He ran on for a couple of yards and pulled up dead: then he backed a bit and pulled in as close as he could get. I'm glad his car's left here—the evidence is absolutely plain."

"Aye, it's clear enough," said Foot, who was cold and sleepy and longing to get home. "Anyways," he added, "'twasn't that big car here ran the chap down: it was a smaller car—more like that old Ensign of Mr. Reeve's. I know that outfit—he leaves it standing outside his house day and night, all weathers. They're a queer lot, them Reeves; always has been."

Inspector Turner was new to the Bramber district: he hadn't picked up the local gossip; it was partly because he *was* a newcomer that gossip did not reach him and partly because his manner seemed a bit starchy to his rural colleagues. In any case, he did not intend to encourage Foot to get chatty in the small hours of a cold January night.

"I take it you know Mr. Michael Reeve's house," he said to Foot. "How far is it?"

"Matter of a quarter of a mile back," said Foot.

"Very well. I'll walk it and you can stay here till I come back. There's a telephone there, and I'll ring through for another man to be sent out to stand by here. There's something I'm not satisfied with about this accident."

"Very good, sir," said Foot glumly. The constable had already done several hours' overtime, but he knew it was no good protesting.

Turner set off at a good swinging pace and he reached Reeve's house within a few minutes. There were no lights showing and nobody answered Turner's rousing knock. Like Brent, he walked round to the back of the house, and found the pantry window open; like Brent, he climbed in while the dog barked furiously in the yard. With his torch to aid him, Turner found an oil lamp in the kitchen, lighted it, and set out to examine the premises. It was a small house, and the ground floor consisted of four rooms only, counting the pantry (or dairy) as one. There was a good-sized kitchen, a parlour, and a smaller sitting room. Turner saw at a glance that this was the room where Brent had suffered his knockout: furniture was overturned, chairs flung about pell-mell, and a tallish narrow bookcase still lay on the floor, the books scattered amid a gory mess which gleamed dully in the lamplight. Turner took all this in at a glance; he also noticed the telephone, but before he rang up his superior officers, he went round the rest of the house. There were four rooms upstairs, only one fully furnished; in the latter the bedclothes were tucked in firmly if not elegantly, and it was obvious the bed had not been slept in since it was made. Turner then went downstairs and telephoned, not to Bramber, but to the police station in Fordings. He asked if two men could be sent out, one to stand guard in the road, one to be posted in Michael Reeve's house. Turner's request was not popular—he had not expected it would be.

"My own opinion is that this is a case of murder," he said. "One man has been killed and Commander Brent was savagely attacked and probably left for dead. That he wasn't killed too may be due to the fact he's got a thicker skull. We ought to see that the wheel traces on the road aren't interfered with and that things in this house aren't moved until they've been properly investigated. And I suggest an all-stations call be sent out on account of Mr. Michael Reeve. He's got a car, and his car's not here."

After that, Inspector Turner was promised the cooperation he asked for. He was a careful and ambitious officer, and
he cared much more about his job than about his comfort.
He had been just going off duty when he was called out to
a shocking road accident in which a bus had been hit by a
heavy lorry; after that he had come out to investigate Brent's
report, and brought Foot with him. Turner decided to stay
in Michael Reeve's house until reinforcements arrived—and
Foot would have to stay on the road until he was relieved.

III

When Dilys Maine left Brent, her one preoccupation was to
get home as fast as she could—before Alice Ridley got home.
Not that Alice would give Dilys away: Alice was stout and
good-natured and very fond of Dilys, but she was a gossip.
When Alice got together with her cronies, things just "slipped
out," and once a good story has slipped out in the country, it's
surprising how far it travels in a short time. Dilys only paused
once—to bunch up her tulle skirts more securely, so that she
could hurry. She was a country girl, and the dark fields held
no terrors for her; she knew the path well (she and Michael
Reeve had strolled this way on many a summer evening), and
her eyesight was good in the dark. She panted a little as she
hurried up the slope of the downland, but once over the top
it was easy going, and she ran down the last half-mile feeling
that she had a good chance of winning her race. She could
see the old house in the hollow well before she reached it:
there was no light in Alice's room, and neither were there any
headlights in the lane approaching the house. Dilys slipped in
by the back gate, crossed the orchard and was soon reaching
up to the old nesting box where she and Alice hid the key

of the kitchen door on occasions like this one. The key was there and Dilys knew she had won.

She opened the heavy old door as carefully as though someone might be listening and slipped into the warm kitchen, glad of the comfortable smell of woodsmoke and the welcoming warmth which still came from the ashes in the range. She knew the big kettle would be hot, hanging on the crane above the embers where she herself had put it before she went out, but she didn't wait to get a hot drink: she crept up the back stairs as silent as a ghost and went into her bedroom with nothing but thankfulness in her mind. In a trice she had unzipped her long frock, pulled it over her head and bundled it into a cupboard. "I can send it to be cleaned, but it was worth making it if I never wear it again," she thought. "It *was* fun, simply heaven…" Off with slinky petticoat and nylons ruined by her helter-skelter in the dark, on with her nightgown and off with the bedspread and then—an afterthought—off with her modest makeup, the lipstick and rouge and powder whose use her father forbade. Dilys was sitting on her bed, wrapped in a warm, sensible dressing gown, busy cleaning her face, when the telephone rang. The unexpected sound brought her heart into her mouth and for some seconds she sat irresolute. Who on earth could be telephoning at this hour?

"Idiot… go and answer it," she told herself. "It may be Father—he's done it before, just to see if I'm really at home."

She tied her dressing-gown cord round her, caught up her torch and ran downstairs, telling herself there was nothing to worry about: she was at home and everything was all right.

"Hullo, who is it?" she demanded, trying to sound sleepy as she spoke into the receiver. She needn't have bothered—it was Alice Ridley.

"Oh, Miss Dilys, I'm that sorry but there's been an accident and the road's blocked," came Alice's anxious voice. Dilys nearly said "I know it is," but Alice hurried on before she gave herself away. "It's on Cookbourne Bridge, just outside Stenfield, miss. A lorry hit a bus and the bus went over the parapet—it's dreadful. We couldn't get by and my taxi man hadn't enough petrol to go the long way round and I can't get home unless I walk it, and I haven't the heart to walk at this hour. So I'm going to stay the night with Mary Huggins and come out early, as soon as it's light."

"That's all right," said Dilys. "Nobody need know, Alice," and the other went on:

"There's just a chance the master might travel by the early train, Miss, the newspaper one. He's done that before; and I thought if that's the case you might tell him I went to see my friend and stayed the night, her being poorly, and that'll save any fusses."

"All right. I'll say that," said Dilys. "Don't worry. I'll tell him Miss Huggins is bad with bronchitis again." Even as she spoke, Dilys heard a sound at the front of the house and realised the front door had opened: she knew it must be her father—he alone had a key to the front door. Deliberately Dilys went on speaking: "I'm terribly sorry about Miss Huggins being so ill, Alice. You're quite right to stay with her and thank you for letting me know." Then she hung up the receiver, just as her father's harsh voice demanded:

"What are you doing? Who are you talking to at this hour?"

Dilys shivered a little as she heard the rasping voice: it meant that her father was "in a taking" as Alice put it, in one of those black unreasoning moods which seemed to be growing on him, alienating his friends, terrifying his household. "But thank heaven I got home in time!" she thought, even as she called out to him:

"It's all right, Daddy. It was Alice. She went to see a sick friend and she rang up to say she was staying the night because she can't leave her friend alone."

"What is she dreaming of, leaving it till this hour?" rasped Robert Maine.

"What time is it?" asked Dilys innocently. She was not by nature a liar, but life with her father was making her more and more adept at the sort of answer which might save trouble. She suddenly realised they were standing in the dark, with only the beam of her torch lighting the room, and she went across to the light switch and put it down. Standing there in her blue dressing gown, pushing her tumbled fair hair back from her pale face, she looked like a startled child.

"I don't know if Alice rang up before, I only just heard the phone," she went on. "Is it very late? and would you like a hot drink or something? You look tired, Daddy."

Robert Maine looked not only tired—he looked gaunt and strained and dirty. He was a big man, with thick grizzled hair and weather-beaten face, but now he looked pallid and there was a stain down one side of his face and his collar was crumpled and awry.

"No, no. I don't want anything," he said hastily. "Go back to bed, child. It's close on midnight. I had trouble with the car or I should have been back earlier—I got my business settled quicker than I expected. Off you go—and I'll speak to Alice in the morning. She'd no business to leave you alone in the house."

"But I don't mind being alone," said Dilys quickly. "I think Alice was quite right to stay with her friend if the friend was ill. Don't be cross with her—she's such a good soul."

She shivered again as she met her father's sombre gaze: something about his aspect frightened her and she added quickly: "If you don't want anything, I'll go back to bed. It's cold, isn't it? I expect the kettle's still hot if you want some tea or anything." She slipped past him with a quick "Goodnight, Daddy," afraid for a moment that he was going to stop her, and a moment later she tumbled into bed.

IV

Dilys went to bed—but not to sleep. Curled up, with the bedclothes close round her, her mind worried over events of the past hour. She heard her own voice asking "What time is it?" and her father saying "It's close on midnight." It was after one o'clock, nearer to half past one, when he said that. "He must have known," thought Dilys. "He always knows the time, his watch is always right." Then came the thought "He wanted me to believe he was home by twelve o'clock... Why? What had he been doing, why did it matter what time he came in?" Then, unbidden, a picture flashed across her mind: the picture of a body sprawled across the road, and Nicholas Brent bending over it. In the morning, Dilys told herself she was being silly: she'd got into a panic because of her stolen evening, because of her own evasions and near lies, and it was fear for herself that conjured up nightmares. That body in the road: it was a man's body. It had been lying less than a mile from Michael Reeve's house, and her father had had a bitter quarrel with Reeve not very long ago. With the dreadful clarity that accompanied troubled thoughts in the small hours, Dilys connected up the two pictures and then thought of a policeman coming to ask her questions: when did she get home? when did her father get home? how had she got home?

"Oh, why did I go, why didn't I stay at home?" she thought.

And then sleep came on her suddenly, the sleep of the young and healthy, but it was troubled by grim dreams of driving through miles of misty narrow roads, and headlights that lit up a dark body and a car that bumped hideously as it lurched over an unknown obstacle.

Chapter IV

I

WHEN INSPECTOR TURNER HEARD A CAR DRAW UP outside Michael Reeve's house some half-hour after he had telephoned, he confidently expected it to be a police car. He was so sure about this that he went to the front door to meet his colleagues, setting it wide so that the lamplight gleamed out on the misty air. Instead of the uniformed figures he expected, Turner found himself confronting a tall young fellow with a white scarf round his neck and a gleam of white shirt front showing through the topcoat the wearer was unbuttoning as he came up the path. For once the Inspector was so taken by surprise that he let the other fellow get a question in first.

"What the dickens…?" began the newcomer, and then added: "Police? What's happened?"

"I hoped you could tell me that," retorted Turner, nettled at being caught off his guard. "Might I have your name, please?"

"My name? Use your wits, officer," snapped the other.

"This is my house. I'm Michael Reeve—and I don't propose to ask your permission to enter my own house. It's up to you to explain what you're doing here: if there's been a burglary, say so."

So calm was the voice, so peremptory the tone, that Turner was taken aback, and Reeve pushed past him into the small hall and stood facing the open door of the room where the furniture still lay pell-mell on the floor.

"Hell!" he exclaimed. "So that's it. Burglary and a general bash-around. What did they hope to get?"

Turner had had a good look at Reeve by this time: he was a big, powerful fellow, but by no stretch of the imagination could it be said that he looked as though he had been engaged in a "general bash-around" recently. His dark hair was not the variety to be "mastered" by hair cream, but it was neatly parted and as tidy as its nature allowed; his collar was uncrumpled, his bow tie in place and his shirt front clean. In short, if this really was Michael Reeve, Turner had to think again.

"If you'll answer a few questions, sir, instead of asking them, we might get things sorted out," said Turner. "I am here on duty, having had a report concerning events in this house this evening."

"So I assumed," interrupted the other coolly. "Who reported, anyway?! The dog?—or the burglar? It looks a fair shambles to me. Is that blood?"

"Will you state your whereabouts during the course of the evening, please?" snapped Turner.

Reeve gave a long sigh, as of a man whose patience is sorely tried. "Where do you think I've been? Do you imagine I put on a boiled shirt for my dinner every evening? If you're a police inspector in this district, you ought to jolly well know where I've been—at the Hunt Ball in Fordings."

"You claim to have been at the Hunt Ball the entire evening, sir? Might I ask when you got there and what hour you left?"

Reeve took his time over answering: he stood with his hands in his pockets and looked at Turner as deliberately as Turner might have studied an old lag—and with about as much respect. During that interval of silence Turner had time to wish he'd encouraged Constable Foot to indulge in a little local gossip. Turner had heard of Reeve as a smallholder and a successful cattle breeder: now he remembered that he was a son of some local gentry—Hollydown Manor, was it? Who was it had said there had been Reeves at Hollydown before the Conquest? This chap had neither the voice nor manner of a smallholder—but Turner wasn't going to let him get away with it because his people had been gentry.

"I didn't say that I claimed anything, Inspector—if that's your rank. I said I was there," replied Michael Reeve at length. He picked up one of the chairs, righted it and sat down on it, completely self-possessed. "And now say you tell me why you're here, in my house, without obtaining my leave to enter: it's time you did a little explaining, and an apology wouldn't come amiss. This *is* my house, and I've a right to ask what's been happening here." ("Them Reeves—a rum lot"—so had said Foot.)

Turner was in a quandary: he realised, rather belatedly, that he had jumped to his conclusions too fast, and he remembered Nicholas Brent saying "I *thought* it was Reeve... Maybe I was wrong. Fact is I'm a bit fuddled and my head aches like the devil..."

"You have the right to ask the reason for my presence in your house, sir," said Turner. "A man's body was found in the road a short distance from here. Commander Brent, who found the body, came to this house to telephone the police."

"When did he come here?" asked Reeve.

"Shortly after midnight," said Turner. "He was anxious—and rightly so—to report to the police, and it is a considerable distance to a telephone booth. When he got no answer to his knock, he went round to the back of the house and obtained access by a window."

"Housebreaking, eh?" said Michael Reeve. "Is that an offence in the eyes of the law, or is it not? I hope you've charged him with it: if not, why not?"

"Commander Brent entered your house with no felonious intent," said Turner stiffly, but Reeve retorted:

"How do you know? If a man breaks into my house, I expect the police to deal with him, not to argue about intents. Go on."

"Commander Brent rang up Brambledene police station and reported finding the body," went on Turner. "As he replaced the receiver he heard someone enter the house by the front door, and a man called out to him to know what he was doing. Commander Brent said that he recognised your voice, he replied, giving his name, and was immediately attacked and knocked out, the furniture falling on him in the ensuing struggle."

"Well, as a story it sounds damned odd to me," said Michael Reeve, "but let's get one thing clear. You say Brent recognised my voice; he knows me—did he say he also recognised my face?"

"No, sir. The room was in darkness, because the Commander dropped his torch and he had not lighted a lamp."

Again Michael Reeve stared at Turner, eyebrows raised, mouth twitching. "Of all the god-darned silly stories I've ever heard, this is about the silliest," he retorted. "Brent broke into my house in my absence; he then says he was attacked in a dark room and he and his attacker started to break the house up. Where do you come in on this, Inspector?"

"I came out to investigate the body reported to be lying in the road," said Turner. "Commander Brent's car was by the roadside and Mr. Tom Hudson was also at the spot—he was driving home from Fordings. Shortly afterwards Commander Brent arrived, having recovered consciousness in this room; his head was cut open."

Reeve glanced down at the mess on the floor. "So that was it. Well, apart from the damage done to my premises, the story of Brent's adventures is no concern of mine. As for the corpse on the road, I know nothing about it. Who was it, anyway?"

"Two witnesses have claimed to identify the deceased," rejoined Turner, feeling that he was now on firmer ground, "and it is my duty to ask you to accompany me to the mortuary in order that you may identify the body."

"Why on earth drag me out?" demanded Reeve, and Turner answered:

"It has been stated that the deceased was known to you, sir. It would be more satisfactory from the point of view of this investigation if you would confirm or deny this statement independently."

Michael Reeve yawned: a large, face-splitting yawn, showing his excellent white teeth. "He's a tough," thought Turner, "hard as nails... He may belong to a family which was gentry, but he's got fists like iron."

"It's all very well for you to talk about what's satisfactory," said Reeve. "I've got a point of view also, and I'm the injured party, as I see it. My house has been broken into, my property damaged, and you ask me to go out again in the middle of the night to identify a mysterious casualty. I tell you I don't like it—any of it. What's to prevent another housebreaker getting in—apparently there have been two of them on the job already, not counting yourself. And from what I know of police work, you've shown more zeal than discretion. It'd have been better for you if you'd had a witness before climbing in at a window, and you should know it."

In one sense, Reeve was perfectly right in his statement, and this infuriated Turner: he knew that under cross-examination his activities might be condemned as irregular from the point of view of strict police procedure. Careful to keep his temper, Turner replied:

"The police have been in difficulties tonight, sir: we've had other calls in addition to this one. I have telephoned for reinforcements and there will be a man along shortly to keep this house under supervision."

"Then your man can do his supervising from outside," said Reeve. "I'm not going to have anybody mucking around in here until I've had a look to see what's been pinched. If Brent's telling the truth and somebody did go for him, that means another chap was in this house for reasons of his own. And I'm going to see where the blokes got in and make sure it doesn't happen again." He got up and strode to the door. "Seems to me Brent was pretty nippy over getting in: I suppose bloke number one left a window open for a getaway."

II

Turner was certainly having a night of it. He arranged for one of the relief constables from Fordings to stand by Reeve's house—and keep an eye on Reeve's car. Turner then had to telephone to report that Michael Reeve had returned home and the all-stations alert for him could be cancelled (a matter which brought some terse comments from Turner's Chief Inspector). There was then some argument with Reeve on the matter of transport, Reeve saying that he could drive himself to the mortuary, having no desire for a lift in a police car. Turner managed to get that one sorted out and eventually he drove a very disgruntled and supercilious passenger to the mortuary in Fordings.

It was nearly three o'clock on that cold misty night when Michael Reeve stood and looked down at the body which lay on the mortuary slab: Turner watched the young man's face closely, but Michael showed neither emotion nor surprise.

"I don't know who the chap is—or was. I've never seen him—not to my knowledge."

Turner played his trump card. "Mr. Hudson and Constable Foot have both stated that this is the body of Mr. Norman Reeve."

Michael turned and looked at the Inspector, still with that cool expressionless calm.

"Then they're wrong: both of them—if they mean that this is the body of Norman Reeve who is my brother. This man was much older than my brother, and he doesn't resemble him except in the most superficial way. Did you ask your constable—or Tom Hudson—when they last saw my brother Norman?"

Turner had to answer: "No, sir."

"Norman left this district and went overseas ten years ago. If Hudson—or anybody else—claims to identify this man as my brother, they should realise that ten years is a long time. And as regards you, Inspector, I take it you've got something more substantial to go on? Presumably, you've examined the chap's pockets and clothes?"

"Barring a few coins there was nothing in the deceased's pockets."

"I see. Well, that's your headache, not mine," said Michael. "You asked me to identify the body and I am unable to do so. I certainly deny that this man was my brother Norman."

"Very good, sir," rejoined Turner evenly. "It would be satisfactory if we could clear up the other matter—Commander Brent's statement that he heard your voice just before he was attacked. We can time this assault by the telephone call: doubtless you can substantiate your statement that you were at the Hunt Ball at the time—half an hour after midnight."

"Doubtless I can," retorted Michael. "Until I have much better reason to do so, I shall do nothing of the kind. If you imagine I am going to give you a list of the people I danced with and sat out with and drank with, you're much mistaken. If Brent is prepared to swear that he saw me when he was attacked, then let him bring an action for assault. I shall be happy to meet him in court, where the evidence can be properly examined."

Turner was tired and angry—and more than a little confused: he realised that he had tried to rush his fences and he wasn't going to do it again. He rejoined quite evenly:

"Very good, sir. We will leave it at that for the time being. The car will drive you back. We shall call on you tomorrow to investigate the possibility that your house was broken into previous to Commander Brent's entry."

"You'll find me somewhere around the place," replied Michael Reeve. "It occurs to me that you have an impetuous mind, Inspector: if optimism leads you to the belief that I shall do a bolt in the night, you couldn't be more mistaken."

III

After Michael Reeve had gone, Turner spoke to the elderly constable who had stood by during the identification—or denial of it. "You've been in this district a long time, Shaw. Do you know anything about the Reeves?"

"I was born on the Hollydown estate, sir. They were a wild lot then, and I reckon they're a wild lot now. The old Squire—Mr. Michael's grandfather, I mean—he was a bad 'un, and Mr. Simon Reeve, who died last year, weren't much better. What I'm getting at is this, sir: there's more chaps with Reeve blood in their veins than answers to the name Reeve. This one now," and he jerked his head towards the now-shrouded body, "he's got a look of them. I know what Foot meant, but he ought to've thought before he spoke. He's got a look of Norman Reeve, this one has, I grant that, but he's older, like Mr. Michael said. Norman—why, he'd be under forty. There was five of them, all told. Norman was eldest; then Geoffrey— killed in the hunting field, he was; then Robert—a proper wild one, he is; then Rosemary—the girl who disappeared eighteen months ago; and this Michael. He's said to be the steadiest of the lot: never heard aught against Mr. Michael, save that he's a quick temper—but they all had that."

Turner went back to the station to give his report and found Sergeant Hallam waiting for him. Hallam was in the county C.I.D., and it was he who had examined the body of the unknown man, as well as his clothes.

"Hullo, Turner—got the chap identified?"

"No. Rather the reverse. I've been told who he isn't."

"I'm not surprised. When a man's pockets have been emptied, and there's nothing on him to identify him, it doesn't seem reasonable that his face should be familiar in the district where the body's found," said Hallam, and Turner looked at him enquiringly.

"Looks to me as though a nice set piece had been arranged for you," went on Hallam. "My own belief is that this bird was coshed earlier on—maybe not killed right out—and then his body was put in the road and a car run over it."

"Why do you think that?"

"Well, it's the surgeon's job really, not mine: they'll sort it out at the P.M. If a pedestrian's run down by a fast-moving car, the impact generally leaves bruises or lesions some-where between the knees and pelvis, and in nine cases out of ten some flakes of paintwork—cellulose from the wings or whatnot—got caught on the fabric of the clothing, espe-cially if it's an old car. The lab people are very hot on finding traces of that kind. I couldn't spot anything of the kind on this bloke's coat, but the lab people may. I gather there was some suggestion that a local car might be involved?"

"Yes a suggestion," agreed Turner. "We're keeping the car under observation."

"An old car, is it?"

"Yes—pre-war Ensign; wings all cracked, been resprayed dozens of times."

"So much the better. If it was the Ensign that hit him, they'll find traces."

"But if the Ensign didn't hit him—if it was just driven over him as he lay?"

"Harder to prove: you wouldn't find any bits or pieces on the bumpers, and the wings wouldn't have touched the body. There's tyre marks, of course."

"Yes—and how many old cars round here have moderately worn Dunlop tyres on a mass-production body of the 1930s? Seems to me it's easier to say what car it wasn't."

"Not Brent's outfit, for example?"

"Definitely not. If only it doesn't rain in the night, I'm going over that road pretty carefully tomorrow—or maybe you chaps will do it for me. It's a narrow road with grass verges, and I reckon you ought to be able to get a good idea of what vehicles passed along that stretch last night. There can't have been many."

"Don't you be so sure," said Hallam. "It was the Hunt Ball, remember, and every farmer in the district was on the road—they all follow the Hollydown, Lord Timberlake's a popular Master—and that road's often clear of mist when the main road gets thick."

"Maybe there could be another answer to this problem, then," said Turner. "If the dead man was left lying in the road, someone who was speeding may have bumped over him before they saw him—and decided not to stop. But that doesn't explain who went for Brent when he was in Reeve's house. I still think it was Reeve himself: he knocked Brent out and then realised he was in a spot. Thought he'd killed him, perhaps, and went and poshed himself up and cooked an alibi."

"Reeve was at the Hunt Ball all right: I saw him arrive," said Hallam. "I was on duty there, looking out for a bloke who's suspected of pinching stuff from the cloakrooms."

"When did Reeve arrive?"

"A bit latish: half past nine. I didn't see him again, I was keeping an eye on cloaks."

"You'd have seen him if he'd come and fetched his coat— before midnight, say?"

"Not of necessity: it's not as easy as that," said Hallam. "Quite a lot of chaps—the farmers particularly—don't leave their coats in the cloakroom: they leave them in their cars and lock the car. I reckon there's more than one reason for that. They'd tell you it saves time at the end, when it's liable to be a bit of a scrum. That's true, of course, but I believe there's another reason." Hallam chuckled to himself and then went on: "They all get an evening suit—dinner jacket or whatnot: they have to, or they wouldn't be allowed on the floor, but it's only the nobs who run to a topcoat of the sort they like to hand over to cloakroom attendants at the Prince's Hall, if you take me. If they leave their coats in the car, it's nobody's business if it's the same coat they go to the stock market in—and anyway, a coat in the car has its uses. Plenty of petting parties in the car park and these old cars haven't got any heaters." Hallam laughed—an amused, tolerant laugh, as he looked at Turner's glum face. "Time you turned in, old chap—you look as though you've had enough of things. You'll feel better able to cope after you've had a bit of shut-eye. But do remember this—the Hunt Ball's an occasion. If you get trying to collect evidence about who sat out with who and whose car they did it in, you'll be asking for a thick ear and you'll get it, uniform or no uniform. This is a rural district and you'll have to get used to country ways."

Turner went home to his diggings at last. He hadn't liked Hallam's last crack. He considered that a police officer who'd been trained to use his wits in a town was more alert and resourceful than a man whose experience was confined to a rural district, and he resented any suggestion to the contrary. Then he remembered Michael Reeve saying: "If you think I'm going to make you a list of who I danced with and who I sat out with, you're mistaken…" (or words to that effect). Turner was beginning to realise that perhaps it wasn't "as easy as that"—as Hallam had said. In fact, at that glum moment in the small hours, when depression can get a tired man down,

Inspector Turner remembered all the awkwardnesses which Michael Reeve could point out, and he found himself wondering if the army wouldn't have been a better career than the police force. A policeman's lot—well, it didn't seem a very happy one to Turner as he turned hungry into bed.

Chapter V

I

WHEN JENNIFER VERITY WOKE UP ON THE MORNING after the Hunt Ball, she sat up in bed with her arms round her knees and indulged in the pleasure of retrospection, gurgling with laughter over some of the absurdities, hugging herself over some of the thrills of the best dance she had ever been to. Jennifer was twenty-two and as pretty as she was ever likely to be; she was an eminently practical young woman who knew just what she wanted—and she was prepared to put all her energies into getting it. It was Mrs. Weldon (who had three married daughters) who had once said to Jennifer: "My dear, if a girl wants to get married, she should work to that end. It's a mistake for her to just sit around and think the young men will do all the trying. Chances come the way of most girls—the pretty ones anyway—but the chance can be developed into a certainty if the girl shows a little gumption."

Jennifer had protested, laughing that this was a very unromantic viewpoint, but Mrs. Weldon's comment had stuck in her mind, and Jennifer thought there might be a grain of truth in it. Anyway, on this sunny January morning, Jennifer Verity sat up in bed and considered what was the neatest way of organising a meeting between Ian Macbane and herself before Ian went off to town again.

"Of course, he's crazy over Dilys," she thought to herself, "but all the men are the same and Dilys can only marry one of them, and anyway I think she's made up her mind already—and Ian isn't the one. And Dilys wouldn't ever want to live in London, and she'd be no good as a barrister's wife, although she's a darling in her own way…"

And here Jennifer laughed to herself and grew pink in the face, because she believed she herself would do rather well as the wife of a rising barrister, and to be quite honest with herself, she intended to "have a go."

"I'll ring him up and ask him if he'd like to try the new car," she said to herself. "I know he adores driving, and Daddy won't want the car today—old Barrat's fetching him out to play golf over at Setterdean."

Having made up her mind over this, Jennifer got dressed quickly and knocked on her parents' door to tell them she'd bring up their breakfasts in bed—a Sunday-morning indulgence which her busy parents loved.

"Bless the child, why so early after a late night? Was it a nice dance, darling?"

"It was heavenly!" replied Jennifer. "The best ever. You were so sweet over my frock and letting me wear your pearls, Mummy. I thought the least I could do was to give you breakfast in bed."

"Bring me up the papers when they come, poppet," called her father. "I can hear Bert's abominable bike about half a mile away."

"Righto, Daddy. I'll bring them," Jennifer called back.

Bert Marling, an employee in the garage at Bramber, added to his weekly earnings by fetching the Sunday newspapers from Fordings and delivering them (for a consideration) in the scattered households of Bramber. Bert's "abominable bike" was notorious in the district: it made so much row that his clientele were generally woken from their Sabbath slumbers before he knocked at the door with the papers.

"Hullo, Bert!" called Jennifer as he came up the path. "It's quite a decent morning—it was misty last night: some people must have had quite a time driving home from the ball."

"Reckon some people did have a time," said Bert. "There was a chap killed on the low road, they had police out there till all hours."

"Goodness, how awful!" said Jennifer. "Who was he?"

"They don't rightly know, miss, but there's all manner of stories going round. Some says it's murder, and Commander Brent tried to catch the murderer and got knocked over the head. Mr. Tom Hudson saw the body, and that Mr. Macbane who's staying at Stenfield—he was in the car with Mr. Hudson. And I'm told the police brought Mr. Reeve into Fordings in a police car. Reckon the Sunday papers'll be fed up not getting the news into today's paper—too late, it was—but they've got a bit in the stop press about the smash on Cookbourne Bridge. 'Several dead' it says."

"Good heavens, how ghastly!" exclaimed Jennifer, but Bert was already rushing back to his bike, anxious to spread his grim news in other quarters.

Jennifer stood in the hall with the papers in her arms, trying to sort out what Bert had said: "a chap killed on the low road"—that was the road which ran by Michael Reeve's farm, and Nicholas Brent had driven Ian Macbane by that route when they came into Fordings—Jennifer knew that, because she had asked Ian if he'd run into fog on the way, and he had said: "No: Nick avoided it by coming on the low road; he says there's always less mist on that one than there is coming by the Rose & Crown or by the Bramber Down Road." But Brent's name had been mentioned—and surely Nick Brent had driven Dilys home? Jennifer (who had known that Dilys was aching to go to the Hunt Ball) had herself offered to drive Dilys home, but the latter had said: "No, it'll only spoil your evening—if I do go, I shall have to get home early and Commander Brent said he'd drive me."

Jennifer had laughed to herself a little: she knew that Nick was in love with Dilys. "And perhaps he'll persuade her to marry him if he drives her home from the ball; she'll be an idiot if she doesn't say yes," had thought Jennifer, who was only too anxious (in the friendliest way, of course), to see lovely Dilys safely married. And where did Dilys fit into this dreadful story of a dead man on the road and Nick Brent getting knocked over the head?

"Jennifer darling, bring Daddy the papers up," called her mother's voice from upstairs. "You know what he's like—he'll never stay in bed without his awful old papers."

"Sorry, Mummy. Bert had got some ghastly story about a dead man on the low road and I was trying to make out what he meant. Perhaps it's all moonshine."

"What's that?" shouted her father, as she ran upstairs. "Another road casualty? I told you what it'd be with that treacherous fog last night. That's the last time I'll let you drive into Fordings on a foggy night."

"Don't fuss, Daddy! It wasn't really bad at all," retorted Jennifer, "and I expect Bert was making things up. He's as bad as some of your awful papers."

All the time she was busy making the coffee and grilling the bacon (her father was very fussy and insisted on his bacon being grilled), Jennifer worried away at the problem. She thought of ringing up Dilys, but decided against it in case Mr. Maine had returned home. He listened to all his daughter's telephone calls on the extension in his office when he was at home, and Dilys's friends had learnt to be very careful about ringing her up.

"I'll ring Ian—I can say I heard he was hurt," she thought. "After all, with Bert spreading these ghastly rumours, anybody can get worried over their friends."

Jennifer needn't have bothered: she had no sooner taken the breakfast tray up than the telephone rang, and Ian Macbane was on the line.

"Oh, I'm so glad to hear your voice!" she cried (quite truthfully). "Our newspaper ghoul has been spreading the most appalling stories of road smashes and sudden death, and I'm full of alarm and despondency imagining you and Tom Hudson were killed in the fog. Whatever is it all about?"

"Oh, Tom and I weren't hurt—though there was an accident. It's all rather a mess, and I don't want to talk about it over the phone," said Ian. "It's terribly nice of you to have worried about us," he added hastily. "If I biked over, would you be at home?"

"Yes, of course—and perhaps you'd like to try the new car," she said. "I've been wondering about Dilys, you know. We might catch her—she always goes to church at Steadham. You see, I was told that Nicholas Brent was—well, you know. It's all a bit difficult, because I swear that girl at Exchange listens in—and I jolly well hope she hears me say so."

"Yes, rather…and thanks a lot. I'll be over in half an hour," said Ian.

"Of course he's in a flap about Dilys," said Jennifer to herself (she was nothing if not a realist). "But he'll soon get over it when he knows that Nick is the one and only—and thank heaven I got my best coat back from the cleaners. That rough oatmeal effect suits my style much better than Mummy's old musquash. And now I've only got to fix Daddy about the car—and he knows Ian's a wizard driver."

II

Before eleven o'clock, Ian and Jennifer were on the road in the new Humber, and Jennifer felt she had "done her best with herself" and earned Ian's "I say, how nice you look." The creamy blanket coat and a little Cossack pillbox hat on her reddish curls looked just right with the gleaming beige car and its chestnut-brown upholstery—and Ian fitted the decor very nicely, being clad in pleasant country tweeds and a tawny shirt.

"How nice we both look, then," laughed Jennifer. "I do like your tweeds; Daddy will always dress in a sort of clerical grey and I do love nice colours. And now for goodness' sake tell me what happened last night: I've been feeling awful over it and having to put the parents off with 'I expect it was just Bert's awful lies,' in case I let out anything I shouldn't."

"I want to tell you," he replied. "What time will they come out of Steadham Church?"

"Oh, not before twelve. I thought we could catch Dilys up on the hill as she walks home—it'll save giving some of the old biddies more to talk about. It's that tiny church, down by the river—you know, one of the 'smallest churches in England'—there must be dozens of them, and there are only about ten in the congregation, and they're mostly ancient. That's why Dilys's father likes her to go there, poor darling."

"She does seem to have the dickens of a poor time," he said. "Look, would it be a good idea if we parked up on the down—where we can see the river, I mean? It'll be easier to talk if I'm not driving."

"Yes, that's a wizard idea. I'm terribly sorry you're so worried, Ian."

"Jolly nice of you. I'm frightfully cheered you could come out—I really am a bit worried, and you've got to be so jolly careful whom you talk to in the country. That's one of the things that gets me down a bit in villages—everybody knows everybody's business."

"It's awful," she agreed. "I'd give anything to live in London, but Daddy just won't."

Ian handled the car very skilfully, and after a long climb up the chalk down, he turned the car on to the dry downland turf, where they could see the pale waters of the Channel gleaming under the wintry sunshine, and the curving course of the Cookbourne meandering out to join the sea by the bluff where Nick Brent's Mermaid Inn shone whitely on its chalk headland.

Jennifer longed to cry "Isn't it absolute heaven?" because the world looked so beautiful, but she settled down with a serious face to listen while Ian Macbane told her the events of the previous evening. "It was all pretty grim anyway," he concluded, "but one of the things I worried over a lot was what happened to Dilys Maine. Have you any idea how she was going to get home? I know she left early."

"Yes—she had to: Commander Brent had said he'd drive her. I know that, because she said so when I offered to take her back."

"I'm so glad you know," said Ian. "You see, Nick Brent told me he was going to drive her home, but it's important not to tell other people that. We don't know he did drive her, but if he *did*, she'd have seen the body in the road—she was bound to have. If that was the case, and the police knew it, she'd be called as a witness at the inquest."

"But that would be simply awful," said Jennifer. "She didn't tell her father she was going to the Hunt Ball, and he's a man with the most frightful temper. I can't think what would happen."

"Look here, isn't this all just early Victorianism?" said Ian. "All this business of the autocratic father bullying his daughter—it's plain bats. Daughters of today don't have to put up with that sort of bullying."

"Of course they don't—not ordinary daughters," agreed Jennifer. "I mean, if Daddy got bullying me, I just shouldn't stand for it, I'd walk out and get a job—but Dilys isn't quite ordinary, there's something old-fashioned about her. I expect it's being an only child and living with that grim parent. But let's leave that alone for now. What I can't help wondering is what she did—got out and walked home, I expect. After all, Nick Brent would have wanted to save her all the fuss and bother, wouldn't he? Though come to think of it, it might have been more sensible to face the fuss and bother and get it over in one."

"I think I rather agree with you over that," he said, "but I'm a bit worried in case the story gets out and the police make a fuss. That'd be much more unpleasant than Mr. Maine getting in a rage."

"Well, it's really Commander Brent's business, isn't it?" asked Jennifer. "He's the chief witness and everything else depends on what he says. It seems to me the best thing we can do, as Dilys's friends, is to lie low and say nothing."

"Quite," said Ian hastily. "That's why I wanted to talk to you about it: Dilys told me you were one of her best friends."

Jennifer screwed up her charming face a little: "She's a darling," she said, "but honestly I think it'd be a jolly good thing if she got married and left that ghastly old father to bully the furniture. After all, I'm not being a snake in saying that Nicholas Brent's crazy over her—everybody knows it."

"The point which seems to matter is whether Dilys is in love with Nick," said Ian, and something in his voice made Jennifer feel she'd got to be very careful.

"You can't expect me to tell you that," she answered quietly. "Dilys isn't like most girls—she doesn't rush round confiding in people—not even in her best friends. But do tell me something else about last night: our ghoul of a newspaper man said that Michael Reeve was somehow mixed up in all this. Is that true?"

"I should say it is. It's the dottiest story," said Ian. "My own belief is that Reeve had a poor deal, just because the Reeves always seem to be hitting the news or having disasters in the family."

"They're all a bit mad," she said, "but where does Michael come in?"

"Well, the story's bound to be all over the county, so I might just as well tell you," said Ian Macbane, and Jennifer said reproachfully:

"I'm quite trustworthy—honestly I am. That's why Dilys tells me things: she knows I don't go telling other people when I've promised not to."

"I'm sure you don't," said Ian hastily. "It's because I felt in my bones that you *are* trustworthy that I wanted to talk to you about all this—because it does look like being a fair-sized mess."

"That's all right then," said Jennifer. ("And that's the nicest thing he's said to me so far," she thought to herself.)

Ian told her about Brent's appearance, staggering along the road, and his accusation against Michael Reeve. "Not that I believe Nick was really responsible for what he was saying," said Ian. "He'd had a wallop over the head and it had happened to him in Reeve's house, and in his muddled state he'd just made up his mind it was Reeve who went for him. The more I think about it, the more improbable it seems to me."

"But Nick Brent must have been wrong, I know he *must*," declared Jennifer. "You see, I stayed to the end of the Hunt Ball and Michael was there—I saw him in the final gallop— you know they always end up with a gallop. Why, he asked me to dance with him again. I've forgotten what time it was exactly, but it was after you and Tom Hudson had gone. I wouldn't dance with Michael, but that's because he's a rotten dancer, he just doesn't know how—but I know he was at the ball until the very end and other people will know it, too."

"Well, that seems to be that," said Ian. "Actually, I did think Brent's story was pretty improbable, and I think he realised it himself, because he hedged a bit at the end and said, 'I *thought* it was Reeve's voice, but I was a bit fuddled.'"

"Didn't he *see* Michael?"

"No, he'd dropped his torch and he hadn't bothered to light a lamp—the place isn't wired—and he was in the dark."

Jennifer laughed—she couldn't help it. "It does sound crazy, all of it. Do you think Nick Brent was a bit delirious— some people talk an awful lot of nonsense when they're concussed."

"Well, I admit that occurred to me: you see, Nick was obviously in a bit of a flap, and I wondered if when he dropped his torch he barged into a bookcase or something and it came cracking down and split his head open. After all, if you're in a dark room and something hits you, you always imagine you've been bashed by somebody."

"Yes—I think that's quite an idea," said Jennifer. "I shall be awfully sorry if Michael's muddled up in all this fantastic story. I know he was what Daddy calls 'a wild fellow' when he was quite young, but he's worked awfully hard to get that place of his going, and I do think there's something nice about him, even though he is a rotten dancer."

"Well, if he was at the ball right up to the end, he couldn't have biffed Nick over the head," said Ian, "and I have an idea that it was because Nick said Michael had gone for him, and the wild Reeves were to the fore, so to speak, that Tom Hudson went and said he believed the dead man was Norman Reeve; there must have been some sort of resemblance, of course, because Foot—the bobby—said the same thing, but personally I should have been very chary of identifying a man I hadn't seen for years in conditions like last night's. In any case, the poor devil was bashed about too much to identify with certainty—Tom admitted that later."

Jennifer made a little movement of alarm and Ian said, "Look—I'm sorry. I oughtn't to be giving you the horrors, Jennifer, it's not fair."

"But don't you see how frightfully interested I am, Ian?" she cried. "I know all these people—Nick Brent and Michael, and you—and if Dilys really has got involved in it, through no fault of her own, she's my friend: I'd do anything to help her out. And it's such an extraordinary story—doesn't it look as though somebody who'd got a down on Michael might have worked the whole thing?"

"Well, that's a jolly interesting idea," said Ian Macbane. "Believe it or believe it not, the same thing occurred to me—but it seems a bit steep. It involves some awfully cunning planning."

"But wouldn't it work?" asked Jennifer. She was an intelligent girl and her wits were working hard. "You say the same thing occurred to you," she went on. "Do tell me exactly what you mean. You've experience of criminal cases: it's much more likely you can make sense of it than most people."

"Well, I don't know about that," said Ian, "but I'll tell you how I thought it *might* have been worked."

III

Sitting in the sunshine, having lighted cigarettes for Jennifer and himself, Ian said: "You have to assume that somebody wanted to liquidate an enemy—call the dead man X, as a change from calling the murderer X. Perhaps the whole scheme was suggested by the fact that X does resemble Norman Reeve: then the idea was to murder X and leave the body somewhere near Michael Reeve's place. It doesn't seem to me too tall an idea to assume that the person who found the body would walk back to Reeve's place to telephone the police—it's the obvious thing to do, because it's miles to any other telephone. So the murderer hung around by Reeve's place, ready to pretend he was Reeve if anybody came to phone, and make it look as though Reeve were involved in the crime. Of course," added Ian honestly, "we don't know for certain that this was a murder: it might have been an ordinary road casualty, but the way the police behaved made me pretty certain they 'weren't satisfied,' as they say—and anyway there's all this extraordinary business about Nick Brent being attacked."

Jennifer nodded, still thinking hard: "It's queer you should have been driving along that road, both going and coming," she said, and Ian replied,

"I know it is: one thing that's satisfactory is that it does let Brent out. You see, I can corroborate that the body wasn't in the road when we drove to Fordings, and—if necessary—Dilys can give evidence that the body was there when Nick was driving her back."

"Yes, I see that," said Jennifer, "and I'm certain Nick was driving her back, but all the same, I do hope she won't have to give evidence. She'd be so unhappy about it all, and she's tried so hard to get on with her father. She's a much more dutiful daughter than I am—she never answers back."

"It might have been better if she did," rejoined Ian, "but look here, if we're going to waylay Dilys coming home from church, we'd better get moving."

Chapter VI

I

WHEN JENNIFER SAW DILYS MAINE WALKING UP THE hill in front of them, Jennifer's first thought was: "She really is marvellous, her clothes always look right—and she doesn't spend half what I do."

In a neatly tailored black coat, with a tiny hat beautifully perched on her shining hair, Dilys looked as stylish as an illustration in *The Bystander*. It wasn't until Jennifer jumped out of the car and came face to face with the other girl that she saw how white-faced Dilys was, and how shadowed her eyes, but there was no doubt that she was glad to see Jennifer.

"Oh, Jenny! how lovely—I've been longing to talk to you!" cried Dilys.

"Then come and get in the car. Ian Macbane's trying it out, and it's really rather super," said Jennifer. "We'll drive you round by the chalk pit and drop you in your lane. Did you get home in time last night, Dilys?"

"Yes. I got home in time—but it was grim. Did you hear?" asked Dilys.

"I didn't hear anything about you," said Jennifer, "but I've been hearing quite a lot about Nicholas Brent." She glanced at Dilys's face and added quickly: "If you don't want to say anything about it while Ian's here, I'll come over another time and you can tell me then."

"But I want to know what happened," cried Dilys. "Alice came back with the most incredible stories, and she said Mr. Macbane and Tom Hudson drove home by the low road and that Commander Brent was badly hurt."

"Well, if you want to hear what happened, Ian'll tell you," said Jennifer, "but look, Dilys, you haven't got to say anything about yourself."

"But I've *got* to talk to someone or I shall go quite mad!" exclaimed Dilys. "I've not dared to say a word except 'Good gracious!' ever since Alice came in."

"All right, then come and get in the car, and we'll talk when we get up to the quarry," said Jennifer. "If we don't get a move on we shall have to give a lift to old Mrs. Hoskins and she's the world's worst gossip."

With the car pulled up again by the chalk quarry, Dilys told her part of the story without hesitation: "Commander Brent drove me back last night: soon after we'd crossed the culvert he pulled up and I could see there was something—or somebody—lying across the road. He got out to look, and when he came back, he said he'd have to ring the police and it'd be better if I walked home, because if I stayed I should have to give evidence about finding the body. So I went by the field path and got home before Alice or Daddy came in—and they've no idea I'd been out at all, and I feel simply frightful over it all."

"You poor dear!" exclaimed Jennifer, and Ian put in,

"It was just sheer bad luck: I'm terribly sorry about it all—but can you tell us this: did anybody else except Jennifer know that Nick Brent was going to drive you home?"

"No, nobody. I'm certain they didn't," she said. "I didn't tell anybody I was going to the ball—I never thought I should be able to go. It was Commander Brent who gave me the ticket—he came over to see Daddy one day on business, and he came out and looked at my geese—he often buys my birds—and I said, 'I don't think I can possibly go,' and he laughed and said, 'You never know; keep the ticket anyway,' and then things worked out marvellously and I let Commander Brent know I could manage it and he said he'd drive me home. I didn't tell a soul except Jennifer."

"Who drove you into Fordings?" asked Ian.

"Oh, I went by bus, in the afternoon, complete with suitcase, and changed at Margot Venning's flat. She went to the ball, too, but when she asked me to stay the night, I told her Jennifer had offered to drive me home—which was true."

Ian laughed a little. "All very well organised—you seem to have a complete cover story."

"It must sound awful!" said Dilys. "But if I didn't plan things like that I should never get out at all—and I do adore dancing."

"Well, don't let's worry about that," said Ian. "The only thing that bothers me is the thought of some person saying that you were in Nick Brent's car after he's said on oath that he was alone when he found the body. Is there any chance anyone saw you get into his car?"

"No. I know they didn't. I went out by that door the staff use, and there wasn't a soul about. I'm quite sure of that. And now won't you tell me what happened later to Commander Brent?"

Again Ian told his tale, quite briefly, and Dilys cried out: "But what does it all mean? It sounds mad—Michael would never have attacked him. Why on earth should he?"

"I don't know," said Ian. "The only thing one can say is that the whole wretched business seems likely to cause trouble for everybody—and I hope that doesn't include you, Dilys. May I give you one piece of advice?"

"Yes, of course you can."

"Don't discuss this business with anybody—not a soul. And if the police do come and ask you questions, tell them the exact truth without hesitation. It's simply not worthwhile—to put it at the lowest estimate—to try to hoodwink the police."

Dilys laughed, ruefully. "I deserved that, didn't I? I've been hoodwinking all round—but I'm not really a liar, even though you find that hard to believe. If the police do ask me questions, I promise I'll tell them the exact truth."

"Good girl—and now I wonder if you can tell me something I want to know: did you ever see Norman Reeve?"

"Oh, yes—I knew them all. The Reeves all hunted, and I went to see the meets at Hollydown and Bramber. I was only ten when Norman Reeve went abroad—it was the year after the war and they said he went to Australia. I don't remember him very well, but I often saw him, and he was always nice to me: he often gave me a ride on his mare."

"Do you know how old he was?"

"Oh, that'll take some working out: he was much older than Michael; Michael's twenty-six and Norman was more than ten years older than that—he'd be about thirty-eight now, I should think."

Jennifer put a word in here: "I think we ought to drive Dilys home, Ian—I'll show you the way to the old lane; she mustn't be late."

"Goodness, no—or Daddy will be in a proper rage," said Dilys, as Ian drove on. "He's still angry because Alice couldn't get home last night. It was awful: Alice rang up about ten minutes after I got home and said the road was blocked and she was going to stay the night with Mary Huggins, and I was still talking to her when Daddy got home and was all in a flap about who was ringing up at that hour."

"But didn't you say Mr. Maine was going to be away for the night?" asked Jennifer.

"Of course I did, but he said he got his business done early and he drove home and had bother with his car or something. Thank goodness he did, or he'd have caught me creeping into the house with my ball dress all bunched up round my waist, and I can't think what would have happened. He was in one of his bad moods anyway. Jenny, I sometimes feel I shall give up and just run away: it really is a bit hard."

"Well, if you ever do run away, you know where to run to—I'll see you through," said Jennifer.

Just as Ian pulled up at the entrance to the lane, Dilys spoke again to Ian. "It isn't true that the police took Michael away, is it?"

He sensed the nervousness in her voice and replied: "I think he had to go to Fordings to see if he could identify the body, but he went home afterwards: old Brandon, who drives the milk lorry for the Co-op, saw Michael this morning and asked what all the excitement was about, and Reeve said the police had gone all haywire and he was going to make a complaint to the Chief Constable."

"Oh, thank goodness!" cried Dilys, and then, catching sight of Jennifer's surprised face, she added quickly, "I know it's nothing to do with me, but Daddy hates all the Reeves, he says they're bad right through. I don't think that's true—I know they've always been nice to me, and I loved poor Rosemary." She turned quickly to Jennifer. "Thanks tons, Jenny. You've been terribly good: I can't tell you how awful I was feeling—as though I were a criminal myself, and talking about things *does* help."

Dilys ran off along the lane and Ian turned the car at the next gate, saying: "I'd better get you home now, Jennifer, or your father will be creating, too."

"Only if you scratch the wings of his beautiful new car," laughed Jennifer. "Daddy's lots of sense, he never fusses about me. I think it's just too frightful for poor Dilys, having a father like hers: and she tried so hard to please him—she said she promised her mother to look after him." Jennifer gave an exasperated whistle. "I'm not really cynical, Ian— and I adore my own parents—but I do think some of this dutiful daughter business is simply sick-making. Dilys isn't really a flat—she's much cleverer than I am in most ways— but when she talks about her father, I always feel she goes moronic."

"I know what you mean," replied Ian, "but it must be pretty hard for a girl who's been brought up in that awful repressed puritanical atmosphere: she really showed quite a lot of spunk in going to the ball, and it's damned hard luck that she got caught up in this mess, just because Nick chose the low road to avoid the mist. If he'd only taken the Greenham Road by the Rose & Crown, none of this would have happened."

"I wonder if Nick Brent often uses the low road," pondered Jennifer, and Ian said:

"Why? What are you thinking about now?"

"Well, it somehow all seemed so pat, leaving the body there for him to find," said Jennifer. "You see, it wasn't left there for Michael Reeve to find, because everybody knew he would have gone to the Hunt Ball and he'd have driven in the other direction and not seen the body. But if anybody knew that Nick Brent used that road quite a lot—well, they might have argued things out as we suggested earlier on."

"You're full of bright ideas, Jenny," he laughed, "but let's hope it's not going to turn into a criminal case at all—just a traffic accident, with some poor devil of a tramp run down by a short-sighted driver in the mist—and the driver failed to stop, as we're always hearing."

"All right—but then who attacked Nick Brent after they'd pretended to talk in Michael Reeve's voice?" asked Jennifer.

"Oh, Nick knocked the furniture over, and imagined the voice because he was concussed," replied Ian.

"Do you really believe that?" asked Jennifer, and Ian replied:

"I'm dashed if I know what I believe: the whole story gets curiouser and curiouser, as Alice in Wonderland said. But I do know this—you've been an absolute trump, Jenny. It's been wonderful talking to you like this, and I'm frightfully glad Dilys has got you for a friend."

When Jennifer thought this over later, she said to herself: "Well, it wasn't really a hundred per cent, as Daddy would say: he was thinking about Dilys much more than he was thinking about me, but he's beginning to like me quite a bit."

II

After he had had lunch with his aunt and uncle in their pleasant house at Stenfield Green, Ian Macbane said: "I think I'd better push over to the Mermaid and see how old Nick's getting on, Aunt. He really was in rather a poor way last night."

"Oh, Ian dear, must you?" asked Aunt Caroline. "We were

looking forward to having you so much, and we hardly seem to have seen you."

"Well, you can't blame the boy," said her husband. "It's not often a rising young lawyer plunges head first into a case of assault and battery—and anyway, I think he ought to go and enquire after Brent."

"Couldn't you telephone, dear?" asked Aunt Caroline, but Uncle John replied,

"Let the boy go, my dear. I admit I want to know what it was all about, and you can't expect to get all the details over the phone."

"Look, Aunt," said Ian, "how would it be if I stayed another night or two—if you'd like me to. There's nothing on that makes it essential for me to be back in town tomorrow morning—I haven't got to be in court or anything like that—and the old man might be quite interested in this story down here: he's always saying it's a mistake to be purely academic in our job."

"That'd be lovely, Ian," said his aunt comfortably, "and I expect this dreadful story will just turn out to be another traffic accident. Very sad, of course, no matter who the poor man was, but I always think things seem so much more lurid in the middle of the night, and I daresay you were all a bit elevated after the Hunt Ball. Now don't laugh, dear: I *know* that a few extra drinks can enliven the imagination quite a lot, and they do say that Commander Brent isn't exactly a teetotaller, you know."

When John Macbane came to the door to see his nephew off (on pushbike again), he chuckled: "One thing, the exercise will do you good, Ian: and there is a spot of sense in what your aunt says—things do tend to get exaggerated in the small hours, and I shouldn't be surprised if Nick Brent had lowered a few. I don't mean he was drunk, I'm sure he wasn't, but nobody's judgement is improved by either alcohol or Hunt Balls."

"Well, Uncle, the corpse wasn't a defect of Nick's judgement: it was damned real—and that Inspector bloke seemed to think it damned fishy."

"Turner—a good man, but a touch zealous," said John Macbane, "and there's this to it. Turner knows all about the case of that poor girl—Rosemary. The police got nowhere in that case and my own belief is that they get suspicious at the very name Reeve. My bet is that Turner lost his head a bit because the whole problem last night seemed to involve the Reeve family again, and Turner hasn't been in the district long enough to know all the ins and outs pertaining to that family. But Tom Hudson ought to have thought twice before he identified the corpse as Norman Reeve—and that's where Caroline's remarks are applicable: Tom probably wasn't in the state of mind to think carefully."

"Well, dash it all, Uncle, you may think the whole lot of us were semi-binged—elevated, to use Aunt Caro's nice word— but the bobby wasn't—Foot. He was stone sober."

"Foot? Damned old fool," said John Macbane cheerfully. "If you had the cross-examining of him, Ian, you'd pull his evidence to shreds in a brace of shakes. Foot hasn't seen Norman Reeve for years. Well, off you go—and talk a bit of sense to Brent: he ought to be feeling a bit chastened by now."

After a ride which he found quite exhilarating, Ian Macbane arrived at the Mermaid Inn and found Nicholas Brent sitting in the deep bay window, watching the shipping on the sunlit Channel, binoculars beside him. Apart from some strapping across his forehead, Brent showed no consequences of his fracas.

"Hullo, Ian! Decent of you to come over. I thought you were packing off home again, else I'd have been on your tracks before."

"I'm stopping on for a night or so, Nick. I shall have to show up at the inquest anyhow, I take it—and I'm so damned interested in the whole business I just can't leave it alone. But how are you, Nick?"

"I'm O.K. The cut's nothing—I had a bang over the boko, all right, though how it all happened, I admit to being a bit vague. I had the D.D.I.—Divisional Inspector—round this morning—a very nice chap—and he was trying to pin me down. By the time he'd finished with me, I was beginning to wonder if I'd imagined the whole story, so far as being knocked out was concerned." He fingered his scalp tenderly and went on: "The D.D.I. seemed to me to be wondering if I'd been drunk enough to trip over the furniture and start shadow-boxing on my own."

"You should know," rejoined Ian, and Nick Brent snorted.

"I haven't been drunk since V.E. Day," he said, "and if I'd swallowed all the drinks in that bar last night I shouldn't have been drunk—but if it's going to save trouble all round for the cops to think I was tight, well, let them."

"How much could you actually swear to?" asked Ian.

"I walked back to Reeve's house after I'd had a look to see if the chap were dead," said Brent. "I knocked on his door and got no answer: I went round to the back and levered the pantry window open—not that it took much doing. I telephoned the police—and if the constable on duty says I sounded drunk, he's a ruddy liar. All that's perfectly clear—not in dispute. It's the next bit I'm more doubtful about. I remember knocking down my torch and then realising somebody else was in the house. When the chap bawled at me, I thought it was

Reeve—in fact, I was certain it was Reeve. But I admit this: I expected it to be Reeve because I was in his house. After all, if you take liberties getting into another chap's house and then somebody starts creating, it's natural to suppose that it's the householder who's mad at you."

Ian nodded: "That's all perfectly sensible," he said, "and you know in your own mind that another man was in the house, and this man came at you?"

"I know it as sure as I'm sitting here," said Brent. "The only bit I've hedged over is recognising Reeve's voice: I may have been mistaken. I don't say I was, but I may have been."

"Fair enough. Now when you first heard the other bloke, had you heard his footsteps approaching the house? or had you heard a car? Reeve went to Fordings in his car, and it's obvious he'd have driven back home in his car."

"No, I didn't hear a car and I didn't hear footsteps outside the house; my impression was I heard a door open, and I thought it was the front door—and that's damn all I can tell you. All I can say is the whole business is an infernal nuisance—both to Reeve and to me. As you know, I don't care for Michael Reeve or for any of his clan, but I'm prepared to offer him an apology. I broke into his house—though I think I was justified there—and I got him in wrong with the cops by saying he attacked me, when it seems he couldn't have. If he's got a sore head over it—so have I."

Brent reached out for his pipe and added: "Have they got the dead man identified yet? I hear Tom Hudson put his foot in it, claiming to recognise the poor devil."

"Well, no one can blame Tom for that—the constable made the same identification," said Ian. "It's up to the police to sort that one out. Another thing, Nick—you can tell me to keep my trap shut if you want to—but did the police ask you to state if you were alone in the car when you first saw the body?"

Brent looked back at Ian Macbane with a long leisurely stare: "Oddly enough, they didn't ask," he said. "I didn't make any actual statement to that effect, but I certainly gave the impression that I'd only got myself to rely on in reporting the casualty. Are you asking?"

"No. No need to. I know," rejoined Ian. "I saw Dilys Maine this morning—to use your method of suggestion, I happened to meet her on her way back from church. I gave her two pieces of good advice and I offer the same to you—gratis. A: Don't discuss the business with anybody if it's avoidable. B: If the police do ask any questions, don't try telling lies."

"Excellent advice," said Brent. "Did she get home all right?"

"Yes—she got in first by a short head, I gather. Her father turned up unexpectedly about ten minutes or so later."

"Well, I'm damned!" exclaimed Brent. "He'd said he was going to be away for the night."

"Changed his mind and came back," said Ian. "He's a damned peculiar parent, I take it."

Both men were silent for a few moments and then Macbane said: "Look here: you said you were prepared to offer Michael Reeve an apology. If you'd like me to act as envoy, I'm prepared to go along and see him, and express regrets if the climate seems propitious. If, on the other hand, he's out for your blood, I might do a little explaining and cooling down—"

"Go, by all means," agreed Brent, "and I leave it to you to express regrets if you think it's worthwhile. You're in a good position: as a comparative stranger in the district you're not involved in any of the local feuds, and you may even pick up some interesting items by the way."

"I admit that occurred to me," grinned Ian. "While it's

generally considered that Tom Hudson and Foot were mistaken in their identification, it does occur to me that a corpse which resembles the Reeve family sufficiently to be mistaken for one of them may yet be related to the family in some way: and if that's the case, young Michael probably knows more about it than he was prepared to admit."

"Of course he knows," said Brent, "but I don't blame him for refusing to wash the family linen in the police station, so to speak. If you're going over to see Reeve, Ian, why not borrow my motorbike? It's all ready in the garage. I won't suggest you using the car on this trip—you don't want to get identified too closely with me when going to call on Reeve."

"I take you: the sight of your oar might give Reeve the pip before I'd time to utter my diplomatic advances."

"That's it—and come back and stay to supper," called Brent, as Ian set out for the garage.

Chapter VII

I

"Macbane? Oh yes, I think I know your uncle over at Stenfield. Weren't you at the Hunt Ball last night?"

"I was and all."

Ian was much relieved when Michael Reeve's face looked a little less surly, for when Michael had opened his front door his expression was almost thunderous. Taking the bull by the horns, Ian went on:

"Tom Hudson offered to drive me home last night and as it happened we saw the casualty lying across the road just before the police turned up. I was sorry for the poor devil, but I'm also sorry for all the people who've got involved—particularly you, if I may say so: you seem to have had your name taken in vain all round."

"That's about the first civil word I've heard since I got home to find a particularly obtuse cop on the premises," said Michael. "Come in, won't you? I'm interested to know you were the first to find the body—after Brent, if he did find it. Take a pew."

Reeve had led the way to the larger of the two sitting rooms, where there was a good wood fire burning in a pleasant fireplace. Ian guessed at once that the beautiful old furniture had come from Hollydown Manor, and he found the small house much more attractive than he had expected to. As Reeve offered him a cigarette, Ian was able to have a good look at the fellow whom everybody seemed to describe as "a tough." Michael Reeve certainly had quality—something that marked him out from the generality of big young farmers: he had a fine, massive dark head, jutting out well at the back, and clear-cut features: his eyebrows were too heavy, and he tended to scowl, but his eyes were surprisingly clear grey-blue under the black brows. "He makes most of the chaps round here look commonplace," thought Ian, "but he's got a nasty temper, or I'm a Dutchman."

"The whole story struck me as capable of many variations," said Michael. "The police have boiled up this theory that the dead man was possibly killed—or stunned—first, and put in the road second and run over later. Well, apart from the original coshing or what have you, who's to prove that Brent didn't do a little rearranging before he telephoned—or that you and Hudson didn't get busy after Brent came barging along here?"

"Of course, in a sense you're quite right," said Ian cheerfully, determined to take this slightly aggressive opening in his stride. "If I were acting for the defence—"

"For me, for instance," put in Michael, and Ian promptly replied,

"Have it your own way: if you needed defending and I were your counsel, I should point out just the possibilities you've noted. Brent was alone, so there was no corroboration of what he did until he phoned the police; Hudson and I might have been in collaboration—incidentally, as I expect you know, it was Hudson who identified the body as your elder brother Norman."

"So I heard, as did also the moronic constable," said Michael, "thereby concentrating attention on my affairs. Brent started it, by saying he recognised my voice, and other witnesses chimed in."

"Look here, I know just how you feel about this business, and I don't blame you," said Ian, "but don't imagine Brent was difficult for the sake of being difficult. He's practically withdrawn his statement that he recognised your voice: he says—and it's quite reasonable—that when he heard someone yell out to him in your house, he simply assumed that it was you and no one else. And afterwards, when he'd certainly had a bang over the head, he just felt mad—and so should I have done and so would you, in the same circumstances. Actually, Brent's pretty sick about the whole thing and quite definitely sorry if he let you in for anything."

"Very handsome of him," said Reeve, but Ian judged from his tone that Brent was still a sore topic, so he left the apology theme alone for the moment and altered the angle of the conversation.

"Look here, Reeve: I wish you would tell me your own opinion about this affair of Brent being attacked. Can you swallow the theory that a hard-headed ex-Marine Commando got so drunk at a Hunt Ball that he was capable of knocking furniture over and cutting his own head open?"

"No. I can't," said Reeve. "Brent was swiped by somebody, and my own belief is that there was a housebreaker in the place who lost his head and went for him."

"But was there any actual evidence of a housebreaker?" asked Ian eagerly. "Have you missed anything?"

"No, but I'm assuming that the thief was interrupted: he heard Brent get in through the pantry window and thought, 'What ho! we're having company.'"

Ian Macbane began to laugh: "The farther you take this story, the more ludicrous the possibilities it opens up," he said, and Reeve replied:

"Well, I've said all along that it was crackers: thief number one, in the house somewhere, hears thief number two (Brent) get in at the pantry window; number one is intelligently interested, listens to see what number two will do—and hears him telephoning the police. This being against number one's principles, he decides to deal firmly with number two—hence both authoritative voice (recognised as mine) and subsequent violence. And if you tell me that you don't believe a word of it, I suggest you make up a better one."

"There's more sound thinking in your narrative than might be imagined," said Ian, "but tell me this—do you ever have thieves or housebreakers in a district as rural as this one?"

"If you're asking do local characters go thieving, the answer's no," replied Reeve, "but I always remember my father saying the likeliest time for thieves is a time when everybody's known to be out of the house for one reason or another, and the Hunt Ball is an occasion when thieves might count on a good many houses being empty. Of course, the police know all this—it's part of their A.B.C. They probably know where is the likeliest haunt of potential thieves—that old caravan site behind the Rose & Crown on the Greenham Road: but if they don't, it's not my business to tell them. I got so mad with that ruddy Inspector last night I hadn't the least desire to assist him in any way whatsoever."

"The real object in assisting the police is the usual one—it saves trouble all round," said Ian diplomatically. "While I agree with you that the story of Nick Brent and his experiences can be reduced to low farce, there's still that corpse in the offing—and there's no farce about that. Flippancy apart, Reeve, what do you make of it and who do you think it was?"

"As to who it was—search me: some poor devil who had a row with another bloke, and having batted number one over the head a bit too hard, said bloke laid his victim out in the road and hoped some driver might oblige by bumping over the victim: and it happened. It can, you know: there are plenty of chaps driving old cars at night who ought never to drive after dark at all—and it was misty. Oh, it could happen all right: and the driver felt the bump and decided to go on and hope for the best. That's all simple enough: the complication occurred because it was Hunt Ball night and a chap like Brent found the body and decided he'd got to phone the police—and so started all the ballyhoo."

"All right," agreed Macbane. "There were lashings of cars on the road last night—and old cars at that—"

"—and old drivers in charge of them," put in Reeve, "very old, some of them."

"All right again—I'm not disputing any of it," said Macbane, "but we've got two stories: one is about the bloke who was put in the road and later run over, and the other is about Nick Brent being laid out after he'd telephoned for the police. Do you connect the two stories, or do you think they're nothing to do with one another?"

"Oh, you've got to connect them," said Michael. "Melodrama is so foreign to this neighbourhood that I refuse to believe in two unconnected bits of frightfulness. I've suggested there was a gang who decided to cash in on the fact that a number of houses were left empty on the night of the Hunt Ball—that's a situation well known to the police: and at some stage, the thieves fell out. Further instalment already suggested, concluding with Nick Brent climbing in here and phoning the police."

He sat up, stretched, and turned to study Ian's thoughtful face. "Having chewed over every possibility, do you feel satisfied we've got anywhere near the actual facts at all?"

"As to that, I don't know," said Ian, "but you've given me some jolly interesting ideas."

"Well, what's the question you're being so careful not to ask?" demanded Reeve.

Ian Macbane lighted another cigarette and took his time before he answered; then he said, "I'm what might be called an interested outsider. I'm interested in the first case because I was one of those who saw the body *in situ*, and shall presumably be called on to give evidence to that effect. I'm doubly interested because it happens that Nick Brent drove me to Fordings by the lower road—so I can also give evidence that the body wasn't in the road between 8.15 and 8.30. And I know—as the police know—that Brent did not drive over the body and then reverse his car off it: the tracks of his big Heron were perfectly plain, from the spot where he first braked."

"Lucky for him," said Reeve dourly.

"As you say," replied Ian. "Well, after that, Brent walked to your house and phoned the police; up till then his movements are quite clearly established."

"You seem to be a clear-headed sort of bloke," said Michael. "More so than I am, I admit. Do you mind telling me exactly what you mean by Brent's movements being clearly established?"

"Certainly: I mean this. Brent picked me up at Stenfield at 8.0. He drove me to Fordings by the low road—and the body was not then in the road. Brent was in evidence at the ball until he left, about 11.45, and he telephoned the police reporting the body just before 12.30. Now Brent's a friend of mine: not an old friend or a particularly intimate one, but I've reason to like him, and I'm glad the evidence is clear so far as he is concerned. Since the whole story seems capable of boiling up a lot of trouble, I should be glad to say the same thing about you that I do about Brent: as I see it, both of you have been involved, through no fault of your own, in somebody else's crime."

"All on the highest level," said Michael sardonically, and then suddenly his voice altered. "Look here, Macbane: you're not only a clear-headed bloke, you've been damned decent over all this. I admit I got in a bate over things: I found a God-almighty sort of police inspector doing the high and mighty—in spite of the fact that it was my house which had been broken into; I was told that Tom Hudson, who ought to have known better, identified the dead man as my brother Norman—which is a damned lie—and, to cut it short, I come of a family who've been notorious for their filthy tempers and general lack of control. I've tried to live here like a responsible man—and live down some of the stories. You've heard them—everybody in the district's heard them. And I'm fed up."

"Good Lord! don't imagine I can't see all that—I can!" exclaimed Macbane. "When I said I was sorry about all this—and tried to convey that Brent is sorry, too—I was admitting that you'd had enough to make you see red. It's enough to make any chap fed up. And there's this to it: you demanded: 'What's the question you were so careful not to ask?' You've only got to answer one question to get the whole thing tidied up from your point of view."

"And what's the question?"

"Where were you exactly at half past twelve, when Brent was in your house, when he thought he heard your voice, after he'd telephoned?"

II

"Where was I?" echoed Reeve. "I was in my own car, in Fordings—parked well away from peeping Toms: and I wasn't alone. And I am not going to say who was in the car with me, or how long we were there. And that is that. If the police make up their minds that I was in this house, and that I knocked Brent down and then knocked the furniture on top of him—well, they'll have to. I'm not calling a witness to prove they're wrong."

"I see," replied Ian. "It seems a pity—but you've got to make your own decisions."

"Like Brent," said Reeve unexpectedly. "There are occasions when a man has to face his own troubles, without calling in corroborative evidence to please the police."

Again Ian said: "I see." And he did see—and he knew that Reeve had made his point. Reeve knew that Nick Brent had driven Dilys home—or part of the way home, and was keeping quiet about it.

"Not that Brent's got anything to worry about," went on Michael. "He doesn't enjoy the reputation of being a member of a family who're capable of anything."

Ian looked across at the big dark fellow opposite to him and thought: "Well, why not risk it? If he's ever likely to talk, it's now, when he's met me halfway, and if he kicks me out, who cares?"

Aloud he said: "Look here, Reeve: you're quite capable of telling me to mind my own ruddy business if you think I'm trespassing on what's not my affair, but it's you who keeps on bringing your family into it, as though the fact of being named Reeve is halfway towards being suspected by the police."

"It's probably more than halfway," said Michael. "You see, the police have had two unsolved mysteries connected with the Reeve family and they've never forgotten it. One was several years ago when a man's body was found in the coppice which borders the manor garden—apparently, he was a vagrant and he died of exposure, but they never found out who he was or what he was doing there—and more recently, my sister disappeared. You'll have heard about that—everybody in the county heard about it. Well, again, the police discovered nothing—absolutely nothing—and they were sore about it. So when that hulking great fool Tom Hudson says that the dead man you found on the road was my brother Norman, and when Brent says I bashed him over the head and left him for dead, it's not surprising the police concentrate their attention in my direction. More especially as I haven't a ghost of an alibi for the time when the bloke on the road was killed."

"Do they know the exact time he was killed?" put in Ian.

"No, of course they don't. It's never possible to fix the time of death accurately unless they examine the body quite shortly after death—you must know that. They take general probabilities, including temperature and degree of rigor. And the probability is that this chap died five to six hours before the sawbones examined him, that is, between 7.30 and 8.30 in the evening."

"Well, if it was being run over that finished him off, it looks as though he were killed quite soon after Brent and I drove past the spot where he was found," said Ian.

"Quite—and there were two of you to corroborate each

other's doings, but I was by myself from 6.30 to 8.30, in the cowshed most of the time—no corroboration at all. In fact it's a damned sticky wicket."

"Well, I don't see that you've got much to bother about to date," said Ian, "no more than any of the rest of us—Tom Hudson and myself—and Brent, for that matter: we all used the same road, and, as you pointed out to start with, any one of us could have monkeyed with the evidence. But that sort of statement's no good to the police: they've got to have copper-bottomed factual evidence before they can think of making a charge, even."

"They're doing their damnedest to get it," said Michael—gloomily. "They had a couple of C.I.D. blokes more or less crawling along this road this morning, making notes of tyre tracks. They certainly found plenty of mine: I've got an outlying pasture up the road—the last field near the signpost—and I always take the car up there when I go to look the cattle over."

"Incidentally, where was your car standing while you were busy in the cowshed yesterday evening?"

"Outside, on the verge, where it generally is," replied Michael. "You're beginning to use your wits, laddy—like our cops. My car's next door to being a farm implement; I use it for everything, and it stands where it's wanted, on the verge outside the yard gate, and nine times out of ten I leave the ignition key in it—save's fiddling, and car thieves don't function round here."

"Well, damn all, you do ask for trouble!" exclaimed Ian. "It means that anyone knowing your habits could have counted on finding your car all ready for use, as they say, and used it for the dirty work up yonder and put it back before you'd even missed it."

"Quite: didn't I tell you it was a sticky wicket?" rejoined Michael.

"Did you notice if the engine was warm—if it started up easily?"

"Of course it started up easily: I'd been using the car all day, moving stuff on the trailer. I lent my tractor to Jim Hoyle at the Rose & Crown to shift some timber. Incidentally, the car was standing outside here when you and Brent passed, or it ought to have been. Did you see it?"

"No—but that doesn't mean it wasn't there," replied Ian. "It was misty and the windscreen was fogged up inside. But Nick may have seen it—I know he said that was your place, with the new fencing beyond. Hullo—you've got a visitor. Who's the lovely?"

"Oh, Lord—that's Betty Hoyle, from the Rose & Crown. Her mother comes and 'does for me'—or doesn't, as the case may be. She didn't turn up today, so I suppose Betty's come to make excuses."

Michael got up, adding, "I'd better shove her off, and then I'll have to go and see to the stock. It was decent of you to come, Macbane. Come in again sometime—how long are you staying?"

"Oh, a day or two—until the inquest, anyway. I'll certainly come and have a jaw after that—we may hear a few facts to straighten things up."

Michael went to the door, and as Ian got into his coat he heard Betty Hoyle saying:

"Oh, Mr. Reeve, Mum's that sorry she let you down, but she was out late last night, helping in the bar at the ball, and she's sent you some pasties for supper, and if you'd like me to clean up in the kitchen, I'd be glad to."

"Don't bother about any cleaning up—it can wait," said

Michael. "It was decent of you to walk over, Betty, it's quite a step. If you ask Mr. Macbane, he might give you a lift back on his pillion seat."

"Ooh…that'd be lovely, I do hate walking," she exclaimed. "It'd be ever so kind if you would," she added to Ian.

Betty was a dark, high-coloured wench, "bold and blowsy" was Ian's reaction, but he was a good-natured fellow.

"O.K.—provided you're used to it and promise not to fall off," he said.

"I've never fallen off yet," she grinned, and Ian asked:

"Which way did you come, down the road from the pointer?"

"Not me: I came by the bridle path—cuts off half the distance."

"Oh, does it? That's a new one on me. Would the bike do it that way?"

"Sure, it's not a bad path," she rejoined. "The gentleman who lived here before Mr. Reeve came, he always came to our place on his motorbike by the bridle path: it's seven miles return by road, and we're the nearest local."

"Sounds a thirsty farmhouse," rejoined Ian, grinning back at Michael. "See you again before I leave," he said and wheeled his bike out on to the road.

"Ooh…it's Commander Brent's motorbike," shrilled Betty. "It's posh, isn't it? I've always wanted a ride on this one, but the Commander, he's too highty-tighty. He and Dad are like dog and cat, trade jealousy, I call it."

"How do you know it's Brent's machine?" asked Ian.

"Oh, I notice things like that, I'm mad on motors. That's a lovely car he's got, the Wild Heron—smartest car for miles: he gave you a lift last night, didn't he?"

"Noticing girl, aren't you?" said Ian. "It's along at the back, our path, isn't it? Hold tight, we're off."

There was no opportunity for conversation as the machine roared up the bridle path: Betty held on like a limpet—she was evidently experienced in this manner of transport, and experienced in other ways besides, thought Ian. When they reached Betty's home—a cheerful-looking pub—Betty promptly said:

"Thanks ever so—and won't you come in and have one on the house? It's not opening time yet, and Dad'll be no end pleased to have company."

"Well, thanks a lot—I don't mind if I do," said Ian.

Chapter VIII

I

"Drat the thing," said Alice Ridley, as the plate she was wiping slipped from her hands and crashed in pieces on the stone flags of the kitchen floor. "I knew it'd happen—today's one of those days."

"Never mind," said Dilys, "it's only a kitchen plate, not one of the good ones. Put the pieces under the ashes in the dustbin, Alice, and no one will ever know."

"Taking to hiding things at my age, it isn't seemly," said Alice, "but what's coming over your dad these days, I just don't know—he gets more and more crotchety. If it weren't for you, Miss Dilys, I'd answer him back and be done with it, and walk out afterwards."

"Oh, don't do that, Alice," begged Dilys. "I can't think what I should do without you."

"That's all very fine and large," retorted stout Alice, "but it's getting beyond a joke. And today's been one long worry: I dared not open my mouth in case I let out something I shouldn't, and today of all days, the master's been in and out of the kitchen, chatting—a thing he's not given to. Really, I sometimes wonder if he's going queer in the head. You never know where you are with him."

"Perhaps he's falling in love with you, Alice," suggested Dilys mischievously. "I wish he would. You'd make a wonderful wife."

"The things you do say!" scoffed Alice. "Not that he mightn't go farther and fare worse, but not me! I want a little peace as I get older, not to be worried from morning till night. But I can't make him out, and that's flat. He comes into the kitchen while you were at church this morning—if you *were* at church," she added severely, and then hurried on, "and there was I basting the joint in that sinful old oven and he's got to tell me about how his car broke down coming from the station last night."

"That car's past praying for," said Dilys. "Daddy was in the garage the whole afternoon messing around with the carburettor or whatever it was."

"That's as may be, Miss Dilys, but if he came back from Southampton by train, same as he said, having parked his car at the back of Fordings station, like he always does, how did he get home? I know the road was blocked over Cookbourne Bridge, so he couldn't have come that way, and I as near as said so, and that'd have been a pretty kettle of fish after I'd told him how I'd spent the evening poulticing Mary Huggins's chest."

"I expect he crossed the bridge before the collision happened," said Dilys. "He was quite near home when the car broke down."

"I just don't understand it," said Alice, polishing the silver teapot vigorously. She and Dilys were washing up the tea things. "If he came back from Southampton by the last train, he'd have had to change at the junction and take the train I was on," went on Alice. "Makes me cold all over to think of it," she said. "He might have seen me—and then there'd've been trouble. We can't go on the way we've been doing lately, dearie: it's dreadful. He's making liars of both of us."

"Well, it's terribly difficult," said Dilys. "It's only fair you should have a day off sometimes, Alice, and get up to London if you want to."

"So it is, dearie: and it's only fair you should have some fun sometimes, and go to dances like other girls. Not that I'd have said anything—least said soonest mended—but the way we're heading isn't right, not for either of us, telling fibs to save ourselves trouble."

"Whatever do you mean?" cried Dilys.

"Now don't go getting worked up, dearie," said Alice. "I know you meant it for the best, so that I could say 'I don't know anything about it' if the master turned on me: but that net stuff you made your frock of—tulle they call it, don't they?—the little cuttings and bits and pieces cling to the mats and that just like teasels: I can't tell you how long I spent cleaning them all out of the way."

"Oh, Alice—and I thought I was so careful."

"So you were, dearie, but dressmaking's like that—the snippets or bits of thread and all that get into everything. Some people mightn't notice, but I've done too much dress-making not to know what was going on, and I sweep the carpets on my hands and knees, as you know, your dad not holding with Hoovers or suchlike. And if you were making yourself a new dance frock, well it must have been because you were going to a dance, mustn't it?"

"And you thought all that out for yourself and never asked me a single question!" exclaimed Dilys, and Alice went on:

"Nothing like knowing nothing when there's likely to be trouble—and I've never held with the way your dad keeps you away from the fun other girls have," said Alice, "and you know I couldn't help noticing how you never said a word about the Hunt Ball—never said, 'Oh, I do wish I could go…'"

"Oh, Alice, what an ass you must think me," said Dilys. "I did go—now you know. Commander Brent gave me a ticket."

"I thought as much, when he came over to see your geese," said Alice complacently, "and it was because I was so sure you'd be going, I took my day in London—saved you doing any pretending and saved me knowing what you were up to. And it seems to me we're both out of the frying pan and into the fire, because if Commander Brent drove you back, and I've no doubt he did, a fair old time you must have had of it. Not that I'm asking questions if you don't want to tell me."

Dilys carried the tray of clean china over to the dresser and then sat down at the kitchen table.

"Alice, I'll be thankful to tell you! I'm so worried I just don't know how to bear it. It all looked so easy, and now I seem to have got into one big muddle."

Alice took off her apron and then went and sat down in a chair by the fire. "Well, if that's the way of it, you tell me what happened and we'll think it out together. Seeing the sort of muddle we've all got into, it'll be better if you and me get our bits straight—and now's a good time, because your dad's driven into Fordings to post his letters at the general, and he can't go there and back much under an hour, not in that car, he can't."

Dilys told Alice about her drive back from Fordings the previous night, about seeing the body in the road, and how she had run home by the field path after Nick Brent had said it would be better for her to do that.

"Well, that was decent of him, trying to keep you out of trouble," said Alice. "It all depends if there was anybody about who saw you get in and out of his car."

"I'm certain nobody saw me get in the car at Fordings—and there wasn't anybody about when I got out of the car and ran home."

"Let's hope there wasn't," said Alice, "but with such goings-on as there were last night, well, you just never know. There's this story of the Commander being attacked by somebody—and who that was, goodness alone knows—unless it was that Michael Reeve had had a drop too much."

"Oh, Alice, that isn't fair," protested Dilys. "Michael never gets drunk, and anyway, he stayed right to the end of the ball. Jennifer was there, and she saw him."

"Never's a long time," said Alice, "but let's leave that and get the times sorted out. When did you leave Fordings?"

"A quarter to twelve—I knew your train didn't get in till midnight, so I thought that'd give me plenty of time to get in before you did."

"So it should have," agreed Alice. "Now I reckon it took the best part of half an hour to drive to Flusher's gate, where you had to get out, and all of twenty minutes running over the fields—anyway, call it an hour by the time you got your frock off and that. I don't know exactly what time it was I telephoned, but if we say soon after one o'clock, we shan't be far out. When did you hear the master come in?"

"While I was still talking to you, Alice—I hadn't hung the receiver up."

"Well, it beats me altogether," said Alice. "He said he went to Southampton by train, and if he did that he must have got back to Fordings by the midnight—it's the only late train there is that stops at the junction. And yet by the time my taxi man found the road was blocked and I got out and telephoned to you, the master had got back home—with a breakdown and all."

"Then he either came back by an earlier train, or else drove home by a different road," said Dilys, and Alice sniffed.

"And which road would that be? We know he didn't come by the low road."

Dilys sat and stared at the stout practical soul for a moment, and as their eyes met they each recognised a dawning apprehension in the other's gaze. Then Dilys said:

"He could have come by the Greenham Road, past the Rose & Crown—he must have done that, unless he arrived by an earlier train."

"The only other evening train from Southampton gets into Fordings at 9.0. I've looked and I know," said Alice, "and you say he got home after 1.0. Doesn't sound very likely to me."

"No. I suppose it doesn't," said Dilys, "so the only other thing he could have done was to come by the Greenham Road—and why he did that, goodness knows: it's the longest way of all if you drive from the station."

Alice suddenly realised that the expression in Dilys's eyes had changed from puzzlement to real fear, and the older woman said quickly:

"Don't look like that, dearie: there's nothing to be frightened about. It's queer and I can't make sense of it, but there's nothing to look like that over."

"But Alice, I *am* frightened. I know there was something queer last night: Daddy said something about it being late for you to telephone and I said, 'Is it? I don't know what time it is'—as though I'd just been woken up, and a little later he said, 'It's close on midnight'—and it must have been nearly half past one. He *must* have known, Alice, and he wanted me to believe he'd got in by twelve o'clock."

"Well, it's a puzzle and no mistake," said Alice. "Seems to me he *must* have come by the Greenham Road: he couldn't have got past on Cookbourne Bridge, and come to think of it, if he got home after one o'clock, he couldn't have come by the low road because they'd got police and goodness knows what out there." She paused and then added: "Those three roads and the river—they're a bit like fingers: there's the main road, across the river, and the river itself, then the low road and farthest from us is the Greenham Road: they're all parallel, you might say, and they all run into Fordings, and they're all connected up our end by the Brambledene Road which runs down to Cookbourne Bridge."

"What's that got to do with it?" asked Dilys.

"It's only that I'm trying to puzzle it out, dearie. If your dad drove home by the Greenham Road, past that pub he's so often complained of, he'd have had to turn right to get home and come by the Brambledene Road, which is the one you'd have come by if all had been well: and I reckon by that time the police were on that road, going to see about that accident you nearly got tied up in."

"Yes, but why did Daddy want me to believe it was only twelve o'clock?" burst out Dilys. "It just doesn't make sense."

"Well, I don't know, I'm sure," said Alice. "He's all against late hours, and maybe he wasn't anxious for you to know just how late he was."

"Alice, were there many people on that train you came by when it got into Fordings?"

"That there weren't: January's not a popular month for going up to town and coming back by the midnight."

"If Daddy had been on that train, wouldn't you have seen him at Fordings station?"

"Well, I might and I mightn't. I wasn't looking out for anybody—only for the taxi I'd ordered. Peak, it was, and he drew up by the platform and I just jumped in and thought, 'Thank goodness, I'm as good as home.' And he doesn't waste any time, Peak doesn't. That's a fast car he's got." Alice sat and thought for a moment; then she said, "I've often thought it was time you spoke up, for yourself, dearie. You've carried it too far, always doing the dutiful with your dad. I've been just as bad—anything for a quiet life and no backbiting. And this time we seem to have got into a fair old muddle—but he has, too. Seems to me, if he gets awkward, you and I can be awkward, too."

"Oh, I hate quarrelling and arguing," cried Dilys.

"I know you do, dearie—but you've got to make a stand sometime, and if you've any sense you'll make up your mind and settle down in a home of your own. And do for goodness' sake see to it that you don't let your husband bully you, all for the sake of peace and quietness."

Dilys sat silent, her face cupped in her hands, and Alice Ridley went on: "If you'll listen to a word of advice from me, you won't marry any of them young lads who've got a long way to go before they can make a home for a wife. You marry Commander Brent, dearie. He's got something behind him— and a lovely home which only needs a wife to make it just so."

"He hasn't asked me," said Dilys weakly, and Alice snorted.

"He'll ask you fast enough if you give him the chance and you know it. Make up your mind, do... Goodness, who's that? We don't often have company on a Sunday evening, coming to the kitchen door, too."

II

"I'm sorry if I've come to the wrong door, but it was all dark on the other side of the house," said a man's voice. It was a nice voice, thought Dilys, but she had no idea who the visitor was.

"Is Mr. Maine at home?" he went on.

"No, sir. The master's out: he's driven into Fordings to catch the post and when he'll be back I can't rightly say. If you'd leave your name, I'll tell him when he gets back."

"My name's Waring—Inspector Waring, County C.I.D. We are investigating this case of the man who was run down on the lower road last night, and I'm trying to find out which local cars were on the road late in the evening. Could I come in for a moment? I'm sorry to bother you, but I won't keep you long."

"Very good—step in, sir," said Alice sedately, and Dilys had time to marvel at the matter-of-fact calmness of the older woman's voice.

The first man to enter was a well-set-up, healthy-looking fellow with a cheerful face which was still a young man's face; his dark eyes were almost merry, his mouth wide and good-tempered; he wore a goodish-looking Burberry and no hat. Behind him came a stolider fellow, mousey-coloured and commonplace, but somehow very deliberate.

Dilys stood up and faced Waring. "I'm sorry that my father is out," she said. "You really want to see him, don't you—if you want to learn his route last night."

Meeting his eyes, Dilys was aware of the quickened interest in them, one swift flicker of surprise and response before he replied, very correctly:

"Miss Maine? Yes, I want to see your father if he was on the road last night, but it's possible you may be able to answer the first question—and that renders the rest of the questionnaire redundant."

"Won't you sit down?" she said evenly, as he drew a notebook from his pocket.

"Thanks very much. Here is my warrant—just in case you think this visit may be a confidence trick."

Dilys glanced at the police card in his wallet. "I shouldn't know if the card itself were a confidence trick," she replied, "but I'm not worried about it. What is it you want to know?"

She sat down at the kitchen table, and Alice sat down by the fire and said:

"Well, I never did. Two policemen in my kitchen on a Sunday evening—I don't know what we're coming to."

"Oh, don't take such a gloomy view of us, ma'am," replied Waring, and this time Dilys could see the merriment in his eyes—he certainly wasn't one of the policemen who believed in bullying, she meditated.

"We're a very ordinary lot of chaps," went on Waring. "Personally I think it'd be a good idea if we did more in the public relations line—police and public getting together, to develop more confidence on both sides."

"Get along with you!" said Alice. "If you set up as ordinary human beings, nobody's going to be frightened of policemen any more. Why, the first thing I can remember is my mother telling me, 'I'll give you to a policeman,' because I stole the apples."

"Oh, but we don't want people to be frightened in that sort of way any longer," replied Waring, flashing a smile at Dilys. "It's bad psychology," he went on blithely. "When we call on good law-abiding people like you, we want you to feel 'That's fine.' You see, we've learnt by now that the frightened witness isn't a good witness."

"Well, maybe there's something in it," said Alice comfortably, and Waring turned to Dilys.

"I wonder if you can answer the operative question," he said. "Do you know what time Mr. Maine got back last night?"

"I'm afraid I don't know exactly," she answered slowly. "You'll have to ask him. I heard him come in—it was after I'd gone to bed—and I came down and asked him if he'd like a hot drink and he said no, it was very late. I think he said it was nearly twelve o'clock, but I don't really know."

Waring turned to Alice, his bright eyes twinkling. "Did you hear Mr. Maine come in?" he asked, and Alice groaned.

"Dear oh dear," she said. "I knew it'd come out. It's all very well for you to talk about 'public relations' or whatever it was and not being frightened of policemen, and the one time I'm out when I ought to be in, blest if a policeman doesn't come along and ask me what I was doing."

"That seems just too bad," he said, and Alice went on:

"I'd say it is. Seems to me the best thing I can do is to tell you all about it and hope you don't give me away. Maybe I could have got away with it if I'd just said, 'No. I didn't hear him,' but I suppose you'd have gone on asking questions. You see, the master was out all yesterday, so I took the day off. Not that the day wasn't due to me—one day a month, by arrangement, that's what's due."

"Very reasonable," said Waring.

"Well, it seemed to fit and Miss Dilys agreed," said Alice. Dilys was listening intently: she had a feeling that Alice was talking deliberately, drawing Waring's attention to herself, so that questions about Dilys shouldn't arise.

"I went up to London and came back by the late train," went on Alice, "and then I found I couldn't get home because the road over Cookbourne Bridge was blocked by that smash, and not fancying a midnight walk I went and stayed with my friend, Miss Huggins, for the night, and came home on the milk lorry at seven in the morning. And if you think I'm given to coming home with the milk, well, you're wrong. It's the first time it's happened and it's not going to happen again. So I can't tell you what time the master came home because I wasn't home myself. I knew Miss Dilys wouldn't tell on me—and she didn't."

"Of course I didn't," said Dilys. "I told my father that Alice had stayed with her friend, who was poorly. You see, my father's very strict," she added, "and he doesn't approve of going up to London and coming back by the midnight train."

Still with that same amused air, Waring studied the girl's serious, lovely face, and then Alice put in:

"You might as well know the rest: the master had said he was going to stop in Southampton for the night, and he came back home instead—midnight, or whenever it was—and me and Miss Dilys, well, we tried to save trouble. And see what it's led to!" concluded Alice, in a fine rhetorical outburst. "Policemen asking me questions in my own kitchen. And if you go and tell him all I've told you, well, I don't think much of your public relations or whatever you call it."

"It's not part of our duty to pass on information given to us in confidence when it's not relevant to our enquiry," said Waring solemnly, though his eyes were still amused as he studied Alice's wholesome, buxom face. "I take it that as Cookbourne Bridge was the cause of your trouble, ma'am, you came from Fordings station by the main road on the other side of the river?"

"Of course I did," she replied. "No driver in his senses chooses the roads this side of the river, nasty narrow country lanes they are."

"Well, it's the roads this side of the river which interest us, ma'am," went on Waring. "What we are trying to do is to check up on all local drivers who were out last evening, hoping to get reports of any vehicles noticed in the district. It isn't too easy, because so many drivers were in Fordings at the Hunt Ball and didn't return until much later."

"Well, you can be sure of one thing—the master didn't go to no Hunt Balls," said Alice firmly. "He was out on business—Southampton he said he was going to, didn't he, Miss Dilys? But as to how and when he came back, you'll have to ask him."

"I think he said he had a breakdown or something—or perhaps it was just the car wouldn't pull—it's an awful old car," Dilys added. "It's pre-war and it's always going wrong, but Daddy won't change it."

"Some men get attached to their old cars," rejoined Waring. "Well, I won't bother you any more now. Perhaps you will tell Mr. Maine I'll call and see him in the morning."

"I will," replied Dilys, and smiled straight at the Inspector. "I'm sorry we haven't been very helpful—and we do hope you won't have to enter poor Alice's night out as evidence."

"Well!" exclaimed Alice, when Waring had left. "When he mentioned the Hunt Ball I thought we were for it—I just waited for him to ask you if you hadn't been there, too. Beats me why he didn't."

"Because you put him off, Alice dear, telling him about your night out."

"That? Lor, if he wants to ask questions about me, he's welcome and much good may it do him. But one thing I never would have thought—that the police might get on the track of your goings-on when they came to ask about your dad's."

"Alice—I hate it. I'm frightened."

"Bless you, dearie, no need to be frightened. You've done nothing wrong—and I hope your dad hasn't, neither."

Chapter IX

I

"It's a teaser, sir," said Waring, but he said it cheerfully. Waring was an optimistic extrovert, and it took a lot to get him down. Inspector Thorn (the Divisional District Inspector, County C.I.D., an officer of standing) glanced from Waring to Turner—the latter a very ordinary police officer, who would like to have been in the C.I.D. and considered himself wasted in the humdrum of police work. In reply to Thorn's questioning glance, Turner said:

"As I see it, sir, the case has a common-sense solution. I think it probable in the highest degree that Michael Reeve killed the deceased, or stunned him, put the body in the road and ran his own car over it. While we cannot prove beyond doubt that the wheel tracks on the deceased's clothing were made by the tyres of Reeve's car, there is the strongest possibility that this is the case."

"I quite agree," put in Waring, as cheerful as a cock sparrow. "In fact, I'm dead certain that it *was* Reeve's car, but that's quite a different thing from saying that it was Reeve who drove the car. Reeve habitually leaves his car standing on the verge by his gate, and as often as not leaves his ignition key in the slot. And in spite of all that, I'm quite sure he isn't any sort of fool."

Thorn turned his head slowly (reminding Waring of "the eldest oyster" in "The Walrus and the Carpenter"). "And so?" he enquired.

"Well, sir," went on Waring, "let's assume that Reeve did the original coshing—on his own premises, perhaps. Do we also assume that he then moved the bloke a quarter of a mile up the road, ran his own car over the body and went home? It doesn't make any sort of sense to me. The deceased has sufficient facial resemblance to the Reeve family to be mistaken for one of them: if Michael killed him, would he have been fool enough to leave him in the road, close to his own house, with the Ensign's wheel tracks on the clothing? He could have buried the body, put it under the dungheap or the silage, or bunged it in a barn, or driven to the cliffs and flung it over. If Michael did this job, he must be weak in the head—and I don't think he is."

He paused a moment and then added: "It must have seemed a gift to someone—person or persons unknown. The deceased resembles the Reeve family—in all probability was a member of the Reeve family; then leave his body close to the residence of the only surviving Reeve—being Michael—finish the job with Michael's car and Bob's your uncle. Moreover, the ensuing moves could have been calculated with quite a degree of probability."

"Go on," said Thorn, and Waring took up his story, quite indifferent to Turner's glum, sceptical face.

"On most nights of the year, particularly in the winter,

no one would have driven along that road—the low road, as they call it—at all. It seems to be very little used at night in the ordinary way. The body would have been discovered by the postman, or the milk-lorry driver, next morning. But Saturday was the night of the Hunt Ball and all the farmers were out—also fellows like Brent and Macbane. It was all Lombard Street to a china orange the body would be found, and a cert that Michael Reeve would be on the road himself. Moreover, seeing where the body was found, it could be argued that if a law-abiding man found the body, that man would probably go back to Reeve's house to telephone the police, because it's the nearest place to go. But if the man who happened on the body had been a bit tight, he might have run over it again before he even saw it—which would have made things even more mixed than they are."

Thorn nodded. "I admit the story suggests various solutions," he said, "and I think you've got a point when you say that if a law-abiding man found the body, that man would have gone to Reeve's house to telephone—as Brent did."

"And a reception committee waited in the house to see what happened and knocked the law-abiding bloke over the head, just to make it more confusing," added Waring blithely.

Turner made a sound of protest, and the D.D.I. turned to him with a curt "Well?"

"As I see it, sir, Waring is using his imagination too freely. Countryfolk, particularly farmers, aren't imaginative. I don't believe for a moment that any farmer worked out this elaboration of ways and means and times and seasons."

"And I just don't believe in assuming that other men are so much more foolish than I should be myself in given circumstances," said Waring. "If Reeve did this thing, then he behaved like a fool, and I don't think he is a fool. He may now be a smallholder, and not a resident at Hollydown Manor, but he's an educated chap and a pretty competent one."

"We're not getting any further arguing about Michael Reeve's qualifications," said Thorn drily. "What we need, first and foremost, is to get the deceased identified." He glanced at Turner. "Aren't there any other members of the Reeve family who can be called in for that purpose?"

"No, sir. The older generation have all died. The daughter, Rosemary, disappeared last year and is still listed as a missing person; Norman Reeve went overseas and nobody has seen him for ten years, and the remaining brother is in Hong Kong. It is still my belief that the deceased *is* Norman."

"It's no use having beliefs about a man you've never seen unless you can bring reliable witnesses to swear to identity," said Thorn tartly. "Both your original witnesses—Hudson and Constable Foot—have gone back on their original opinions."

"I agree that our first job is to get the deceased identified," put in Waring. "I've been putting in a bit of time with the local gossips, particularly some of the old chaps who were employed on the Hollydown estate while Norman Reeve was still living at the manor. None of them think the deceased is Norman, but I got a suggestion out of an old boy named Ben Grubb, who was once employed in the Hollydown stables. He says he believes the deceased was the son of the old Squire, born out of wedlock, and that he once lived on the caravan site behind the Rose & Crown."

"That doesn't get us much farther," said Turner gloomily. "There used to be an encampment of caravans on that bit of rough land behind the Rose & Crown, but they were evicted years ago. There are caravans there now, but they are used by holidaymakers who pay rent to Hoyle—the landlord. None of them has ever heard of the Reeves."

"Quite true," agreed Waring, "but Hoyle himself has lived at that pub all his life." He paused a moment and then added: "I'm interested in Hoyle. You see there's an old bridle path connecting Hoyle's pub with Reeve's land—the path is a shortcut from the Greenham Road to the lower road. It's only a matter of a mile across the fields."

Again the D.D.I. turned his ponderous head and put in his monosyllable: "Well?"

"There seems to be a link," said Waring meditatively. "Ben Grubb's suggestion gives the caravan site as the birthplace of the deceased; Rosemary Reeve, when last seen, was walking towards the cliffs behind the Rose & Crown—it's rough gorse land, and she often walked that way with her dogs. She was crazy over her dogs, but that day she didn't take them with her. Finally, Michael Reeve's house is only a mile or so from the Rose & Crown if you take the bridle path. And any big tough could shift a corpse for a mile if he needed to."

Thorn grunted, and Turner looked exasperated. Still quite casually, Waring went on: "Mrs. Hoyle went to the Hunt Ball—she helped in the bar. Miss Hoyle helped in the ladies' cloakroom. Mr. Hoyle stayed at home to look after his own bar, though I gather there wasn't much custom, and Bob the potman served the locals. I don't know, but I have a feeling they might repay a little concentrated attention. And there's Mr. Maine, of Foxlea Mill," added Waring.

"Where does he come in?" enquired Thorn.

"I don't know," admitted Waring, "but he was out in his car that evening and got home around midnight—though everybody seems very vague about the time. He says he drove over Cookbourne Bridge before it was blocked by the smash and had a breakdown later. I only mention him because he's been at loggerheads with Jim Hoyle—some little argument about Hoyle being open after hours and allowing gaming on the premises. And Maine's daughter, who is a poem to look at, was in a flap about something: very quiet and nicely behaved, but definitely in a flap. I wouldn't mind guessing she was vague about her father's return because she wasn't there when he did return."

Thorn raised his dark eyebrows, looking more saturnine than ever. "I'm accustomed to allowing you a bit of licence, Waring, because I've often found that some of your disconnected statements do lead somewhere, but I think you might be more explicit on this occasion."

"Sorry, sir," said Waring, with his endearing grin. "It's a sort of mixed grill—all these people, associated somehow, hiding something, worrying about something. I told you I was interested in the Rose & Crown lot because the place is only a mile or so away from Reeve's place by the bridle path. Foxlea Mill—the Maines' place—is also about a mile from Reeve's place, to the north of it, by the field path. Come to think of it, these two paths are probably sections of the same ancient bridle path, leading from the mill to the sea. And if Miss Maine and Michael Reeve don't sometimes meet on those field paths—well, it's just too bad. You see, there's a connection, sir, and my local gossips have it that Maine and Reeve are at loggerheads."

The D.D.I. listened to young Waring's rambling discourse with a patience that Turner found incredible, but Thorn knew from experience that Waring had a lively awareness which enabled him to get the "feel" of contacts in a case in a manner which had often borne unexpected and valuable fruit. Instead of the curt dismissal which Turner expected, Thorn meditated over Waring's observations and then said:

"You certainly have a knack for picking up odds and ends

of information quickly, Waring. The next step is to correlate them—if they are susceptible to the process."

"Yes, sir: the point is that the truth is somewhere if we can only sort it out—one of them, or perhaps more than one—Reeve, Maine, Hoyle, Hudson, Brent, Macbane, their girlfriends, wives, daughters, families, and dwelling houses—the truth is there somewhere, or the facts which will lead us to the truth. It's in their locality."

With a twitch of his shaggy dark brows, Thorn turned to Inspector Turner. "Any comment, Turner?"

"Well, sir, I've heard a bit about what's called intuition, or psychic bids as some of the intelligentsia say, but I haven't much patience with the method. To me, police work must be based on facts, the sort of facts which can be sworn to in court and stand up to cross-examination."

"O.K.," said Waring cheerfully, "and how many such facts have you got?"

Turner hesitated, and Waring cut in again, quick and purposeful: "Brent rang you up and reported finding the body that you can swear to; but was there anybody to corroborate Brent's statement about finding the body? Brent said he heard Reeve's voice after he telephoned—or *thought* he heard it. Brent was attacked—but can you or he swear to his assailant? Hudson and Macbane were by the body when you arrived—you can swear to that. Can you swear to what they were doing before you arrived?"

"All that is quite true," put in Thorn. "You have the body of an unknown man, dressed in labourer's clothes, with nothing in his pockets to identify him. The problems are: who is the dead man, who killed him, who removed any papers or identifying marks, and finally—where was he killed?" He looked at his two officers with a slightly sardonic gaze and then added: "I suggest that Turner should continue checking up on the times that drivers left the Prince's Hall and the times they arrived home, and Waring can follow up his ideas about Hoyle and Maine and the possibilities of the bridle path and the field path between the Rose & Crown and the mill." He turned to Turner again, adding: "Try to check Reeve's movements, and find out exactly when Hudson and Macbane left the Prince's Hall, also when Brent himself left."

"And why he left so early," murmured Waring. Thorn turned again and studied the lively face of the younger man.

"Do we really know that Brent was alone when he found the body?" asked Waring.

"If there had been a witness, Brent would have been glad enough to produce one," retorted Turner. "He had a witness for the outward journey: it's plain enough that Brent is clear of suspicion from the time he picked up Macbane until the time he discovered the body in the road. If he had a witness to that I'm not prepared to believe he wouldn't have produced him or her in order to clear himself of any suspicion at all."

"O.K. If you're satisfied," said Waring, and Thorn cut in again.

"I'm not belittling ideas, Waring, but ideas must be subject to the discipline of proof. Since you have raised this notion of a possible connection between the Hoyles at the inn, via the bridle path to the lower road and on by the field path to the mill, I'm prepared to let you have the time to collect evidence—if it exists—to support your idea. Report again this evening, and we'll consider both your findings."

After Waring and Turner had left him, the D.D.I. sat and meditated for a moment. He was thinking about the two officers: Turner, routine-minded, concrete, his feet firmly on the ground, his method based on the ascertainable details of police evidence—times, places, prints, and all the rest of it: the methods which, admittedly, had been the foundation of police work since the force was inaugurated. And Waring— imaginative, aware, sensitive: able, by some odd quirk of his lively mind, to obtain confidences and acquire impressions which were beyond Turner's scope. Thorn had to admit, from past experience, that Waring had a lively and unexpectedly sound judgement over people of whom his observation had been of the slightest: when Waring had said, "Seems to me there's a connection somehow; so-and-so was being cagey..." it had often proved that there was a connection, and later in the case Waring had produced some unexpected observation which showed that his logical powers had not been in abeyance while he soaked in awareness of human nature.

"Makes you wonder what *is* the basis of detection, after all," pondered Thorn. "Timetables or human nature? After all, criminals are human and maybe young Waring's getting back to basic detection. They ought to make a good pair, Turner with his conscientious routine, Waring with his awareness of humanity."

But it was not Turner's careful facts that exercised Thorn's mind: it was remarks of Waring's. "Reeve's not a fool... If a law-abiding man found the body that man would probably have gone to Reeve's house to telephone... I'm interested in Hoyle... and the old bridle path connecting the mill and Reeve's place and the pub... and Maine has been at loggerheads with Hoyle... and Maine's daughter is a poem to look at... and do we really know Brent was alone when he found the body? Why did he leave the Hunt Ball so early?"

Detection? Perhaps not, but it was from observations of this kind that the police had, on occasions, got a fresh lead when routine led them to a blank wall—and the D.D.I. knew it.

II

On that same Monday afternoon, when the D.D.I. had talked to Waring and Turner and sent them out again to follow their own lines, Dilys Maine decided to walk up the hill by the field path—the same path she had followed after she left Brent on the Saturday night. Her father was out, at his office in Fordings, and Nicholas Brent had rung up shortly after lunch; Dilys had answered the phone and she recognised Brent's deep voice at once.

"Is Mr. Maine at home? Commander Brent speaking."

Dilys felt her heart thumping a little but she replied sedately: "My father is at his office, Commander: if you ring Fordings 681 you'll get him."

"Thanks. I'll ring him there, Miss Dilys. How are you keeping—all well at home?"

"Quite well, thank you," she replied, guessing at the real meaning of his question.

"Good," he replied. "I'd been meaning to come over to see you. You said you'd like a puppy when Lassie obliged—my cocker. She's got a lovely litter. If you'd like to choose one for your own, perhaps you could manage to get over here sometime."

"Oh, thank you very much—I'd love one," she said. "Perhaps I could get over tomorrow."

"Well, give me a ring when you can manage it," he replied. "I could pick you up at the top of the hill and save you the last mile or two over the downs—it's a perishing cold walk with this wind blowing off the sea."

"Thank you very much indeed," she answered, and Brent rang off with a quick "Not at all. It'd be a pleasure. Goodbye."

Turning from the phone, Dilys saw Alice Ridley standing by the door, her eyes wide with enquiry.

"A fine old taking we're in," said Alice. "I can't even hear the phone go without expecting it'll be police asking this, that, or the other. That nosy parker we had here last night was a bit too bright and noticing for my peace of mind. That was Commander Brent wasn't it, dearie?"

"Yes. He's promised me a puppy—his pedigree cocker's just had a litter."

"Has he indeed? Those pups are worth a lot of money—no end of prizes that bitch of his has won. They say he knows more about dogs than any of the vets do." She looked at Dilys with her shrewd blue eyes. "All the same, maybe it'd be better not to go traipsing over there just yet. If he's promised you a pup, he'll keep it for you, all right. Wait a week or so, until there's not so much backchat being handed round."

"Yes. I think it'd be better," said Dilys. "Anyway, I was going to walk up the field path this afternoon. I must have dropped my pearl brooch last night. I can't find it anywhere, and it might have dropped off while I was running."

"Goodness! That brooch of your mother's?" exclaimed Alice. "There'll be trouble with your dad if you've lost that— and let's hope it didn't come off you know where—where all the trouble was."

"I don't think it can have," said Dilys. "They'd have found it—Tim says they searched the road by inches. Anyway, it's much more likely to have come undone when I was running. I'd got my frock all bunched up round my middle and I could easily have got the brooch unfastened."

"Well, if you're going, for goodness' sake go now," said Alice. "It'll be half dark in an hour or so—and I never did like that old path, anyway. It's too lonely, and that bit between the big gorse bushes always gives me the miseries."

"Why, Alice? It's a lovely path."

"Maybe it is, dearie, but I've never forgotten how that poor girl Rosemary went by that path, the last day of her life it was. I saw her and I've never forgotten it."

"But Rosemary was seen after that: they saw her from the inn, walking towards the cliffs."

"So 'twas said—and I think your dad's right over one thing, when he says those Hoyles are liars, the whole pack of them. Well, it's no use talking, but if you've got to go, go quickly while it's still daylight—and don't you stay out too long. I shall get imagining things if you stay out after dark."

"But Alice, I've never heard you say things like this before," protested Dilys, and Alice replied:

"Maybe you haven't, but things have never been like this before—police all over the place and a murderer around somewhere. I don't like it, any of it, so you be careful and don't go asking for trouble." Alice broke off and walked to the door; then she paused for a Parthian shot. "We don't know who it is—remember that. It might have been anybody."

Chapter X

I

IT WAS A BLEAK, GREY JANUARY DAY WHEN DILYS SET
out through the orchard and climbed the field path to the
ridge of the down above the mill. She walked slowly, with her
eyes on the ground, looking for her lost brooch. She knew it
had been pinned safely to her dress when she left the Prince's
Hall and got into Brent's car on Saturday night, and when she
first missed it she could not remember if she had unpinned
it when she tore her dress off so hastily when she got home.
But she knew that it was nowhere in her room now—she had
shifted everything to look for it. "It must have come undone
while I was running," she thought, staring down at the rough
ground, hoping to see the gleam of gold and pearls among the
bents and dry leaves which rustled in the cold wind.

Perhaps it was because she was so intent on the ground
and could not lift her eyes to the lovely curving lines of
familiar downland that she felt troubled; perhaps it was
Alice's gloomy words which had made her uneasy, but Dilys,

who was never frightened by the solitude of the country in which she had been reared, found that she was suddenly aware of being very much alone, and she began to think of Alice saying "There's a murderer about...and it might be anybody." Then came the thought of Rosemary Reeve, walking up this same path the day she had disappeared. Some said she had walked to the cliff edge, two miles beyond, and thrown herself over at the point where the sea washed the base of the cliffs; others said she had gone deliberately to meet someone on the lonely Greenham Road, got into a car and been driven away. She had been an odd, silent girl, beautiful in her dark, glowering way: ill-tempered and resentful of restraint, reticent to an abnormal degree, confiding in nobody. It was that fact which had made it so difficult for the police to get any information about her, for she seemed to have no friends—only the casual acquaintances of hunting field and point-to-point, most of whom she had offended by her arrogant ways. But Dilys knew that the country people had gossiped about Rosemary among themselves, even though the gossip was never repeated to the police. Old Sally Friston, who lived by herself in an ancient hovel by Down Coppice had once said, "No man'd wed her, for she was a real vixen, but no man could pass her by."

As Dilys walked between the dark gorse bushes, which grew so high on the northern slopes of her path, she thought of Rosemary climbing this same path, and of Alice saying contemptuously, "Them Hoyles is all liars."

Even to Dilys, who had no detective quality in her make-up, there was something ominous about the way this path, and the bridle path which continued it on the other side of the low road, seemed connected with trouble—first Rosemary, and now the dead man who "favoured the Reeves," and at the far end of the path lay the Hoyles' place: the Hoyles, who her father said were bad to their marrowbones.

Dilys had reached the highest point in her walk: the ground sloped downwards now, towards the low road, and she realised with a shiver that she could see the dip in the road where the body had lain, and away to the west the warm tiled roof of Michael Reeve's house. It was at this spot, she remembered, that she had paused to pick up her tulle skirt again and to bundle it more securely so that she could run down the far slope, and she could almost feel the tug of her slender shoulder straps as she had struggled with the windblown folds of frock and cloak. "If I *did* drop it, it was probably here, when I was wriggling," she thought to herself, and went down on her knees to hunt more closely. It was then that she heard a footstep, behind the thorn hedge which bordered the path, and she felt a moment of panic. Into her mind there flashed the thought, not of a murderer, but of a detective with bright, amused, observant eyes: young Waring asking her: "Are you looking for something?... What is it and when did you lose it?... And why did you come this way?"

II

It wasn't a detective: it was Michael Reeve. When Dilys heard his voice, she was so much relieved she cried out, "Oh, Michael, I'm so glad it's you—I seem to have got the horrors and I keep on expecting to see policemen behind every gorse bush."

She heard him crash through the hedge, careless alike of damage to the fence and damage to himself, and he said quickly: "Some of them are still around there, on the road and the bridle path. Let's walk back, over the top—then they won't see us and we shan't see them. Is this what you were looking for, Dilys?"

He held out his hand, and lying on his hard brown palm Dilys saw her brooch. "Michael—wherever did you find it?"

"Further down, not far from the road. I started along the path, thinking I might meet you—and then I thought I'd better not meet you. You know what they're all saying, don't you?"

"How should I know?" she asked unhappily. "I've hardly been outside the house, except to go to church yesterday."

A moment later they were over the ridge, hidden by the gorse bushes, and Dilys cried out: "Michael, who was he? The man they found in the road?"

"Not who they said he was—not my brother Norman," said Michael. He seemed to tower above her, dark and brooding against the dark, brooding gorse, which showed never a gleam of yellow on this chill midwinter day. "You've got to believe that, Dilys—he's not my brother Norman. As to who he is—let them find out. I don't know: I don't know anything about him, who he is or how he got there. Do you believe me, Dilys?"

She stood and looked at him, her face tilted up, so that her eyes met his: his face was tanned brown, square and hard, his eyes black and shadowed, unhappy under heavy brows, his lips compressed and jaw set. Michael, for his part, looked down at her tilted, heart-shaped face and marvelled again at the exquisite petal-like texture of her skin, silk smooth and untouched by the biting wind, pale as apple blossom with faint shadows under eyes which were blue as violas were blue, blue like harebells, blue like the wild hyacinths he had seen her gather under the beech trees in Maytime.

"You know I believe you. I've always believed you—and

believed in you," she replied steadily, "no matter what people said. But what does it all mean, Michael? Was it only by chance the man was killed just there and that people say he was like your brother?"

She saw his face lighten as she spoke, as though the brooding shadow were lifted from his eyes and his tense lips eased into the curves which she had so often thought were unexpectedly gentle in his hard, square, nut-brown face.

"Of course it wasn't chance," he said. "It happened like that because somebody is trying to down me, trying to tie a dead man round my neck, as they tied the albatross round the ancient mariner's neck."

"But why?" she cried, her eyes wide with distress.

"Because I'm the one Reeve left," he said. "You know, Dilys, it's no use pretending you don't—the whole county hated us: hated my father for his disregard of other men's rights; hated my brothers because they cheated and swindled; hated my sister for her pride, because she wouldn't be pitied and wouldn't show pity. And the hate's passed on to me, because I've stayed here and tried to make a decent thing of my life here, instead of bolting abroad as my brothers did." He broke off and looked down at the girl's troubled face: "Oh, my dear, it's not fair to plague you with all this—"

"But I want to know," she cried. "I want to understand what's happened, and why it's happened. Michael, why was it that you quarrelled with my father?"

"I didn't, Dilys. He quarrelled with me. Someone told him that you and I were friendly, and that we sometimes met on this path. Anyway, your father came and warned me off. That was fair enough, in its way, considering what he thinks of my family, but he started in on Rosemary—and I couldn't stand that."

"What do you think happened to her, Michael? I've never asked you before, but now, with all this horror happening… so close here… I've started wondering again."

"You're not the only one," he said drily. "I don't know, Dilys—I've never known, and honestly I didn't want to know. Rosemary—she was a law unto herself, she lived in a world which you don't know about, and if she took her own way out—well, it's better not to know." He looked unhappily down at the girl's pale face and added: "Rosemary got herself involved with so many men round here that none of them dared talk. They all kept mum—and thank God for it."

"Do you think this…" (she made a gesture with her hand towards the road, hidden behind them by the ridge of the down) "…is anything to do with what happened to Rosemary?"

"I don't know, Dilys. How can it be?—and yet I keep on asking myself. And every answer opens up some more hideous possibility." He stopped, frowning again, his eyes full of trouble, and then went on: "I don't want to worry you with all this, Dilys. I did want to see you, and to tell you that I hadn't anything to do with the man's death and that I don't know who he is. If you'll only believe that—I swear it's true, swear it by everything I hold sacred—and if you'll believe it, then I can stick it out and face whatever is coming."

"I do believe you," she said quietly, and he added quickly,

"Bless you for that. Go home, now, Dilys—and don't come over here again, not till all this horrible business is settled, one way or the other. It's better for you to keep away."

"All right. I'll do as you say: I only came today because I thought I must have dropped my brooch here; but, Michael, before I go, can't I ask you about some of the things that puzzle me—I worry, too, you know."

"You can ask me anything: you know I'll do my best to help."

"The Hoyles, Michael: are they really wicked, as Daddy says? Or is it that he's just gone queer himself? He frightens me sometimes—it's as though he'd turned against everybody and thinks the only person who is good is himself."

Michael laughed a little at that, his eyes gentle again. "My dear, what's good to one man is bad to another. Hoyle's a publican: he drinks and he gambles: some say he still smuggles, and for all I know it's true—that inn of his was a smuggler's refuge in the long ago. He lets out camping sites to questionable customers; everything he does seems poisonous to that father of yours. Hoyle's not all bad, but I do think there isn't much he'd draw the line at if he were up against it."

"Do you think he's connected with all this trouble?"

"Again, I don't know, but I think it may have started way back among the riff-raff who used to camp there. But don't you worry about it, Dilys. It's nothing to do with you. I should hate to think you'd got involved in worries because you'd been friends with me."

She looked up at him again, her eyes wide and questioning: "It's not only...because I'm friends with you. Didn't you guess...when you found my brooch?"

"No!" he cried, his voice almost violent. "I didn't guess anything, and I'm not going to guess. Go home now, Dilys. Sometime, when all this is done with, I'll come and talk to you again. Goodbye now—and bless you." With that he strode off up the down, and Dilys, clutching her brooch, turned towards home.

III

Michael Reeve strode back home. When he reached his own gate, he walked round the side of the house, meaning to fasten up some of the outbuildings, and it was by the far fence that he met Inspector Waring, who had come by the bridle path from the direction of Hoyle's inn.

"Good day," said Waring cheerfully. "I've been learning the lie of the land. Do you use this path much?"

Reeve leant against the gate, farmer-wise. "The track runs along my meadowland, so I use it quite a lot. If you're asking do I walk over to the inn by this path, the answer's no. If I want a drink I go in the car—it's quicker, and no farmer walks for the sake of walking."

"Got a motorbike?" asked Waring, and Reeve laughed.

"You should know—you've had plenty of time to find out. I've never had a motorbike. If you've been boy-scouting over the wheel tracks, they were made by Macbane: he rode over here on Sunday and gave Betty Hoyle a lift back. She and her mother do a bit of cleaning and so forth for me."

"O.K.," said Waring cheerfully. "I just wondered. The Hoyles are your nearest neighbours, aren't they?" He paused and then added: "It's my business to pick up the odds and ends of gossip which float around. I gather that old caravan site had an unsavoury reputation at one time."

"If you want to gossip, don't expect me to oblige," retorted Michael, and Waring looked at him coolly.

"Aren't you being a bit of a damned fool?" he asked. "The man whose body was found in the road was first identified as your brother. You deny the fact—and with reason. The deceased is an older man than your brother Norman. But I've been told that a chap used to live on the old caravan site who 'favoured the Reeves'—as they say hereabouts. According to Hoyle, and Bob the potman, he hasn't been seen in these parts for years…"

"All right. Get Hoyle and Bob the potman to identify him,

then," replied Reeve. "Seems he's their business—he's certainly not mine. I don't know him—never did know him and he's no concern of mine."

"Hoyle and Bob won't identify him," replied Waring. "That'd be bringing him too near home. If he once lived on the old caravan site, perhaps he took a fancy to revisit the place where he was born—and Hoyle and his potman were at home on Saturday night. It's not that far away," he added meditatively, "and a wheelbarrow would have helped, wouldn't it?"

"It's no business of mine," said Reeve stolidly, "and you're not getting any suggestions from me."

"In spite of the fact that it was almost certainly your car which ran over the man's body?"

"Almost certainly doesn't get you far," retorted Michael, "and if it *was* my car, it was outside, ready for anybody who wanted to use it."

Waring shot another question, suddenly, at a tangent. "Does Mr. Maine, from the mill, often use this path when he sets out to keep an eye on the Rose & Crown?"

Michael Reeve flushed: the hot blood surged furiously up into his face, even suffusing his eyes, so that he looked suddenly, uncontrollably, enraged, and Waring remembered what he had been told of the Reeve temper, the fierce overpowering rage which could animate them all. But Michael had his voice under control.

"Why not ask him?" he retorted. "I can't tell you. I've never seen Maine on this path, never seen him at Hoyle's. Who says they have?—tell me that."

"It's his nearest way, isn't it, if he didn't want to go there in a car which everybody knows from the racket it makes," replied Waring. "And he must have gone there sometimes, because he's reported some of the rowdyism which goes on there."

"Maine's got a bee in his bonnet, but it's not the sort of bee you're interested in," retorted Michael. "He's all on the side of the angels. If you want to know how he went to Hoyle's, ask him—not me." And with that he turned away and went back to his house.

IV

Waring walked back by the bridle path, towards the Rose & Crown. He was getting more and more interested in this case, gradually sorting some sort of pattern out of the confusion of contacts he had made, working out the association of characters and the connections of roads and byways which made a whole of the scattered units in this sparsely populated countryside: they were all tied up together, even visitors like Macbane, distant neighbours like the Veritys, and that one-time Marine Commando—Nicholas Brent. It was surprising how much Waring had absorbed in a short time: not the accurate timetable information of Turner and his fellows, but a far livelier variant—an awareness of human beings and the sort of society they made, through all its various strata. Waring had seen Jennifer Verity and learnt from her that Michael Reeve had danced the final gallop at the Hunt Ball; he had seen Dilys Maine and garrulous Alice; he had seen Betty Hoyle—though only across the bar, getting that quick first impression which Waring valued, before the folks he interrogated had become aware of his own job and put up the inevitable defence mechanism which it always caused. Waring had gone into the pub for a drink yesterday, as any other man might call in at a roadside pub. Betty had smiled at him, and Waring had guessed at once that the stout, blowsy young woman was a talker. Her father was close at hand, a big hulking fellow, once sandy-haired, now grizzled, with a wide rubicund face and many chins: he looked a cheerful, welcoming fellow, did Hoyle, but his blue eyes were too small and too close set, his mouth too pursed and lips too tight. Waring thought from his bulk he might once have been a prize fighter, and his huge fists still looked formidable, despite the creases of fat around their red bulk. Mrs. Hoyle had been there, too: stouter than her daughter ("It'll be a poor lookout for Betty if she doesn't get off soon," thought the lively Waring. "Fat on both sides of the family. Betty'll be a mountain before she's forty"), Mrs. Hoyle was affable enough, but she was worried—Waring knew well enough that the "deep line" between her eyes and her tendency to watch the door were signs of unease.

He walked back along the bridle path in the greying afternoon light, crossed the road (the Greenham Road, parallel with the lower road) and went to the side door of the inn. He hoped that Betty might open it: he was on duty now, and his call had to be official, hedged around by police regulations about the taking of evidence, but he believed that Betty would talk anyway—Waring judged her to be a "natural talker"—and he wasn't often wrong in his judgements of young women.

V

It was the licensee who opened the door, stout Jim Hoyle, and he favoured Waring with a good stare, for all that his manner was affable enough. "Well, sir—what can I do for you?"

"Spare me the time for a chat on local politics, so to speak, Mr. Hoyle," replied Waring, who always found that a light-hearted approach served his purpose better than the official formula. "County C.I.D.," he added. "Inspector Waring. I've been told you know more about these parts than anybody else does."

Hoyle stood back from the door. "Come in and welcome," he said genially. "I've lived here all my life and my dad before me—and had no trouble with no one, police included. Come in the parlour, sir—I've got a nice fire going in there. It's chilly and no mistake." He led the way into a comfortable, fuggy little room, indicated an armchair for Waring and took another himself, one on either side of a nice old-fashioned fireplace where a kettle sang on the hob.

Hoyle didn't wait for Waring to speak, but plunged straight in himself, his voice full of confidence.

"You'll have heard I went to the mortuary as requested, and took Bob with me, Inspector. Bob, he's worked here-around best part of his life; born out yonder he was." Hoyle hitched a wide fleshy thumb in the direction of the old caravan site behind the inn. "No man's land, they call that bit," he added. "Old common land 'twas, right to the cliff's edge."

"Well, if Bob was born out yonder, he's the chap to help us," put in Waring, and Hoyle picked up the allusion at once.

"Yes, I've heard what they been saying, Inspector—and some of 'em ought to know better," he went on. "But let's get this straight: that corpse you've got in the mortuary, he's no one I know; never set eyes on him so far as I can tell—nor Bob hasn't neither; but you can talk to Bob yourself, later. Now I know what Mr. Hudson said and Foot, too—and I'm not saying it wasn't a honest mistake, but that was never Norman Reeve—a sight older than Mr. Norman, he be, and a smaller man. Them Reeves, they're all sizeable, like Mr. Michael—and like the poor young lady who disappeared: a fine tall girl, she was."

"D'you know Ben Grubb?" asked Waring, and Hoyle chuckled.

"Aye, I know Ben Grubb. Eighty-three years old, Ben be,

spry enough, but going a bit childlike at times: remembers what happened sixty years ago a sight better than he remembers last year. Now I call to mind the chap Grubb had in mind, and so do Bob: Stan, we called him. His mother was a Romany lass went round telling fortunes, and his father—well, it'd be anybody's guess: Reeve maybe. But Stan was my age, sir, sixty-two that be: served in the First World War, same as me; and that chap in the mortuary may be older than Norman Reeve, but that's not saying he's over sixty."

The stout licensee broke off for a minute and then spread his hand out towards Waring, a nice, confident, confiding gesture. "When things happen like this here, people all gets gossiping: airing of their ideas, as you might say. There's always been plenty for the gossips hereabouts, with a family like the Reeves as lords o' the manor. See here, sir," and Hoyle leant forward, friendly and confident. "You've heard tell o' the Reeves—and a wild lot they was, some o' them. My dad knew; been here all through history, the Reeves has. Is it aught to be wondered at you get a few fellows that has Reeve written all over their faces? You think it out."

"Well, it's a point," said Waring, and Hoyle went on:

"And you think back a bit, Inspector. You're young: you've had education. You know that in country districts like this, 'twasn't always what's called a welfare state, with inspectors and registrations and welfare officers and fill in forms from the cradle to the grave. No, by heck. There wasn't all them regulations in my dad's time, and if so be a Romany lass or a farm labourer's girl got into trouble, well, no questions asked was the rule them days. And if so be you're surprised to find a down-and-out with a face like Reeve, well, I reckon you're not using the wits the good Lord gave you."

"That's all right, Mr. Hoyle. I'm not disputing any of it,"

said Waring, "but you know I've got to get a bit closer to the facts than what you might call generalisations. A man has been killed—murdered—and not very far away from this place. He was killed on Saturday night, when you and your potman were certainly about these premises, and when most of the farmers were on the roads. Do you expect me to believe you haven't used your wits to guess a bit nearer the mark than you've admitted so far?"

Hoyle rubbed his hands together. "Well, sir, if it's guessing you're asking for, I don't mind obliging," he said amiably.

Chapter XI

I

"AND MAYBE A GOOD GUESS'LL BRING YOU NEARER THE truth than all that stuff Turner and the rest put down so careful in their notebooks," went on Hoyle. "Not but what I've just been telling you hasn't got a bit o' sense in it," he added. "After all, that chap in the mortuary, he favours the Reeves all right, and his body was found nigh Michael Reeve's steading. Now, sir, what've you learnt about the Reeves—this generation of them?"

"Robert, Norman, Rosemary, and Michael," said Waring. "As a family, given to hunting, racing, betting, horseflesh, dogs, and gaming: any sort of gaming, I imagine, from cards to cockfighting. Robert and Norman both went overseas, having quarrelled with their father, leaving a trail of debts behind them, so that no one's got a good word to say for them. That about right?"

"Aye, that's right. Debts—you've said it. Debts to all the tradesfolk who were fools enough to trust 'em: gambling debts—cards and that—and debts to the bookies. Welshers, both of them. Cut and run and left the bookies to snarl. And their dad cut 'em out of his will and left what there was to leave to Michael, not that it was much when they'd tidied it all up, because Michael, he paid his father's debts like an honest man. Not his brothers', though. You mark that, not his brothers.'"

"Then there was Rosemary," went on Waring. "She disappeared—and you were one of the last to see her, Mr. Hoyle."

"Aye, one o' the last—but my girl Betty, she saw Miss Reeve after I did, out on no-man's land there, making for the cliffs. Wild, she looked, our Betty said."

"What do you think happened to Rosemary, Mr. Hoyle?"

"I reckon she threw herself over the ness there: full tide it was, and blowing great guns—storm blew for three days. I'll lay any money that was the way of it. She hadn't got her dogs, see: always had her dogs with her, no matter where she went, big quarrelsome brutes they was, too—mastiffs. I know I've cursed 'em often enough when the fancy took her to call in here for a drink—drank like a man, she did. She left her dogs chained up at home because she knew what she was a-going to do, and didn't want them to follow her. And for why? The same old story, old as 'umankind: she'd got landed, left in the cart, and she was too proud to face it. Who it was left her in the lurch—why, any of a dozen or so. Likely she didn't know herself. But that story's naught to do with this here, don't you believe it."

"And finally, there's Michael," said Waring.

"Aye, Michael: the only steady one o' the whole bunch. He's got a temper, mark you—all the Reeves has that. He's done a bit of gaming and gambling in his time, too, but he's steadied now. A worker, that's Michael. Put all his money into that pedigree herd he's building up. He's a name for being close, Michael has, and he's a rare hard bargainer. I reckon Michael means to build the family fortunes up and make his own place in the world—and that's not so far off this story you're worrying away at as you might think. Or maybe you're sharp enough to see what I'm getting at."

"Well, I could make a case of it, but it mightn't be along your lines," said Waring easily, careful not to let Hoyle realise how closely his every word was being weighed. "You say that Michael paid his father's debts, but not his brothers."

"That's it—not much you miss," said Hoyle approvingly. "See here, sir—when it was known Michael inherited the Hollydown estate, I can tell you one thing of my own knowledge: plenty of them that Norman and Robert owed money to hoped they'd see a bit of it. I've had bookies and touts in this bar cursing Michael, swearing they'd get even with the Reeve family some day. Last year that was. Why, after the last of the flat racing at Sewell's, some o' them came into this bar trying to tap me—to find out how Michael stood. Not that I could name 'em, but it's a fact and I've got witnesses. Bob heard 'em, so did my missis. And if it's a guess you're wanting, I reckon my guess is as good as the next: some of 'em swore to down the Reeves, and this was their way of doing it."

"Well, it's an idea," said Waring, "but how do you think they found such a convenient victim—the dead man who was enough like the Reeve family to be identified as Michael's brother?"

"You think over what I've said and maybe it wasn't that hard," said Hoyle, his shrewd, calculating blue eyes staring back at Waring. "We've a saying round here, 'There's more Reeves around Hollydown than answers to the name Reeve'—aye, and more than I could tell you. And if a fellow favours the Reeves in his face, likely he'll have their temper in his blood, too, if you follow me."

"Go on," said Waring, and Hoyle chuckled.

"Aye, I'll tell you—only guesswork, maybe, but it's got a knowledge of 'uman nature behind it—I reckon it's 'uman nature led to this here peck of trouble."

"Original sin?" queried Waring, who was much entertained by the conversation.

"Aye, original sin, as parson used to say," replied Hoyle. "Passed on from father to son, with the looks and the temper, and gambling in the blood. Isn't it plain common sense to reckon the sort of fellow I've got in mind would favour his forebears in that? Haven't they all gambled, all been mad on horseflesh and that?—and half of 'em been cheats and welshers when it came to paying up? You're not slow, sir: you can see through a wall as far as most. Couldn't there be two reasons for that chap's body being where you found it? One, to pay him out for some trick he'd played; two, to get back on the last Reeve of all—being Michael. Bring off a double. That's how I see it."

"Well, you've done some logical thinking, Mr. Hoyle, but I've got to get closer to facts. You say some of the bookies from Sewell's came in here, asking questions about the Reeves."

"Aye. October that was, after the Prince's Handicap. Bob'll bear me out—a dirty-mouthed lot they were, too. I know I told my womenfolk to go out o' the bar—thought there might be a bit of trouble before we were through, but I managed."

"Why did they come here, Mr. Hoyle? You're a tidy distance from Sewell's."

"Because this is the nearest public house to Reeve's place," replied Hoyle. "Not another licensed house for miles—the Mermaid's the next, but I reckon they didn't fancy raising a row with Commander Brent. He's got a short way with rowdies. And if you want to know who they were—well, you go and ask some of the police at Sewell's. They keep an eye on such gentry. No use asking me their names—I don't know them."

"Never go racing yourself, Mr. Hoyle?"

"Never's a long time," said the publican. "I've seen most of the classic races in my time, but these days I have to stay around and attend to business. My wife's not so young as she was, and she don't like being left in charge of the bar any longer—and that girl of mine, well, she's not that much sense."

"Let's get back to Saturday evening, Mr. Hoyle. What time did Mrs. Hoyle go out, and your daughter?"

"You'd better ask 'em," replied Hoyle. He raised himself ponderously and walked to the door, shouting: "You there, Liz? Come here a minute."

Mrs. Hoyle, stout, ponderous, curiously pallid of face, came into the room, and once again Waring got the impression that she was nervous. He stood up politely, and she sat down heavily in the chair her husband had just vacated, saying: "What'd it be now?"

"Can you tell me just what time it was you left here to go to Fordings on Saturday evening, Mrs. Hoyle?"

"It'd have been soon after seven," she said. "Mr. and Mrs. Williams, they was going to the ball and they offered to drive me in, and we left early so as to pick up Miss Baker from Lower Dene."

"And did your daughter go with you?"

"No. She left a bit later. Young Jim Pellant said he'd pick her up on his motorbike, the Williams car being only a small one—and none of us that slim. Betty's mad on riding pillion; I don't hold with it myself, and it was a tiring evening anyhow:

we was neither of us back home till three o'clock. Too much for me, 'twas—late hours don't suit me these days."

"Did you notice any other cars on the road while you were driving?"

"That I didn't. 'Twas misty like, and that old windscreen of Bert Williams's car was fogged up so you couldn't see a thing. Cars there may've been and plenty of them, but I was sitting in the back and I couldn't see a thing."

"Is your daughter in, Mrs. Hoyle? She might be able to help a bit."

"She's not in the house just now: I think she went out to pick up the bus at Broomberrow—there's none passes on this road."

Waring was thinking hard, his quick mind playing with a theory which was only half-formed.

"When you left here in the Williamses' car, Mrs. Hoyle, was your daughter still in the house, or was she looking out for young Pellant—outside, that is? I know some of these young chaps on motorbikes are always in a hurry."

Mrs. Hoyle looked at Waring with her large lacklustre eyes, and she hesitated before she answered. "Well," she said slowly, "Betty came outside when Mr. Williams pulled up, just to have a word with him, but I don't reckon she stood out there in the cold for long."

"Course she didn't," said Hoyle. "She come inside in the warm till she heard the motorbike—she can tell the sound of every motorbike around here, and that old Rudge of young Pellant's makes row enough to wake the dead. There's another point I might mention while you're here, sir, just to clear up any misunderstandings. I gave Inspector Turner a list of all the chaps that looked in for a drink Saturday evening— local chaps, all of 'em, farm labourers, quarrymen, and one or two old codgers from Netherdown. No strangers at all there weren't, not Saturday evening. I've no doubt he's checked up on some of them, him being careful like, but there's nothing to help you there."

"It was quiet for a Saturday evening, I gather," said Waring.

"Quiet? Of course it was quiet: all the farmers, and the young fellows who'd got the money to posh themselves up, they was at Fordings," replied Hoyle. "Only the old chaps and the labourers left to come in for a pint."

"Yes—come to think of it, it was a good evening to choose for a crime," said Waring thoughtfully. "Everybody with a car heading for Fordings, getting there by half past eight or so; then a few hours with the roads clear, then everybody driving home again."

"Aye," said Hoyle. "You're right there—and whoever did it probably reckoned the body wouldn't be found till the small hours, especially on the lower road. There's not many uses it."

"Oh, you do give me the proper 'orrors," complained Mrs. Hoyle. "I can't see why you're so sure it was murder. Seems to me the poor wretch might 'a been knocked down by accident: it's shocking how careless some drivers are, and on a misty night, with an old car whose headlights weren't that good, it's none too easy to see a man walking on the road in front of you. I wouldn't drive myself in some of these cars the farmers go out in, that I wouldn't."

"Well, you may be right after all, Liz," agreed Hoyle. "It could 'a happened that way—but there's this story of Commander Brent being knocked over the head."

"I don't believe it!" she exclaimed. "I reckon he was more mixed than he thought he was: there he was, in a strange dark house, blundering round where he'd no business to be, knocked things down as likely as not and took a tumble—that makes more sense to me than all this crime stuff." She turned to Waring. "Sorry if I've been speaking too free, sir, but all this stuff they're talking—well, I can't see no sense in it. We've never had no trouble in these parts. It's not like towns—and I just don't believe it."

Waring got up. "We've got to look at it all ways, Mrs. Hoyle."

"Oh, I see that—it's what police is for," she said drearily, "but it don't make sense to me."

II

Outside, it was twilight, greying to dusk. Waring had very keen sight and he could see without any difficulty—a colourless world, with the line of the downs dark against a shadowy sky, and the distant sound of the sea beating against the chalk cliffs of the ness. Waring set out towards the cliffs—the old "no-man's land" that had been common ground for centuries, rough grazing, unenclosed, where the camp had been. Beyond the garden wall of the inn there was an acre or two of rough land, fenced in: this was the caravan site, on which Hoyle let standing room to motor caravans during the holiday season. Two of these "homes from home" stood there now, chilly-looking pallid rectangles, unsubstantial in the fading light. Beyond the fencing, gorse land stretched to the cliffs.

As Waring made his way towards the cliffs in the fading light, he thought of some of the points which had emerged when he talked to Hoyle: first, and most obvious, was the publican's determination to shift the responsibility for the crime away from the immediate district. Hoyle made no suggestion that any of his neighbours could be responsible: not Michael Reeve (though local gossip had it that there was no love lost between Hoyle and Reeve); not Mr. Maine—though Hoyle had every reason to cause trouble for Maine, since the latter had certainly tried to make trouble for Hoyle. There had been no mention of Tom Hudson, though several people had said that Hudson's original identification of the dead man as Norman Reeve had been based on malice. ("Tom Hudson, he's jealous because Michael Reeve's beasts always get placed higher than his in the show ring, and then Tom, he's been trying to ape the quality since he bought his own steading, and Michael laughs at him"—so ran the gossips.) Hoyle's only allusion to Nicholas Brent had been fair enough, too: "Got a short way with rowdies."

"Hoyle wants to shift the onus: he offers a red herring of bookies' touts from Sewell's Racecourse," thought Waring, "knowing quite well that we're likely to get bogged down over that one—though I'll have a word with the Sewell's men and get them to send some of the racecourse attendants over to try to identify the deceased. And I wonder if Betty Hoyle really *was* out when I asked for her just now—or if Mamma hustled her out of my way. If Betty *did* stand at the door to wait for Jim Pellant and his bike, or even watched from a window, she may have seen something she hasn't told us about."

As he meditated, Waring drew near to the cliff edge, and as he stared he had a feeling of satisfaction. In the half-light, clear against the dark, stunted gorse and withered grass, the chalk cutting showed surprisingly light. Here, where the cliffs dipped to a mere twenty feet in height, there were steps cut in the chalk to give access to a little beach, sheltered by the steep headland of the ness to the west and the bluff beside the Cookbourne River to the east.

"So that's why the bridle path is there," thought Waring. "It leads to a sheltered beach where you could land a boat—or shove off in one. And if smugglers didn't take advantage of it in the long ago, I'll eat my hat—or perhaps it wasn't so very long ago."

Standing there, listening to the pounding of the waves, Waring thought again: "A quiet Saturday night... Did Hoyle take advantage of it to do some business, with his womenfolk out of the way, and precious little custom to keep him in the bar? Was that it?—and some nosy parker saw more than was good for him?"

Smuggling: the word was evocative of old-time stories, preventive men and desperadoes; but had smuggling ever been more profitable than today, with spirits and tobacco taxed as never before? Even an occasional case of duty-free whisky and brandy would yield a nice profit to a publican serving it at retail prices today.

"It's an idea," thought Waring, "and if trouble cropped up on Saturday night, it'd be good policy for Hoyle to spin a yarn about the wild Reeves and their rows with the bookies."

He turned back from the cliff edge and made a quick decision. "I'll go and see Brent. He must know what the chances of smuggling are, and he ought to know a bit about Hoyle, too."

III

"Hoyle: well, he's no friend of mine and you might as well know it first as last," said Nicholas Brent.

He and Waring were sitting in a small panelled room which had a fine open chimney where logs blazed with blue and green in their flames—sure sign of old ships' timbers.

"Better get it straight," went on Brent. "The fact that I'm here at all makes Hoyle properly mad. He wanted this place for himself, only he was too close-fisted to put in a decent bid for it."

"Why did he want two pubs?" asked Waring.

"He didn't: he wanted to shut this one down to give him a clear field. He tried to get the licence taken away on the ground of redundancy when I first bought the place; then when I'd laid him out over that one, he tried to make trouble with the brewers. All that's an old story, but you might as well know, because it explains why I'm not too fair to Jim Hoyle—wicked old sinner he is too."

"Do you think he wanted to keep you out because he didn't want a naval chap around keeping an eye on his private beach?" enquired Waring, and Brent hitched up one eyebrow. Waring liked the look of Brent, a big fair fellow, looking remarkably clean and healthy: close-cropped fairish hair, weather-tanned skin, aggressive jaw, and long-sighted keen grey eyes; he gave an impression of abounding vitality and of a purposefulness that was the more impressive for his quiet voice and clipped speech.

"Like to enlarge on that point?" he asked.

"Well, I may be talking through my hat," said Waring. "I'm a proper landlubber and I know it, but Hoyle's got the equivalent of a private beach where it seems to me you could land a dinghy or suchlike—and Saturday night was nice and quiet, from every point of view: quiet weather, quiet roads, family out of the way, the potman there to serve the few locals who came in. Could he have had a cargo landed at the foot of his steps in the cliff?"

Brent chuckled. "Smuggling up to date?" he queried. "I wouldn't put it beyond him: I often wondered if there was more behind his objection to me than was justified by his resentment at 'unfair competition,' as he called it. But if so,

I've never caught him out—and it's not for want of trying. I've got a very nice little craft, and I've often had a look-see on nights when the tide and the weather made a landing possible, and I've never seen a thing."

"But you think it'd be possible?"

"Of course it'd be possible to land a small cargo and dump it by those steps, but I doubt if enough could be landed to make the enterprise worthwhile. It involves shipping the stuff from the Continent, and by the time you'd paid the skippers there wouldn't be much profit. No one's going to run a craft across the Channel, with all the risks involved, without being paid good money for it. You're thinking of spirits—whisky, brandy, or gin?"

"Yes."

"I don't believe it myself," said Brent. "For one thing, the customs and excise men are pretty fly: they have their own methods of knowing what's sold, and it wouldn't be easy to hoodwink them."

"But in spite of your scepticism, you've taken your own craft out to watch Hoyle's private beach?"

"Yes. I have, though I didn't expect to spot any rum-running."

"Then what did you expect?"

Brent laughed. "Don't be too hopeful. I've told you that Hoyle tried to queer my pitch when I first came here, so I did my damnedest to catch him out. You see, the old chap who sold me this place, Jeff Barrow (he's been dead for years, incidentally), yarned quite a bit when he'd decided to sell me the Mermaid. He warned me I should have trouble with Hoyle, and as good as said that Hoyle ran a gambling house, and even organised cockfighting bouts. I doubt if half of Jeff's stories were true, but he did say that Hoyle's clients used to come and go by sea, landing at that cove in the lee of the ness.

Well—they may have done, but if so it was all a long time ago. It certainly didn't happen during the war—the beach was mined and wired off—and I don't think it's happened in my time. Hoyle knows I watch him."

"He could have been pretty certain you weren't watching him on Saturday night," put in Waring, and Brent shrugged his broad shoulders.

"Maybe—but if Hoyle had wanted to commit murder, I'll lay any money he wouldn't have lugged a corpse overland and dumped it in the road. He'd have sunk it somewhere you'd never have found it." Brent broke off and then added: "Got the body identified yet?"

"No—though there's a consensus of opinion that deceased was an offshoot of the Reeve family."

"Likely enough—though that doesn't get you much farther."

"Possibly not. Now before I go, do you mind giving me a few more details about your own drives on Saturday evening?"

"Anything you like—though I thought you'd got it all taped—but fire away."

"You took Macbane to the ball: did you go to Stenfield and pick him up there?"

"No, I didn't. I picked him up at Tim Grant's, which saved a few miles. Tim's an old friend of Ian's. It so happened that Dowson was driving from Stenfield to pick up some lovelies at Greenham, and he dropped Ian at Tim's—about half a mile from the lower-road pointer. Everybody with a car was taxiing somebody on Saturday night. But, for the love of Mike, don't get imagining that Macbane had anything to do with your gloomy story..."

"I'm trying not to imagine anything," said Waring, as cheerfully as ever. "Now you left the ball early, sir—before twelve."

"I did. I reckoned I'd done my duty, and I'm not so crazy on dancing the night through as I was ten years ago."

"Quite. I don't think that Inspector Turner thought to ask you if you were alone in the car."

"I don't think he did—and why should he? I told him—and I'll repeat it on oath anywhere—that I was alone when I found the body. I bent over it, ascertained the chap was dead, refrained from shifting him—though it'd have saved a heck of a lot of trouble if I'd been able to drive on to the upper roads—and the rest of the story you know. The only point I've gone back on is whether it was Michael Reeve's voice I heard before the chap came at me. I honestly thought it was at the time, but I may have been mistaken. It wasn't Hoyle or his potman—I can swear to that."

Waring sat silent for a moment, his lively eyes studying Brent's face. "It seems to me that you and Reeve have got something in common, so far as the events of Saturday evening are concerned," he said, and Brent said,

"What the hell do you mean?"

"When Reeve was asked what he was doing at the time you were knocked out, he claims to have been sitting in his car—'sitting out,' if you like to put it that way. He won't say whom he was sitting out with, though it might save him a lot of trouble if he did. Now you have not claimed that anybody was with you in your car—though I think it'd save you trouble if you did."

Brent stared back at him. "I think I get you. Well, off the record I'm not trying to save myself trouble because I fail to see that I'm *in* trouble. I've told a straight story and I abide by it, and I've nothing to add."

"Right," said Waring. He got to his feet, adding, "Hoyle favoured me with his own version of events on Saturday night;

guesswork, as he admitted—but he's a lively guesser. Owing to the fact that Michael Reeve and yourself decline to answer all the questions put to you, I'm being driven to do quite a bit of guessing myself."

"That's all right by me," rejoined Brent. "You guess away."

"I take it you know the laws covering the giving of evidence in a court of law, and what contempt of court involves?"

"I'll take that hurdle when I come to it," rejoined Brent calmly.

Chapter XII

I

WHEN HE LEFT THE MERMAID INN, WARING DROVE
down to Foxlea Mill. The road he drove on was the north–
south road, connecting up the Greenham Road and the
low road, both of which joined the north–south road about
two miles above the mill. It was dark when Waring left the
Mermaid, and he changed gear punctiliously when his headlights picked up the studded road sign "STEEP HILL. ROAD
NARROWS". It *was* steep, too, he contemplated, a veritable
tunnel of a hill, running between chalk banks and curving
wickedly at the bottom. He took the awkward turn which
led him into the drive of the Mill House; there were no
lights showing in front, but Waring went and knocked at the
front door—though he would much rather have gone to
the kitchen door and had a heart-to-heart with Alice Ridley.
Waring had taken a liking to Alice, and was pretty sure that
the stout housekeeper was a very shrewd body and that little
escaped her.

It was Dilys who opened the door: when he saw her standing there under the harsh white light of an unshaded bulb which she had just switched on, Waring had much-ado to remember that he was a policeman, on duty, and that it was his job to make this girl give exact evidence. (He was pretty certain that her evidence had not been "exact" when he talked to her yesterday evening.) Her pale skin and ash-blonde hair had an almost luminous quality, and her eyes were shadowed and dark, her lips drooping like a child's. She was beautiful after a fashion which no man could perceive unmoved, but it took little detective ability to sense that she was unhappy and afraid. Behind her stood a taller girl, whom Waring knew to be Jennifer Verity, and Waring's detective instinct came to the surface again when a swift thought flashed unbidden through his mind: "They've been cooking something up between them…"

Aloud he said: "I'm sorry to bother you again, Miss Maine. Is your father in?"

"Yes. He came in half an hour ago, but I don't think you can see him, Inspector. He's gone straight to bed: I'm afraid he's ill."

"I'm sorry about that, though I thought he looked off-colour when I saw him this morning," said Waring. "What's the trouble?"

"I think he's got a very bad chill: he's feverish—it may be flu. He really is very ill—he could hardly get upstairs."

"Have you sent for a doctor?"

"No. He told me not to. You see, he's always been difficult about doctors—he doesn't believe in them."

Jennifer Verity came forward. "All the same, I think you ought to get a doctor, Dilys. If Mr. Maine is as ill as you think, it's wrong not to have a doctor."

"Oh, I know, I shall have to send for Dr. Wright—if he'll come," said Dilys unhappily. "Anyway, Alice is with him; she's a very good nurse and she'll know if it's really serious. But you can't go asking him questions now," she added to Waring, "he hardly knows what he's saying. I can't imagine how he drove home; he certainly wasn't fit to drive."

"Look here, Dilys. I'll call in at Dr. Wright's on my way home," said Jennifer. "He'll understand, and then, if Mr. Maine is difficult, you can say it wasn't you who sent for a doctor. I expect he caught a chill on Saturday night when he had all that bother over the car breaking down," she added.

"All right," said Dilys. "I do think he's ill—really ill."

"I'll be off then," said Jennifer. "I'll bike round by Brambledene and see Dr. Wright."

A moment later she was gone, and Dilys turned to Waring.

"Honestly, you *can't* see my father now," she protested, and Waring replied:

"Of course not. Please don't imagine we're bullies who bother invalids—but would you mind answering some more questions yourself?"

"Anything's better than worrying Daddy," said Dilys. "Come in here—I'm sorry if it's cold. Alice and I don't bother about a fire in here every day. I'll switch a stove on."

It seemed a grey vault of a room to Waring, that big formal drawing room: pale-grey walls, dark-grey carpet, sober upholstery, and black-framed pictures. Looking at the slender loveliness of the fair girl in her demure dark frock, Waring wanted to exclaim, "But you don't belong here... It's incredible that this is your home."

Dilys switched a stove on, and then said: "Yes? What is it?"

"You went to the Hunt Ball on Saturday evening?"

"Yes," she replied after a long pause. "I did go. I didn't stay very long, because I had to get back before Alice or my father came in. He didn't know I was going, and he wouldn't have approved. He's very strict."

"How did you get back?"

"A friend drove me back."

There was a moment's silence: Dilys stood with her hands clasped loosely in front of her, very still, very white, and then Waring saw that she was shivering. She went on quickly, before he could ask another question: "That's not quite right: I wasn't driven all the way home. I walked the last mile or so, over the fields."

"By the old bridle path?" he asked, and she stared at him, as though startled, and then nodded.

"Was it Commander Brent who drove you back?"

"I can't tell you," she replied.

"Wouldn't it be much better to tell me, and get it over?" he asked gently. "Policemen aren't inhuman, you know. I don't want to distress you, but you must realise that the question has got to be answered."

She stood there silent, like a frightened child, and he went on: "Commander Brent couldn't drive on, could he? He couldn't get by—so he suggested that you should run home over the fields, hoping that nobody would know you had been in his car when he saw the body on the road—was that it?"

Again she replied: "I can't tell you," and then Waring heard steps on the stairs and the sound of somebody hurrying across the hall and a voice calling:

"Miss Dilys, Miss Dilys...where are you? The master wants you."

"I'm here, Alice," she called, and ran to the door, and Alice Ridley burst out:

"I can't think what's come over him: he's nigh out of his

mind. You go up, dearie, and see if you can quiet him. Oh, my goodness—whatever does he want now?"

The last question was spoken at Waring, just as Dilys ran out of the door. "Goodness, haven't we got trouble enough," burst out Alice, "without you worriting around? The master's that ill, and Miss Dilys worried out of her mind, and now you've got to come, making things worse."

"I'm sorry," said Waring. "I've got my job to do, and you know it. If you'll only answer a few plain questions, Miss Ridley, I shan't keep you long."

"What do you want to know?"

"Miss Maine was at the Hunt Ball on Saturday. Who drove her back?"

"That's not for me to say. I wasn't at home, and you know it. You know I was with my friend, Miss Huggins."

"I don't care where you were," said Waring. "You got to Fordings at midnight and you were on the other side of the river until morning, and what you did there doesn't matter to me. But it does matter if Miss Maine came back in Commander Brent's car."

"It's not for me to say," replied Alice obstinately. "I wasn't here, and I didn't see what she did, and I don't know when she got in—and likely she doesn't know herself. The master said it was just on midnight when he got back, and Miss Dilys was in then."

"If Miss Dilys came in Commander Brent's car, she certainly didn't get back here by midnight," said Waring. "She's told me that she came across the fields—that means by the old bridle path. It must have been nearer one o'clock than midnight when she got back."

"Well, I don't know, I'm sure—and whatever does it matter?" said Alice indignantly. "If you imagine Miss Dilys had aught to do with all this wickedness, you're busy on; it's not in the police force you ought to be, it's a mental home. If you can look at her and still imagine she's been doing something plain wicked, there's something wrong with you. I've known her all her life and she's as good a girl as ever walked."

"I'm not suggesting she's done anything wicked," said Waring, as Alice had to pause for breath. He knew she was fighting a spirited rearguard action, and he realised his chances of getting any questions answered that evening were now pretty remote. Alice plunged in again.

"What it was happened Saturday evening, it's not for decent folks to say, but if there was any evildoings, it's not in a respectable house like this you want to come poking round. If there's aught wrong, it's along of those Hoyles. They're bad—always has been."

"Well, say you tell me a bit more about them, then," said Waring. "It's no use saying they're bad if you haven't got any evidence—any facts."

Alice stood with her hands on her hips and studied him. "You and your facts," she said scornfully. "If you're country-born, there's some things you can smell. But if you must go on talking, you come into my kitchen: it's as cold as charity in here, and I've got the supper to see to, police or no police."

"That's O.K. by me," said Waring. "I like your kitchen."

II

"Hoyles," said Alice, after she had investigated the contents of the oven. "It's time they was bowled out. Every bit of wickedness which ever happened round here was along of them Hoyles. The master knows—he'll tell you when he's better. In the old days it was that lot from the encampment back of the inn. The old Squire, Michael's grandfather, I mean—he was always over there, and they did use to gamble and fight cocks and the dear Lord knows what else. Then, when Michael's father was Squire, 'twasn't much better. We all knew about the goings-on—all of us except the police."

"Why didn't you tell the police, if you knew there was something wrong going on?"

"They was told all right, but they was never there when they should 'a been. Hoyle's much too smart to be caught by police—but the master, he knew. He watched—and if you're going to tell me the police never heard naught from the master, well, somebody's telling lies. But when the Squire was alive, none of the police cared to make trouble for him: he backed Hoyle, the Squire did, and 'twas more comfortable like to believe Squire than to believe the master."

"Well, the Squire's dead now, and it's no use arguing over what may have happened in the past when there's no evidence to prove it," said Waring, but Alice went on:

"Not so long past: what happened to Rosemary Reeve? No one knows; you police may be clever enough, but did you ever find out what happened to Miss Rosemary? I saw her, that day, going up that bridle path you've talked about, and I've never forgotten it. She often went up that path, and you know where it leads."

"It leads to Hoyle's place, and then onto the cliffs and the cliff steps," said Waring. "Hoyle saw her on the cliffs, and so did his daughter. He gave evidence that he saw her."

"Likely he did—and he'd seen her often enough before. Miss Rosemary knew all about the gambling parties at the inn: she'd got gambling in her blood."

Alice turned to her oven again and Waring thought for a moment; then he said, "Go on. You might as well tell me what you're thinking—though you didn't tell anybody when it might have been helpful."

"Tell anybody? Me go to the police and tell them what they should have had the wits to know for themselves?" she cried scornfully. "When the Squire died, he left all he'd got to Michael, didn't he? Debts and all. There was nothing for Rosemary—and she owed a packet all round, to every bookie in the county. Michael wasn't paying her debts—he'd got enough to do to clear his father's, and he wasn't sending good money after bad for her to throw away."

"How do you know all this?" asked Waring, and she retorted scornfully:

"Everybody knew it. I was friends with Mrs. Bates, who was housekeeper till the Squire died, and she told me enough about Miss Rosemary's goings-on for me to know the sort of girl she was—not that I wasn't sorry for her, losing her mother when she was a tiny, and brought up among a wild lot like her elder brothers. And as to the Squire's will—everybody knew about that, how Rosemary was left naught."

Alice came and sat down at the kitchen table. "I've always believed Rosemary went to Hoyle for money. It was the day before the Sewell's Races she disappeared. She reckoned she could get money out of Hoyle by telling him she'd tell the police what she knew about his goings-on—and I've no doubt she knew plenty."

Waring listened with the liveliest interest: with one side of his mind he knew that Alice was sidetracking him, keeping him away from the main issue, but he was much too interested in her story to stop her. He put in a word here.

"If Miss Reeve intended to get money out of Hoyle by threats, wouldn't she have taken her dogs with her? She must have known she was taking a risk, if there's anything in your idea."

"That's just it," said Alice. "It's the one place she wouldn't have taken her dogs, not if she wanted to talk to Jim Hoyle. The dogs hated Hoyle: one of them went for him one day and he hit it over the head with his cudgel. She knew Hoyle wouldn't let her in if she'd got those dratted brutes with her—savage, they were. Michael had them put down after she disappeared—no one couldn't do nothing with them."

"Well, Miss Ridley, I won't say that I'm not interested, because I am," said Waring, "but the job I'm investigating is the death of a man whose body was found on the low road last Saturday night."

"Maybe you are," she said tartly, "and likely you'll go on investigating, as you call it, same as they did over Miss Rosemary—and a lot of good they did. And if you can't see the connection, you're not so bright as you look."

"I could make up all sorts of connections," said Waring, "but the only connection that would be any good to me would be one that had evidence to support it: facts, not guesses."

"Then you'd better go looking where you can find some facts, and that's not here," she declared. "You make me tired. Ben Grubb's told you who the chap was—the dead man. Don't you tell me he hasn't. Ben's told everybody else: he was that chap who was born on the old caravan site and lived there until the police evicted the lot of them. But he came back—always coming back he was, hanging around there."

"Hoyle says that man was his own age—over sixty," said Waring, and Alice retorted,

"Hoyle! If you believe what he says you'll believe anything! I may not have any of your blessed facts, but I've sense enough to see what happened. That chap tried the same game on Hoyle Miss Rosemary tried—getting money. Likely he knew what happened to Miss Rosemary—and Hoyle finished him and put his body in the road for somebody to run over; and he put it near Michael Reeve's place so that the police'd say, 'Those Reeves again. We've got him this time.' And that's just what they did say. That blockhead of an Inspector—Turner, his name is—he just fell for it."

"Don't be too hard on Turner," said Waring, who had his own reasons for keeping the conversation going. "He got off on the wrong foot because Mr. Hudson and Foot identified the body as that of Norman Reeve; besides, there was the added complication of Commander Brent being attacked in Michael Reeve's house. I've no doubt you've heard all about that—you hear all about everything," he added.

"What sort of folks do you think countryfolks are?" she burst out. "Do you think we're all dumb round here? Everybody for miles has been talking about nothing except the dead man on the low road. Mr. Tom Hudson, he got talking to his cowman, and the cowman talked to the milk-lorry man, and the milk-lorry man got gossiping with Commander Brent's man. They're all talking: even Mrs. Weldon—she's housekeeper at the Mermaid and not given to gossiping— she came along to see me to ask about poultry for the season. Poultry, indeed—I know what she wanted—"

"Probably the same thing that I want," said Waring, and Alice Ridley sniffed.

"I don't know about that, but I do know this: I can't get on with my work with you in the kitchen. Haven't we got bother enough without you coming making more?"

"I'm sorry, Miss Ridley," said Waring, and he spoke very soberly this time. "I don't want to add to your worries, but I've got my job to do. You've been pretty clever, haven't you? You called Miss Dilys away so that I couldn't ask her any more questions—oh, I know. I'm not really stupid. You've got Mr. Maine upstairs in bed and you tell me he's too ill to be talked to—"

"That's true," said Alice. "He's a sick man if ever I saw one. My goodness!" she exclaimed. "You're not going to tell me you don't believe he *is* ill upstairs?"

"Oh, yes. I believe that," said Waring. "I don't think Miss Dilys was telling me lies when she said her father was ill in bed—I'm quite sure she wasn't. But I want to know *why* he's so ill, and I'm going to stop here until I've seen the doctor Miss Verity is sending."

Alice stared at him. "Why he's so ill," she echoed, and Waring could hear the trouble in her voice. "He's got a fever on him, and a cough I don't like the sound of. I said he should see a doctor this morning—I knew he was poorly—and he nearly snapped my head off. The bees that man's got in his bonnet!" she cried. "What with his temperance campaigns and his 'I won't have a doctor in the house' he's enough to drive a body crazy. And there he is, fair delirious, and if that's not enough, I've got you to bother with. Can't you let us be when we're in trouble?" And with that she put her apron over her head and wept.

Waring sat still for a minute or two, while Alice sobbed into her apron, and then he said: "Crying's not really going to help, Miss Ridley. It's not going to get rid of me, for one thing—and your saucepan's boiling over, and that won't help."

Alice emerged from her apron and sprang to the stove with surprising agility. "Drat the thing!" she exclaimed. Having dealt with the saucepan, she turned again to Waring.

"You're not going to get anything out of me and that's flat," she declared. "If you want to twist things round and pretend Miss Dilys and the master had anything to do with murdering people, you'll get no help from me. The master, he may be tiresome, and the good Lord knows how often I've said I couldn't put up with things no longer, but one thing I do know. He's a good man. He may be hard and narrow and old-fashioned and plain stupid, but he's done his best as a father according to his lights—though any other girl but Miss Dilys would have run away long ago, him never letting her have a bit of fun like other girls. But he's not wicked, that I swear."

"Well, now you've got all that off your chest, you just listen to me," said Waring. "I've heard a lot about Mr. Maine, and I've got enough sense to know he's about the last man to commit a crime or to help conceal a criminal, but he was out on Saturday night, and he got home much later than he told me. And he did not drive home over Cookbourne Bridge."

"That's as good as saying he's a liar," flared Alice.

"No, it isn't. I'm not suggesting he's a liar, but I am suggesting he's not responsible for what he's saying. When I talked to him this morning I could see he looked ill—not quite normal."

"Of course he wasn't normal," she declared. "He'd got a fever on him. I knew that all yesterday—he wasn't himself."

"Why wasn't he himself?" persisted Waring. "My own belief is that he got into some sort of roughhouse on Saturday night, and got knocked out, and when he came to he may not have remembered what happened. You can't have it both ways," added Waring. "If a man is known to be truthful and sober and upright, he doesn't start telling irresponsible stories to the police without some reason. But if he's had a knock over the head and not had the proper treatment for it, he may say anything."

Alice gave a great sigh and subsided into her chair again. "Maybe you've got more sense than I thought," she said slowly. "It could 'a happened that way. But if he got into a roughhouse as you call it, I know what house it was. It'd've been that Hoyle."

"You can say you know. It's no use my saying 'I know' unless I've got proof," said Waring, "and the first thing I've got to have proof of is Mr. Maine's illness, and I'm staying here until the doctor's told me if there's any ground for my own idea about it."

III

"Delayed concussion; rising temperature; pneumonia," said Dr. Wright, "and off the record, serve the old fool right. If he'd sent for me yesterday, I'd have kept him flat in a dark room for a week, and he'd have got over it. Now he's asked for trouble and he's got it."

"Was he coshed from behind?" asked Waring.

"That's about it—base of his skull. He was probably unconscious for quite a time—may have been for hours: then he might have got up without realising in the least what had happened to him. They say he drove home. I've heard some queer stories about head injuries, but this one beats the band. How he survived I can't imagine."

Wright turned and studied the young detective's face. "Well, here's a ready-made solution for you: if Maine recovered consciousness and drove his car home after he had been coshed, he might have run over anyone or anything without even knowing it."

"It's nice and simple, but it won't wash," said Waring. "The times don't fit. In any case, it doesn't explain where Maine got knocked out."

"Well, if I make a guess, I shall be in good company— everybody in the district will say the same thing," said Wright.

"Maine's got ideas about Jim Hoyle and his activities: it's known that Maine's been watching Hoyle's place on various occasions. Silly fool the man is—Maine, I mean. What are police for? If Hoyle caught Maine snooping on Saturday night, Hoyle may have laid him out."

"'May have' isn't much use to me," said Waring, "but in any case, if Maine were laid out by Hoyle on the Greenham Road, I can't see how he ran over Exhibit A on the lower road."

"No. I grant you that'd take some explaining," agreed Wright, and Waring went on:

"Look here, sir. I gather that Maine is a temperance fanatic, a dyed-in-the-wool Puritan who is anti-drink, anti-gambling, anti-dancing, anti-fun of any kind, but how did he get any information about Hoyle? Did he just go and watch that inn on odd evenings as the spirit moved him?"

"No, not quite like that—though maybe he kidded himself that the word of the Lord came to him, as these fanatics do. Maine helps with a Boys' Club in the lowest quarters of Fordings, and I believe they get some real young toughs in there and try to convert them with the aid of good meals and a better gymnastic instructor. My own belief is that Maine gets information—which may or may not be genuine—from some of the boys in that club, and instead of passing the information on to the police, he tries to play a lone hand on the principle of 'respecting confidences.'"

Waring groaned, and Dr. Wright laughed. "He's more than a bit bats, friend Maine—but all on the side of the angels. Meantime, if you want to know whether he's going to recover, I tell you frankly I don't fancy his chances. There's probably a very slow cerebral haemorrhage, and pneumonia's setting in."

"You're moving him to hospital?"

"Yes. It's his only chance. The ambulance will be here

any moment. And, by the way—leave that girl alone for tonight. She's got about as much worry as she can stand for the moment."

Waring groaned again. "I could shake her!" he said. "She's the most incredibly lovely thing I've ever set eyes on, and she's just an infernal nuisance to a detective."

"Poor child! The sooner she's married the better. Life here isn't fit for a girl like that, with her father going slowly and steadily more insane every day of his life."

"Well, I gather there's quite a queue for her to choose from," said Waring.

"You're telling me! Someone suggested that young Macbane was making the running, but personally I'd put my money on Nick Brent. Ah...that's my ambulance arriving, so I'll get cracking."

"And you think that in all decency I'd better push off?" said Waring, and the doctor nodded.

"I do, indeed. You can't pester that child now—in any case, she had nothing to do with it."

Waring went, but as he sorted his car out from the ambulance (which left him precious little room to manoeuvre) he thought: "Brent and Macbane...and she was having a heart-to-heart with Michael Reeve this afternoon. Nothing to do with it, I wonder..." And he wondered quite a lot.

Chapter XIII

I

"MACBANE," THOUGHT THE INDEFATIGABLE WARING to himself. "I'll have another smack at him. He always seems to crop up—part of the pattern."

Waring drove himself off to Stenfield through a dark and cheerless evening; it was misty in the hollows, the roads were narrow and difficult, and he didn't know his way. As he drove between chalk banks or dark thorn hedges two trains of thought played through his mind: first he concentrated on the actual driving—which was tricky—and then he gave rein to his own imagination and thought how easy it would be not to brake in time if he saw a dark body lying in the road after one of the bends and dips he was negotiating. He thought, too, of Dilys Maine, sitting beside Nicholas Brent in the big Heron… Dilys Maine…she recurred in this story like a theme tune, and he didn't seem able to get to grips with her.

When he arrived at Stenfield, and found the Macbanes' house, the front door opened just as Waring was about to ring the bell: it was a cheerfully lighted hall, with warm-coloured shades on the lamps, and there in the becoming glow stood Jennifer Verity and Ian Macbane beside her. Waring saw the girl's radiant face—and knew that it wasn't only the becoming lighting that made her look so vivid. "Glory!" he thought in a flash. "The girl's fallen for Macbane, and they say he's one of the Dilys aspirants…"

He had no time for further thoughts, for Jennifer exclaimed when she saw him:

"Goodness…it's the Inspector again. We seem to be playing Box and Cox. Did Dr. Wright go to the Maines', Inspector?"

"He did, at the double, Miss Verity—and a good thing too. He got an ambulance and had Mr. Maine moved to hospital at once—he's very ill."

"Oh dear—how awful for Dilys. She's so good about him, and really he's the most difficult parent ever," said Jennifer. "This business about refusing to see a doctor is enough to drive anyone mad."

"Well, I think he was past the stage of being difficult by the time Dr. Wright got there, so you can count it as your good deed for the day, Miss Verity—getting a doctor quickly when one was needed."

"Oh, I'd do anything for Dilys," she said quickly, and then added: "I came on here to tell Mr. and Mrs. Macbane about it all—Aunt Caro, as we all call her, is so helpful when anyone is ill."

"I'm certain she'll do anything she can," put in Ian; Jennifer looked at Waring in a puzzled way, and then asked: "How did you know I was coming on here, Inspector?"

"I didn't," answered Waring truthfully. "I came here to consult Mr. Ian Macbane."

"Oh, then I'll leave you to it," said Jennifer hastily. "I'm so thankful I was at the Hunt Ball the whole time," she added. "I don't know anything about anything, so it's no use asking me questions."

"Well, if any questions arise which you *could* answer, I know where to find you," said Waring.

She gave him a quick glance and then turned to Macbane.

"Goodnight, Ian. I'll ring Dilys later and find out if she wants anything."

"Let me know if there's anything we can do, Jennifer—and for goodness' sake, be careful on that bike. It's a filthy evening—just like Saturday night."

"Heavens—aren't you cheering!" she flashed back. "I'm the world's safest on a bike, I always biked to school. Goodbye for now."

"Come in," said Ian to Waring. "We can use the study if you want to talk—in here. What is it now?"

"It's a very simple question which no one has the common sense to answer simply," said Waring. "I'm hoping I can rely on your common sense to answer it, if you happen to know."

"Well, I'm not fool enough to hold out against the police when they want evidence in a criminal case," said Macbane. "What is it?"

"Do you know if Commander Brent drove Miss Maine home from the Hunt Ball on Saturday evening?"

"He drove her—but not right home," said Macbane, adding, "for obvious reasons," and then looked at Waring. "Didn't Dilys Maine tell you when you asked her?" he enquired. "She promised me she would tell the exact truth if the police asked her."

"She refused to answer, and so did Brent," replied Waring.

"Silly fool," said Ian. "I know he was trying to keep Dilys out of it, because she'd have had to give evidence, but he might have had the common sense to know there's no future in holding out against the police in a criminal case."

"Then why didn't you tell me?" asked Waring wrathfully.

"Because I wasn't asked, and because my evidence on the matter would only have been hearsay," retorted Ian promptly. "It still is, for that matter—I didn't see Dilys Maine in Brent's car: but I repeat firmly that to the best of my knowledge and belief Brent did drive Dilys Maine home—as far as the gate onto the bridle path. She walked the rest. And if Brent tries to brain me because I've told you the truth, I shall still tell him he was a fool for not telling you in the first place. For one thing, it lets him out. Poor Dilys saw the body lying in the road when Brent pulled up—and I can't make out why she didn't tell you at once when you asked: she was perfectly sensible about it when I warned her to tell the exact truth if the police asked her."

"There's nothing perfectly sensible about the Maines now," said Waring. "They're all het up together: Miss Dilys refused to admit she'd been in Brent's car because she didn't want me to know what time she got in. You see, her father was out that evening, and there's some uncertainty when he got home."

"Maine? but that's crazy!" exclaimed Macbane. "He's not in on this. He's a monument of virtue."

"So he may be, but he was out in his car on Saturday evening and the story he told me was distinctly mixed—though I don't think he really knew what he was saying," said Waring. "Look here, Macbane—how well do you know the Maines?"

"I don't!" replied Ian. "I don't know Mr. Maine at all. I saw Dilys at the Hunt Ball two years ago—and I've never forgotten her. That's why I came down this year—I couldn't make it last year."

"I see," said Waring. "Then you don't really know the people around here well?"

"Of course I don't. Good God! Did you think I was a likely suspect?" demanded Ian. "I've only been down here three or four times in my life. I met Nick Brent when I was sailing in a regatta some years ago, so I know a bit about him, but apart from getting to know the Veritys, I hardly know anybody round about. I'd heard of the Reeves, of course—they're a byword—but I'm no sort of authority on folks hereabouts."

"That's a pity," said Waring. "I've had enough local gossip to fill a book, and there's hardly a fact you can pin down. I'm sick of hearing that Hoyle's a bad 'un—even though I'm quite prepared to believe it—but the local men haven't anything positive against him. He's never been charged with a misdemeanour, and they say he's always been cooperative when the police said they'd had complaints of irregularities."

"The complaints being from Mr. Maine, who sounds more than a bit crackers to me," put in Ian.

"Possibly—but that's not much use to me," said Waring. "I've come along to you because you do know what evidence means and now you say, 'Sorry, I'm a stranger here'—or the equivalent—like asking one's way in a strange town and finding an intelligent bloke who can only say. 'Sorry...etc.'"

"Well, I am a stranger here, to all intents and purposes," said Ian. "You don't want me to tell you rumours about the Reeve family, or what the gossips say about Hoyle—it's all hearsay and no substance. The only things I can tell you of any value are the facts you already know—that Brent drove me to Fordings—"

"Let's start a little earlier on," said Waring. "When was it Brent offered to drive you to Fordings?"

Ian Macbane sat and looked at him thoughtfully for a

moment or so, then he said: "All right. Have it your own way, but if you're hopeful about my part in the proceedings, you're losing your way in the dark. However—let's start at the beginning. I reached Fordings at 2.15 on Saturday afternoon and got here about 3.0. My uncle told me Nick had said he could give me a lift into Fordings that evening, and that Tim had said I could have his old Austin if I liked to drive it. I chose Nick's offer: it was jolly decent of him, there were lashings of people wanting a lift. I rang him up and told him I was going to have a word with Tim, and could he pick me up there about eight. It'd save him coming right out here—and that's how we fixed it. Nick called for me at Tim's around eight and drove me to the hall—and I might remind you that from the time I reached this house at three in the afternoon until I spoke to Inspector Turner when he found Hudson and me pulled up by that body on the lower road, my doings are corroborated. I was never alone once."

"O.K.," said Waring. "I only wish I could say the same of everybody else in the case."

"Well, you've got a clean bill for Brent—in spite of the fact that he and Dilys have done their best to look phoney," said Macbane. "Reeve's in the red, I gather, having only a calving cow as an alibi. Hoyle's got his potman and various locals to swear he was never out of sight of somebody for more than five minutes—and five minutes wasn't enough in his case."

Waring put a word in here: "You gave Betty Hoyle a lift along the bridle path on Sunday afternoon."

Ian laughed. "I did—and I don't propose to do it again. I was riding Nick's bike, by the way, greatly to Miss Hoyle's satisfaction. I couldn't make out if her devotion to Nick's bike was as great as her devotion to Nick."

"What's that?" put in Waring, and Macbane laughed.

"Betty Hoyle is crazy on pillion-riding and her great ambition is to get a lift from Nick. I suppose she's got a thing about him because he had a reputation for being a woman hater: he lived alone in that inn of his for years while he was getting it in order—his hermit-crab stage, I called it. So Miss Hoyle sighed in vain. If you want a non-stop gossip, Waring, try Miss Hoyle."

"I'd like to—she looks a talker," said Waring. "Did she tell you any items about Saturday night?"

Ian chuckled. "I tried to lead her on, but as she set out for the ball on somebody's motorbike about half past seven, her evidence wasn't admissible. However, she told me all about Dad being in the bar all the evening—and if you're hoping Hoyle put paid to the deceased, you've got to admit it would have taken him more than five minutes to get the job done."

Waring sat and pondered. "He'd have had to cosh the bloke, shift the body along the bridle path to the low road, fetch Reeve's car, return it, and get back to the inn—he couldn't have done it in less than half an hour—probably more."

Macbane nodded. "All of forty-five minutes I've tried it and I've no doubt you have. And the job was done sometime after 8.15, when Nick and I drove along the low road. So my bright little idea of its having been done earlier, when Mrs. Hoyle and Betty obliged with an alibi for Dad, won't wash."

Macbane sat silent for a moment, then he asked: "Have you got the deceased identified?"

"No, but I reckon his identity's in his face. He's a Reeve—an illegitimate son of the 'old Squire,' as they call him, Michael's grandfather, that is. And I'm prepared to believe he was born on that old caravan site, and that he occasionally came back and saw Hoyle. Although we've nothing official against Hoyle, I think it's probable the countryfolk are right when they say he ran a gambling den."

"Cuts both ways, doesn't it?" put in Macbane. "No one who had been at Hoyle's to gamble would give direct evidence against him because they'd be involved themselves. Anyway, I don't see that you can pin this on Hoyle: he couldn't have been out of the place for more than a few minutes—the chaps who went in for a drink bear that out."

Waring nodded; he was thinking hard, and somehow he found this conversation with Macbane was helping him to sort things out.

"You've been taking what might be called an intelligent interest," he said, and Ian Macbane laughed.

"Admittedly. I've been at a good many murder trials, officially or unofficially, but this is the first time I've ever been mixed up in a police investigation of a capital crime. I'm damned interested and I've been trying to get all the evidence I can."

"Hoping to beat us to it?" asked Waring.

"No. I'm not that sort of fool—only trying to correlate the evidence. You know, in spite of the fact that I can't see how Hoyle could have done it, I still believe he's involved somehow."

"Why?"

"Well, he's the only really questionable character in these parts: he's known to have been mixed up with both Michael Reeve's father and grandfather—both of whom were pretty fair blackguards, I gather—and finally, the general belief is that Hoyle was involved in the disappearance of Rosemary Reeve."

"General belief," groaned Waring. "Too damned general—but go on: haven't you taken it farther than that?"

"Of course I have—though there's no evidence. I'm prepared to believe that the deceased was the chap who was born on that caravan site and that he knew something about the Rosemary Reeve business and Hoyle's part in it. So Hoyle put him out and shifted the chap's body—or had it shifted—near to Michael Reeve's house, because Michael would be an obvious suspect."

"As a theory, it's attractive," said Waring. "It provides a motive and it's a logical train of thought, but not only is there no evidence to prove it, the only evidence we've got proves that Hoyle was never out of sight of somebody for more than five minutes between opening time and closing time—and the potman gives him an alibi for an hour after that."

"Well, couldn't the body have been put where Brent found it between eleven and midnight?"

"It could, of course, but whose car did Hoyle use to run over the body? I'm certain it was Michael Reeve's car which left the marks on the coat, and Reeve's car was in Fordings between eleven and twelve."

"I don't believe Michael Reeve did it," said Macbane, and Waring replied:

"Neither do I—because he's no sort of fool. But the same goes for Hoyle—he's no fool or he'd have got copped years ago. If he'd killed that bloke, Hoyle would have chucked the body over the cliffs, not gone dragging it a mile away and leaving it for us to find."

Macbane sat and thought. "Why was the body left where it was, when was it left—and who left it?" he asked slowly. "It's a teaser."

Waring nodded and said quite casually: "Incidentally, is Miss Verity also taking an intelligent interest in detection? I feel an intelligent girl might help, and it's hard to believe that Miss Jennifer is quite uncooperative when you are so profoundly interested."

Ian Macbane laughed aloud this time. "A palpable hit, Inspector," he rejoined. "You're quite right about the part an intelligent girl can play. I've asked several of the chaps who were at the ball if they could give me any gen about when Michael Reeve was in evidence. They either couldn't care less or didn't think it was the done thing to enquire: but Jennifer has no inhibitions over asking the girlfriends—nor they in answering."

"So what?" asked Waring.

"It seems established that Michael was in evidence from about nine o'clock to midnight, and from 1.15 approx. to the end of proceedings about an hour later. And all the lovelies are completely sceptical about Michael having a petting party in his car for an hour or so, because he isn't that sort of bloke, and there wasn't a single girl at the ball who was missing for over an hour."

"Thanks for the grain of fact—every mickle helping towards the muckle, and my regards to Miss Jennifer," said Waring. "Quite a number of blokes tended to lose interest in that ball round about midnight—including you and Tom Hudson; and the odd thing is that the four of you—Brent, Reeve, Hudson, and yourself all came back by the low road."

"Not so very odd," said Macbane steadily. "Nick Brent told me he chose it because it was often clear of mist when the Greenham and the main roads were thick on top. I told Hudson what Nick had said, so he drove back that way, and Reeve's place is on the low road anyway."

"Yes. How clear was that road when Brent drove you to Fordings?" asked Waring. "As clear as when Hudson drove you back?"

"No. Definitely not," said Macbane. "There was very little mist coming back—it'd cleared a lot. Going to Fordings it was pretty thick in places, and the windscreen misted up my side—we were both smoking and the windows were up—" He broke off and then added, "But don't, for the love of Mike, go cherishing a theory that the corpse was on the road and we never noticed it. It's plain impossible: the chap was spreadeagled right across the middle of the road and Nick's car couldn't have passed it. He'd have had to bump over it—and he didn't. I'll swear in the witness box that the body was *not* on the road when we drove to Fordings, and I've a wholesome repugnance to committing perjury."

"All right—don't protest too much," said Waring, "and thanks a lot for your help. It does help to talk things over," he added, "and you're a clear-headed bloke. I must be off."

II

It was only about ten minutes after Waring had left that Jennifer Verity telephoned and Ian answered the call.

"Ian? It's Jenny. Is the Inspector still with you?"

"No. He's been gone some time. Why?"

"I thought he might like to know something. Bert—the man who brings our papers—says that Betty Hoyle was found on the Greenham Road, badly hurt. She'd either been knocked down by a car or come a spill off a motorbike—they don't seem to know which."

"Cripes…is this another 'incident'—or another accident? Waring will be fed up, he wanted to talk to her. Where was she taken? Hospital?"

"Bert said that Booker found her—the van man from the Co-op, and he took her back home: she was only about a mile from the Rose & Crown when he found her, and he said it seemed the best thing to do."

"Best... I wonder. If she's badly hurt, he may have killed her. Did your chap say how bad she was?"

"I don't suppose he knew, but since he said she was lying almost in the ditch, she must have been unconscious. Of course, we haven't the least idea if this was just a road accident, but I thought that if Waring were still with you, he'd probably want to rush over to see."

"I'm quite sure he would have, but I haven't the vaguest notion where he's gone. Still, they'll have telephoned the local police about the accident—that's obligatory."

"I know, but that van man's a moron and somehow I can't see the Hoyles telephoning the police immediately. It ought to be done at once, oughtn't it?"

"Of course. Look here, Jenny: why don't you do it? You can put it through as an enquiry, saying the paper man told you and you wondered if it were true, because there've been rather a lot of accidents lately."

"All right, if you think I should, Ian—but they'd have to get a doctor and he'd inform the police, wouldn't he?"

"Yes—after he'd got there and examined his patient and all the rest, and that inn's quite a way from any doctor."

"Yes. I see. I'll ring the police and just ask."

"Thank heaven you've got back safely anyway, Jenny. For heaven's sake don't go out again tonight."

"Of course I won't—it's a beastly night anyway. I'll let you know what the cops say—so listen for the phone, won't you?"

"I'll be here—waiting," said Ian.

Chapter XIV

I

WARING HAD BEEN RIGHT IN HIS GUESS THAT ALICE Ridley was a shrewd body: indeed, she had the sort of wits which could have been trained to detection had she entered the police force in her youth (though Alice would have been horrified at such a suggestion—she had a poor opinion of the police). When the ambulance had left, taking Mr. Maine to hospital, with Dilys beside him, and when Dr. Wright and Waring had left too, Alice breathed a huge sigh of relief. She was alone in the house at last and could get busy on her own ideas without fear of interruption. She damped down the kitchen range, moved her saucepans to the side (too thrifty to risk a burnt pan), and then went over and bolted both back and front doors, so that no one could "walk in on her."

"He must have put it somewhere, and upstairs rather than down," she thought. There was not much that Alice missed: she had deduced Dilys's presence at the Hunt Ball from tiny snippets of tulle which had clung to the carpet; she had deduced that the master had been in trouble on Saturday night from other items of evidence—there was the broken glass: minute slivers which Alice had swept up on Sunday morning, one near the telephone, others on Mr. Maine's bedroom floor. The slivers were part of a watch glass—Alice was quite certain of that—and the master hadn't worn his wristwatch yesterday. She had noted particularly, because he always wore that watch. "And he couldn't have realised at the time that he'd broken it, else he'd have taken it off and put it in his pocket, him being a sensible fellow," she thought, "but he wasn't sensible Saturday night. That know-all of an Inspector said maybe he'd been in a roughhouse, and if I can find that watch of his I might find out what time it stopped."

Alice went upstairs to Robert Maine's bedroom and began a systematic search: she knew where he kept all his things—hadn't she cleaned his room ever since Dilys was a tiny tot?—and Robert Maine had kept no secrets from his wife, and his wife had trusted Alice Ridley completely.

His keys were on the bedside table, where he had put them when he staggered up to bed with Alice's sturdy arm round him, only two hours ago. It took her a very short time to realise that the watch she sought wasn't in any usual or obvious place, and she had already looked for it when she cleaned the room that morning and failed to find it. "He's hidden it," said Alice to herself. "Muddled or not, he'd got the time on his mind, as though it mattered a lot."

She took up the bunch of keys: she knew what they all were (as his wife had known) and unlocked an old-fashioned brass-bound box, which opened out to make a writing desk. Lifting a flap, the first thing she found was a photograph, a picture of a lovely, laughing, fair-haired girl—not Dilys, but Dilys's mother, Eleanor. It was Eleanor who had chosen that queer new-fangled name for her beautiful baby... Dilys... Queer, they'd all thought it. As she looked at the photograph, Alice felt a tear trickle down her nose. Eleanor Maine had been very good to Alice in the long ago, when Alice had been sorely in need of help; now Eleanor was dead, and it looked as though her daughter might be in need of help. Quite simply, Alice was prepared to do almost anything to help: to suppress evidence or to invent it, it was all one to her. If the police were prepared to suspect Robert Maine of evildoing, then the police were fools, and Alice was quite ready to throw a spanner in the workings of the law if she could.

"Not that he's not a fool himself," she muttered angrily, thinking of her master. "If he'd only trusted me we'd never have been in this muddle... Ah, there it is..."

The watch was tucked away under some papers and Alice stared at it. Some of the glass was still there, wedged under the hands, and the time it showed was half past nine. "Saturday evening that'd have been," she thought to herself. "There's grit in it, too...as though he'd fallen on the ground, and where he was when he did it, I can guess as well as that know-all..."

After a moment's thought, she wrapped the watch in her handkerchief and put it in her pocket, relocked the writing desk and chose another key. The big hanging cupboard where Robert Maine kept his clothes had been locked when Alice did the room on Sunday morning, and it had made her puzzled. Didn't the master always leave his office clothes for her to brush and see to at the weekend? Why had he put his suit away and locked the cupboard in addition? She soon found the dark suit: coat and trousers were folded into a damp and clumsy bundle in the far corner of the big cupboard. "They must have been soaked," she thought, "and it didn't rain Saturday night."

She hurried downstairs, plugged in her electric iron, got the ironing board out—and a pile of rough dried laundry as camouflage, in case anybody caught her at it—spread the coat on the board and examined it carefully.

Alice was a good detective over matters within her experience: she soon ascertained that there was no blood on the coat; neither was it seawater which had soaked into the good dark cloth—seawater always left a white mark at the edges when it began to dry on material like this. "I reckon it must have been a ditch he lay in to have got his clothes in this state," she thought. "It's not seawater, and if he'd been thrown in the river, he'd have been drenched right through and dripped all over the place... Smells like a ditch, too."

Alice's own idea was to keep her master "out of it"—"it" being the trouble on the lower road. Dry his clothes, hide his watch, make everything seem normal, so that if Waring came along and insisted on searching there shouldn't be anything unusual for him to find.

"Once they prove he's been in a mix-up, they'll go suggesting all manner of things," she thought as the steam rose and the iron sizzled while she pressed the suit under a cloth. It was the back of the clothes which had got wettest. "A ditch, that's what it was: that ditch near the Rose & Crown—maybe he hid in the ditch, watching out for goodness knows what. Why couldn't he have let things be? If that Hoyle's a rogue—and everybody with a ha'p'orth of sense knows that—better have let the police on to him instead of giving us all this trouble. If he hadn't got me to look after him they might arrest him on suspicion, and it's two to one he doesn't even remember what happened."

Alice was not acquainted with the phrase "delayed concussion," but she knew all about the symptoms attendant on that state. A countrywoman born, she had tended accident cases of many kinds, often without any advice from a doctor: she knew that a man who had had a head injury might be rendered unconscious, recover his senses after a period of time and go about his business for a while without remembering much of what had happened to him; she knew, too, that that same man would probably go sick later, and that any head injury should be treated with care. Alice needed no doctor to tell her that a man with a head injury should be kept flat in a dark room.

"If he'd only had the sense to tell me, I'd have looked after him and saved all this bother," she thought angrily. "As things are, Dilys'll go saying something stupid to try to help her dad out of the muddle."

She banged the hot iron down on her sizzling cloth and thought out the likeliest explanation, for the doctors would know all about the head injury. "His car broke down and he tried to push it and slipped," she hazarded to herself. "The roads were slippy and he went backwards and hit his head down in the dip there—there's always frost in that hollow..."

Her ironing completed, she put the suit on a hanger and left it to air by the hot tank; then, as an afterthought, she went upstairs and collected Robert Maine's underwear from the linen basket in the bathroom and put it to soak with the other washing in the wash house. "And if that know-all comes in and notices I'm a day late with the washing I'll tell him he ought to've noticed it was no sort of a drying day today and I use my common sense about when I do the laundry," she thought. "I reckon he can't make head or tail or that there now."

She gave a large sigh when she had tidied up from her ironing activities, glanced round the kitchen to see that everything was in order, and then went to the telephone.

II

Robert Maine had known Alice for so long that he thought—quite mistakenly—that he knew all there was to know about her. Alice Ridley had both acquaintances and relations with whom she kept in touch quite unbeknown to her employers. Alice's cousin Joe had had a variety of jobs in his time: horseman on a farm, van man to the railway (driving the horse vans), drayman to a brewer's, and finally (his present job) odd-job man to the Railway Hotel in Fordings, where his still considerable strength and experience with barrels, bungs, and taps made him a valued employee in the cellars. Alice Ridley was very careful never to mention Joe to anybody, but she never forgot that she and Joe had been playmates on her father's farm in the long ago, and she often asked Joe for advice or for news of old friends, or even to do errands for her on occasion. She rang through to the Railway Hotel without any hesitation and asked if it'd be convenient for Joe Benson to come to the telephone for a moment.

"O.K., ducks," replied a woman's cheerful voice. "I'll get him. Hold on."

"That you, Joe? It's Alice here," she said a moment later. "Any news about you-know-what?"

"Aye. I found out. Jack noticed—he's always hanging around at the back where the cars are parked—you know, along by the goods line. That car you mentioned was moved between 7.0 and 7.30. Can't get it nearer than that. And see here, there's been some other enquiries, like you said there might be, but Jack didn't know nothing: and he won't know nothing. You know how 'tis."

"I know," said Alice. "Anything about the other little matter?"

"Well, it's a spot hard to say for certain, but I'm told there's a firm date for a party that night, things being as they are, and your old man might have picked up the news—been going on for years, that date has, or so they says as ought to know. What's that?"

Alice had been muttering to herself "No fool like an old fool," but she spoke up quickly: "Nothing. Only me grumbling to meself, Joe."

"Aye, likely. 'Tis a proper mess all round," replied the other, "but see here: if it'd help, I know one or two chaps who was on the roads that night might remember summat if it'd be a convenience. I don't like to think of you worrying so, Alice."

"That's all right, thanking you all the same, Joe. Somebody's got to use their heads, things being as they are, and there's only me to do the thinking. Now don't you do aught unless I give you the word, but I'll say this: whatever 'twas, 'twas on our road, this side the hill up to Greenham."

"Arr... I reckoned that'd be best. Well, you say the word and I'll see to it. I never did hear such a pack of nonsense as some folks is talking—and some as ought to know better, too."

"You're telling me," said Alice. "A fool he may be, but a rogue he's not and that I do know. Thanking you kindly, Joe, and that's all for now."

Alice went back into the kitchen after she had hung up and sat down to think things out: Joe's report was all perfectly clear to her. Mr. Maine had driven into Fordings on Saturday morning, parked his car at the back of the Railway Hotel and gone to Southampton by train. He had returned to Fordings shortly after seven, picked up his car—and driven out to the Greenham Road, to the Rose & Crown—Alice was certain of it. The "firm date" Joe had mentioned so cautiously was the day of the Hunt Ball, on the evening of which Hoyle had had a "party." "Just the sort of evening to suit him for his goings-on, with all the police drafted into Fordings to sort out their blessed cars at the hall," thought Alice. "And the master got wind of it and went along to watch, trying to catch Hoyle out, and got knocked over the head for his pains," she went on. "But I don't like it—any of it. That pub of Hoyle's is too close to the lower road, and they'll be asking what the master was doing all that time."

Alice worried away at her problem: there were certain good points about Joe's news: there was Jack, for instance. Jack, a hanger-on at the pub, and the railway station, had once been charged by the police for "loitering with intent." He had got off with a caution and the result was that he had regarded the police as his natural enemies ever since. If the police asked Jack questions, Jack wouldn't know: he would play the moron— and Jack could defeat any policeman at that game. So far it was all plain sailing, thought Alice; and if necessary Joe could oblige with a friend who had seen Mr. Maine's car on the other side of the river. Having reached this stage in her meditations, Alice was startled by the sound of the telephone.

"Drat the thing!" she exclaimed, but even as she hurried to answer it, her mind was busy with conjectures about the caller. "Maybe it's the hospital," she thought. "He looked mortal bad…"—but she checked the thought which came unbidden to her mind: "Wouldn't it be better if he passed on, poor soul, he's been getting queerer and queerer of late… You ought to be ashamed, Alice Ridley," she told herself, "and anyway, things never work out the easy way…"

III

"Is that Miss Ridley? Commander Brent here. I've been told that Mr. Maine has been taken to hospital. Is it true?"

"Yes, sir, it's true all right," replied Alice. "We had to have a doctor, he was that bad when he came home—pneumonia, they say. The doctor ordered an ambulance and had him taken to the cottage hospital."

"I'm very sorry to hear that," said Brent. "What about Miss Maine—is she at home?"

"No, sir, she's not. She went in the ambulance with him, so she could hear the doctor's report when they'd examined him."

"I see—but if she stays late at the hospital, how will she get home? Look here, I could ring the hospital and find out how long she's likely to be there, and then drive out to fetch her back."

"That'd be very kind, sir," replied Alice. "The only thing is there's so much talk... You know what I mean. I'm so worried I don't know what to do for the best."

"I'm very sorry about all this—more sorry than I can say," said Brent, and Alice could hear the concern in his deep voice. "Could I come over and have a word with you—it's easier to talk when you're together, easier than talking over the telephone, I mean."

"I'd be thankful, sir," burst out Alice. "What with one thing and another I'm properly bothered."

"Try not to worry—worrying doesn't help anybody," said Brent. "I'll be along in about quarter of an hour."

Alice went back to the kitchen again, made up the fire, and then took the suit she had ironed and carried it upstairs—it was well aired now, and the good cloth showed very little sign of its rough usage. As she came downstairs, the telephone rang again.

"Never rains but it pours," she thought. This time it was Michael Reeve.

"I'm ringing up to ask about Mr. Maine," he said. "I'm told he has been taken to hospital: is that a fact, or is somebody spreading rumours?"

"If people'd mind their own business, it'd save a lot of trouble," said Alice tartly. "Mr. Maine was taken ill and he's in hospital, and I've got enough to worry about without answering the telephone."

And with that she smacked the receiver down. A moment later she was ashamed of herself for being so abrupt and then spoke aloud in sheer exasperation. "Them Reeves, they're at the bottom of all this trouble… If Michael Reeve hadn't taken that farm, this'd never've happened. It was because Michael was there… Oh, drat the thing! If that's him again, I'll give him a proper piece of my mind."

But it wasn't Michael Reeve; the slow husky voice which spoke was Joe Benson's. "That you, Alice? I've just heard a queer bit of news. They say Betty Hoyle's had an accident—run down and left for dead on the Greenham Road. I thought I'd let you know. Things is still happening it seems, and no one can say it was you-know-who this time."

"What time did it happen?" asked Alice, a new fear leaping at her.

"Reckon nobody knows. After dusk it was—six o'clock they found her."

"Oh, my goodness me, Joe, it's all enough to drive a body crazy," groaned Alice. "Don't you go ringing up no more: I'm in the sort of state when I can't help imagining things. Not that I'm not grateful to you, but you know how 'tis when you start worrying."

Again Alice went back to the kitchen, and sat down heavily, to think. She had a very clear mind, and she went through every piece of evidence with a deliberation which Waring would have appreciated. The last piece of evidence about Betty Hoyle troubled her a lot. "She must have known something," she thought. "I don't believe in all these accidents, we don't never have no accidents hereabouts. And that Hoyle may be a bad 'un, but he'd never have done that to Betty: thinks the world of Betty, Hoyle does." At the back of Alice's mind was Joe's vague statement: "After dusk it happened. Six o'clock they found her." It was shortly before six o'clock that Mr. Maine had come in—and how he ever drove home in the state he was in, Alice couldn't imagine. "It's enough to drive a woman mad," she said to herself.

IV

Considering the state of perturbation she was in, it wasn't surprising that Alice Ridley was thankful to pour out her troubles to Brent. He was a good listener, and his kindly encouragement elicited all Alice's woes: the time Dilys got in on Saturday night; the time Alice telephoned; the time Mr. Maine got in; Dilys's refusal to tell Waring who had driven her home; and Alice's own intervention calling Dilys up to her father. "I know what's in her mind," said Alice unhappily. "Her dad said it was only twelve o'clock when he got in, and she won't admit he was wrong. I'm that afraid she'll say something silly and get mixed up in all the trouble herself."

"I'll see that doesn't happen," said Brent. "I didn't want to let the police know she was in my car because she'd have had to give evidence, but with things as they are, we shall have to tell the plain facts. But why are you so worried about what her father was doing?"

"In case the police try to prove he killed that chap you found," she replied. "He was out in his car all that evening and he must have been in some sort of trouble—though what it was I don't know."

"Look here, Alice: if you want me to help—and you know I'll do all I can—you'd better tell me what's in your mind. Half-confidences are no good. I know that Mr. Maine has been trying to prove a case against Hoyle—are you thinking he went to the Rose & Crown that night?"

"I just don't know," she said unhappily. "I'm trying to find someone who saw his car coming over Cookbourne Bridge—he always drives home from Fordings that way. You see, folks round here don't like going to the police and getting mixed up in a bother like this one, but they'll talk to me because they've always known me."

"Yes, I see that—though you need to be careful that your witnesses are reliable."

"I'll be careful, all right," she said. "If I can only get it proved he came by the road across the river, I shouldn't worry so much. It's not that I'm afraid he did it—anything wrong, I mean—it's the police making things up I'm afraid of. And the master always had a down on the Reeves."

Brent studied her shrewdly. "And to tell the plain truth, you don't want it said that Mr. Maine has been watching the Hoyles' place? You want to prove he came home by the main road, the other side of the river?"

Alice nodded: she was being very careful—even with Brent. "That's it, sir. If the police get it into their heads he came by the Greenham Road, past Hoyle's place, well, it's not far to the low road if you take the bridle path—that's what they'll say. One thing I do know for sure—the master didn't drive by the low road, not between half past seven and half past eight he didn't, and that's the time they reckon the man was killed."

"How do you know he didn't?"

"Because Will Hamden, that works at French's farm, he biked out to Fordings after tea Saturday and came back by the low road, as far as the Hollydown turn, that is, just before Michael Reeve's place. He had a puncture and he had to push his bike, and it took him an hour from the Bramber Head turning to the Hollydown turn and he says that no car passed him all the way. But there's one other thing that's worrying me," went on Alice. "Maybe you've heard about Betty Hoyle being knocked down this evening?"

"I certainly hadn't heard—but what's Betty Hoyle got to do with it?"

"Oh, I know I'm being silly," cried Alice, "but I've got fair worked up. The master drove home from Fordings this evening, ill as he was, and in no state to drive at all. For all I know the police will try to make out he did that, too, being on the road in the state he was. Don't you say nothing to the police about the master watching Hoyle's, sir."

"Pull yourself together, Alice. You're imagining things," protested Brent, and she replied:

"I know I am—and if you knew the comfort it is to be able to tell somebody the silly things I've been thinking…"

"All right," he said, patting her shoulder. "I understand—you've been brooding over things and letting everything get out of proportion. Now don't you worry any longer: when Mr. Maine is well again, he'll be able to give a sensible account of what happened, and I'll talk to Miss Dilys and tell her she's got to tell the police about being in my car. That's all perfectly straightforward. And Alice—don't go cooking the evidence. It won't work—the police are much too shrewd to be hoodwinked."

"I want to keep the master out of it," said Alice obstinately. "He never had naught to do with any of it, that I do know."

"Of course he had nothing to do with it—and we mustn't allow Dilys to let herself get muddled up thinking she's helping her father," replied Brent. "I'd better be off now: the hospital people said there was no object in her staying the night there. Mr. Maine isn't in any immediate danger."

"I only hope he isn't," sighed Alice, and Brent added abruptly:

"You know I'll look after her, Alice—whatever happens. And don't you get worrying and imagining things. The fact is that the pair of you have got in a panic, just because the police asked a few routine questions."

After Brent had left, Alice made herself a cup of tea and sat over the kitchen fire, trying to cheer herself up by remembering Brent's sensible words. At ten o'clock the telephone rang again and informed her that Dilys was being driven home. It wasn't until she replaced the receiver that an odd idea shot suddenly across Alice's mind. "Well, I never did…" she said to herself. "I must be going crazy…" And she went back to the fire and started worrying all over again.

Chapter XV

I

When Waring left Ian Macbane, his intention was to return to Fordings, hand in his report, and knock off. Hours of work and overtime are disregarded by the detective who is hot on the trail, but in a case like this one it seemed to Waring that a good long think might be a more profitable way of spending the evening than further attempts to sort out objective fact from local gossip. It wasn't until he had halted at the main road and was about to turn cautiously in the direction of Fordings by way of Cookbourne Bridge that two sentences echoed in his mind—both uttered by Ian Macbane: "It's a filthy evening—just like Saturday night," he had said, and then, "I'm a stranger here."

"I wonder," thought Waring. "It's worth trying out…"

Very carefully, with due regard for the Highway Code, he manoeuvred his car so that he could return the way he had come. He determined to drive back past Foxlea Mill, then up the hill, turn left down the low road, reverse at the road junction by Bramber Hill, return along the low road and then follow the transverse road, which would take him to the Greenham Road; then turn left past the Rose & Crown, and so on to Fordings again. In this manner he would drive along all the roads followed by his witnesses—and suspects—on Saturday evening, and drive, moreover, in the same weather conditions which had prevailed on Saturday.

Thus it came about that when Jennifer Verity rang up Ian Macbane and told him about Betty Hoyle's accident, and later, when the local police tried to find him to report the same happening, Waring was not to be found. He was driving slowly and carefully through the dank mist by a succession of narrow, difficult country roads, all of which were characterised by switchback hills and mist which varied according to the elevation.

It was, as Macbane had said, a filthy evening, and apparently the rural population thought so too, for Waring saw neither vehicle nor pedestrian for miles—indeed, he saw very little beyond the verge of the road in his fog lamp's beam and the occasional swirl of white vapour on the hilltops. It was one of those evenings when a driver was fully occupied in keeping his vehicle on the road and had no attention to spare for anything else.

It was when Waring had driven four of the seven miles described by local custom as "the low road" that he saw the headlights of a car facing him, pulled up on the verge, with a man signalling to him in the beam of light. Waring pulled up, called out "What's your trouble?" and recognised Tom Hudson, the young farmer who had driven Macbane back from the Hunt Ball.

"The Lord he knoweth: the damned thing's packed up on me," said Hudson. "I've been doing all I know for the best part of an hour and I'm fed up. Can you give me a lift? There's a garage chap I know who lives just beyond the Bramber road junction, and he'll probably come out if I ask him."

"O.K. Hop in," said Waring.

Hudson turned off his headlights, left the spotlights on, and then came and joined Waring. "Thanks a lot," he said. "I could have walked it—but I loathe walking and it'd take a good hour. Rather a rum go," he went on. "Reminiscent of Saturday evening and Nick Brent leaving his car parked way back there."

"Reminiscent of Saturday evening in more senses than one," replied Waring. "Was the mist about the same—patchy, like this?"

"It's a darned sight worse this evening than it was on Saturday and looks like it's getting thicker," replied Hudson. "It was fairly thick on the road across the river on Saturday: I went that way, but I came back by this road because Brent told Macbane it was often clearer on the low road. He was right, too. There was very little mist coming back."

"Sounds as though you don't often use this road," commented Waring.

"Quite true, I hardly ever come this way, but there used to be a shocking bad bit of surface, near the culvert. They've relaid it at last and it's quite passable now. The fact is you get into habits about roads and my habit is to take the main road over Cookbourne Bridge."

"Why this diversion from habit tonight?"

Hudson laughed, a little shamefacedly. "Well, there are really two answers: first, I wanted to test Brent's theory that this road's always clearer than the main road in conditions like this; second, I wanted to drive this way to see how things look if you rush that hill where we found the body. You know how it is: if there's a steepish bit coming you tread on it as you approach it. I bet that's what happened, you know: some-body with inefficient lights went roaring up from the dip and killed the bloke; it's happened time and again when visibility's bad—and the driver said to himself, 'Must have been a sheep or what have you'—and didn't stop to see."

"Well—I won't say that I agree, but it's the most comfort-able explanation for a lot of people," said Waring.

"There's another point in favour of that argument," went on Hudson. "No one in these parts would ever expect to see a pedestrian on this road. It's one of the most unfrequented bits of road in the county—seven miles of it, and the only places you pass are Mike Reeve's and those two empty cottages—ruins, both of them. There are only two turnings—the Hollydown one, which nobody uses since the county made a nice new road for the loony bin, and the turning to French's farm. This road was used by the manor people in the old days, but nobody uses it now. There's no bus along it: the buses—about two a day—go by the Greenham Road."

"Yes. I noticed how little used this road is."

"You're telling me! I was the best part of an hour trying to get my outfit going and devil a soul passed me—till you happened along. Here's the road junction—my chap lives along this lane. You going into Fordings?"

"I'm just cruising around, getting the feel of things," said Waring with a grin.

"Cripes! Rather you than me. Well—thanks a lot."

Hudson jumped out as Waring pulled up, and the latter drove on until he found a turning where he could reverse, and then drove back the way he had come.

Half a mile on, he saw a white blur in the mist which told of approaching headlights. The road was very narrow at this point and Waring pulled in as close as he dared (he knew there was a ditch), dipped his own lights and waited; he reckoned there was just about room for the other driver to pass—if he were careful. A moment later a very old car came cautiously out of the mist towards him, slowed down to a crawl while the driver put his head out of the window to judge his distance, and Waring found himself looking at Michael Reeve. The latter pulled up, his car only a matter of inches from Waring's, and called:

"I say, there's a car pulled up on the verge some way back and no driver in evidence. Since it happens to be you, I might as well say I haven't run over anybody—just in case you have any more ideas."

The voice was cool enough, and Waring noted that Reeve wasn't frightened of the police—far from it.

"It's O.K.," he called back. "It's Mr. Hudson's car: it's broken down and I gave him a lift to the corner."

"Right—thought I'd mention it. Thanks for pulling in— this is the narrowest bit of the whole bloody road. Goodnight."

Reeve moved on, creaking in bottom gear as noisily as an old locomotive, and Waring laughed a little. "That empty car gave him a turn: once again... I wonder. This is a dammed funny mist, thick and thin by turns."

Despite the mist, Waring recognised the spot where the body had been found, and he admitted in all honesty that Hudson's theory had something to be said for it on a misty night. Any driver, knowing the road, would tend to accelerate as he ran down the slope to the culvert in order to get up the hill on the other side without changing down: "...And come to think of it, that was a ready-made explanation for us," meditated Waring, carefully refraining from accelerating and changing right down as he mounted the hill to the pointer.

Again he saw the glare of headlights approaching from his left, pulled up at the T-junction and waited for the other car to pass. It was going in the direction of Foxlea Mill, and Waring just had time to recognise the number plate—Commander Brent's car. "They're all out this evening, driving round in circles," thought Waring. "Hell—here it is again, thicker than ever."

The mist swirled round him as he got going again, noticing the steep gradient at the road junction, turned left, kept on for half a mile and then turned left again, onto the Greenham Road this time. This was at a higher level than the parallel low road and the mist was more uniform, a tiresome white blur which shut out everything save for road verges and occasional fences and hedges. Waring kept an eye open for the Rose & Crown—it was on the right-hand side of the road, standing behind hedges, like a well-kept cottage. He saw the hedge in his own headlights, but the mist was so thick he couldn't even see lights in the windows or door—if there were any lights. "I should think trade's about minus this evening," he thought as he drove on, trying to see what there was to see—occasional glimpses of dark hedges, gaunt trees, and the rough grass of the verge, yellow under his spotlight.

II

It was after nine o'clock that the Macbanes' telephone rang again, and Aunt Caroline said, "Dear, oh dear. I sometimes wish we hadn't got a telephone..."

Ian rushed to answer it, expecting he knew not what.

"Waring here. Sorry to bother you again—"

"Waring!" exclaimed Ian. "Where the deuce are you? They've been trying to get hold of you all over the place."

"Why? What's happened now?"

"Betty Hoyle was run down or came a cropper or something. They found her on the road about six o'clock, somewhere near the bus stop. Some fool picked her up and carted her home in a van and they never thought of reporting it—or said they didn't."

"Where is she now—at home?"

"No. They've taken her to hospital."

"Then there's damn all I can do about it at the moment," said Waring. "Look here, Macbane, are you game to cooperate in an experiment? I want you to come out to Tim Grant's cottage, as you did last Saturday, and follow the route you took then. I'll drive you—pick you up at Tim Grant's, that is."

"Good Lord, what for? It's the hell of a lousy evening."

"I know it is. The point is, as you said, it's like Saturday evening. If you're game to help, I'll send a police car to bring you along to Mr. Grant's. I wouldn't ask if it weren't important, but it is."

"Well, if you put it that way, I haven't much option," said Macbane, "but, as I told you before, if you're getting bees in your bonnet about my part in the proceedings, you're wasting your time and you might as well go home and keep warm."

"I'll have a car along to fetch you as soon as they can make it," said Waring.

Ian Macbane hung up the receiver, aware of a definite sense of discomfort. A police car—well, that might be to save him time and trouble—or it might not. Then his legal acumen reasserted itself and he said to himself, "If Waring tries any funny stuff on me, he'll soon find where he gets off." He went back to the sitting room and told his aunt and uncle about Waring's request. "I haven't the foggiest what it's all about," he added, "but since he asked for my cooperation, I couldn't very well refuse."

"I do think it's too bad," protested Aunt Caroline. "Ian's the very last person to know anything about all this wretched story."

Uncle John hitched an eyebrow up in a quizzical way. "Are you quite sure you haven't the—er...foggiest, Ian?"

His nephew grinned. "Foggiest—not an inapposite word," said Ian. "It occurs to me that Waring might have a theory that when Nick drove me on Saturday evening, the body was in the road and we didn't even see it. Of course, the mist was much thicker going than it was coming back, but I've already told Waring his idea's a washout. The thing's impossible."

"Why is it?" rejoined Uncle John. "It's often easy to miss things in a fog, when visibility's very poor."

"This is nothing to do with visibility," retorted Ian. "The body was sprawled right across the middle of the road, and if it'd been there on the outward journey, even if we hadn't seen it, we should have felt it—we should have bumped right over it. In addition to which the police knew perfectly well that there were no tyre marks from Nick's car on the poor devil's coat—those tyres of his are almost new and the track they leave is unmistakable."

"Well, that sounds pretty convincing," replied Uncle John, "but Waring isn't what you'd describe as a stupid fellow, is he?"

"No. He's a very able chap, but I think it's probable that once he gets an idea into his head, he'd be very pertinacious before he let go again—trying it out all ways and so forth. Listen...yes, this will be the police car; he's been pretty snappy over getting it here. Don't sit up, Aunt. I don't suppose I shall be long, but there's no reason for you to sit up for me."

"All right, Ian. I'll leave you a hot drink in the Thermos and the whisky on the sideboard."

"Bless you! Goodnight!" called Ian.

III

Waring had spent quite a time in the telephone box near the Bramber road junction. He had got what he called "one of those ideas," and he meant to test it this evening, while the weather conditions so closely resembled those of Saturday evening. The reason that the police car reached the Macbanes' so promptly was that Waring had ordered it to be sent before he did anything else, with instructions that if Ian had gone out, he was to be fetched from wherever he happened to be. Next, Waring had rung up Ian, found him at home and got him to agree to come out; after that, he put through another call to enquire about Betty Hoyle. He got very little information, save that she was now in the cottage hospital "doing nicely," though she was considerably damaged, apparently as the result of a fall from a motorbike. This last bit was guesswork, but her injuries and the state of her clothes suggested that this was the likeliest explanation.

"I'd say this," said the Sergeant to Waring. "There's a lot of things said about her father and we're never too sure ourselves—but he didn't do this, of that I'm quite sure. I reckon it's all of a piece with the other story. She saw something or heard something, and someone tried to put her out."

"They don't seem to have succeeded," said Waring, and the Sergeant chuckled.

"No, but if she hadn't been an uncommon tough one, she'd have gone west: the surgeons say it's a bloody marvel she lived."

"Let's hope she'll feel chatty when they give her a chance to chat," said Waring. "Got a man by her?"

"A woman—Inspector Jane Ross: she won't miss much," replied the Sergeant.

"Well, I'll be seeing you later, Sarge," said Waring. "At the moment I'm driving round in circles, but if I have any luck, there'll be some explaining to be done."

A moment later he was on the move again, driving back to Tim Grant's. Grant was a retired schoolmaster of seventy-five; he lived alone in a cottage about a mile away from the low road. Waring had already explored the approaches to the cottage, which was built in a woodland clearing (it had once been a gamekeeper's cottage), and it could be reached by a variety of tracks, all equally rough, which had been used by the tractors belonging to a tree-felling contractor.

When Waring parked his car outside the cottage, he said to himself, "I suppose it's rather a good spot in the summer." On that drear January evening, when every branch dripped lifelessly and the dank mist hung in wreaths around beech trunks which looked like grey ghosts in the headlights, it seemed a melancholy spot.

Waring deliberately turned off the heating device which kept the inside of his windscreen clear from misting, and equally deliberately lighted a cigarette. He wanted to reproduce, as closely as possible, the conditions when Brent and Macbane had driven on Saturday evening, and Macbane had said, "We were both smoking and the windscreen misted up."

Waring did not have long to wait. His timing worked nicely: the police car pulled up a few yards away and Macbane got out, followed by a constable. Waring got out to meet them, saying in his cheerful, normal way:

"Sorry to bring you out: I know it's a foul evening—just like Saturday, as everybody keeps on telling me."

"Well, I hope you've got a valid reason for your goings-on," said Macbane. "I think the rumour's going round that I've been arrested… Hullo, here's Tim. He must think we're all crackers."

The cottage door opened and a white-haired man looked out, his head shining in the light behind him. "Hullo! It's you, Ian, isn't it? What's the excitement? Come along in."

"No such luck, Tim. This is Inspector Waring. He's got a bee in his bonnet, or I think he has, and nothing'll satisfy him but taking me for a drive into Fordings. My own belief is that he's got a bogus corpse on the road and hopes to drive over it without me noticing it."

"Just a matter of timing," put in Waring cheerfully. "When chaps like this one get fresh about the police, they always forget it's no more fun for us than it is for them. I've been driving round in circles for hours and you've only got to do it once. Come along and let's get it over. There's bed for you at the end of it and a large question mark for me."

"Well, let me know if you get home safely," called Grant.

When they were in the car, Ian asked tartly: "Will you tell me exactly what all this is about?"

"I'm going to drive you as far as Bramber Head by the route which, I understand, you followed on Saturday," said Waring. "All that I'm asking is that you should tell me if you notice anything which you didn't notice on Saturday—including bumps or lack of them, corpses or absence of same, approaching or overtaking vehicles, pedestrians or anything else."

"We saw neither vehicles nor pedestrians, and you know it," retorted Macbane. "All right—get on with it. I said I'd cooperate, and I will."

"Good. Here goes. What a road…"

They bumped through the coppice to the lane, along the lane's tortuous half-mile, turned left and then left again—the steep turn which took them in the Fordings direction. Ian Macbane said:

"O.K. This is the low road. The corpse was at the bottom of

this dip—when we came back. It wasn't there when we drove to Fordings." He leant forward, wiped the misted windscreen, and kept his eyes on the road. Waring drove slowly and carefully, and after a moment or two Macbane said:

"O.K. We've passed the fatal spot—no booby traps, fakes, or illusions."

"I never suggested there would be," said Waring. "Did Brent drive at this speed, or faster?"

"Faster—he knows the road, of course, and his headlamps and spotlight are A1. That's the culvert, isn't it, and Reeve's place a bit beyond. Lord, it seems pretty deadly tonight—and I enjoyed it on Saturday."

"Mist conditions about the same?"

"Very much. It was thick on the hills, but quite clear down in Fordings. What was that turn—the Hollydown one?— that's right. They say nobody ever uses this road now except Michael Reeve... The mist's a bit thicker than it was on Saturday, at least I think it is." Again he leant forward and wiped the windscreen—the wipers were going, back, forth, back, forth, but the chill air outside caused the inside of the window to mist up... "just as it did on Saturday," muttered Ian Macbane. "This is a mug's game," he went on. "I can see the road and see the hedges, occasionally, and that's all: but if there had been anything lying in the road, I should have seen it, and if we'd bumped over anything, I should have felt it."

"That's all right," said Waring imperturbably. "All I asked you to testify was whether you noticed any difference in the drive this evening compared with the drive on Saturday."

"No, not really," said Macbane slowly. "The mist's a bit thicker on the hilltops, but otherwise it's the same—in a physical sense I mean. Otherwise it's all different."

"How so?"

"Oh, don't be such a great oaf. On Saturday I was looking forward to the ball and I was yattering away to Brent. I don't suppose I bothered to look at the road—why should I? This evening I've been trying to stare through the mist, trying to make out what the hell you're driving at, and feeling pretty fed up because I think you've gone all astray, trying to tie me up in knots for reasons of your own... This is the last hill, isn't it?—the rise over Bramber, and we shall see the Fordings lights as soon as we run down out of the mist—just as we did on Saturday."

"That's it," said Waring. "Over the top and down we go. There'll be a car to take you home, if that's any consolation."

"Thanks a lot. Could they take me by the main road—across the river? I'm fed up with this route."

"As you wish," said Waring.

They were over the ridge and began to run down smoothly; far below them they saw the first lights twinkling. Macbane was silent for quite a time: then he spoke very soberly:

"Sorry, Waring. I'm there at last. I thought you were being a mug. I was the mug. That's right, isn't it?"

"I think I require notice of that question," replied Waring pleasantly.

IV

It was while Waring was still "driving round in circles" that the local people collected a piece of evidence which sent their spirits up considerably. Their witness was an old man named Patton, who had once been employed on Sewell's Racecourse. He had retired now, and it was probably this fact that made him ready to talk when those whose work kept them in the bookies' eyes found it expedient to know nothing. In short, Patton identified the body found on the low road.

"His ma was a Romany lass, and he was born on that there caravan site," said Patton.

"Mr. Hoyle denies this," put in the Inspector. "He says that the man who once lived on the caravan site was his own age—over sixty—and served in the army with him in the '14–'18 war."

"Mebbe—but there was two of them," said Patton. "This one's younger than t'other. I mind them both—tic-tac men: Alf and Fred they called 'emselves, or Alfred when they was being funny. This is Fred—got a knife scar in his shoulder— that right? Alf knew a lot about hosses, but Fred was a wizard with dogs."

"Dogs, eh?" put in the Inspector. "Greyhounds?"

"Any dogs: he was a dirty dog himself. If so be he wasn't a goner I'd not have been that keen on talking about him. Aye, this is Fred, not Alf. Alf did a bolt after that case when Lord Landon's filly was maimed—I've never seen him since—but Fred's been around at Sewell's once or twice last season."

Patton stopped and ruminated: he was a very old man and couldn't be hurried. Then he said slowly: "Them Reeves—got it in his face, hasn't he? Not that he was a killer—too fond of his own skin. There's some'll pull a knife among those racecourse rowdies—you know that. Some won't. But barring that, there's no sort of dirty work he wouldn't try on."

"What are you getting at?" asked the Inspector encouragingly.

"That girl who disappeared…not that Fred would 'a touched her, he wasn't like that, but he was around these parts then. Reckon he knew something. That'd be like Fred—try to raise the needful."

"Look here: say if we sort this out a bit," said the Inspector.

"If there were two brothers, as you say, how was it that Ben Grubb didn't know them both?"

"This one, Fred, he was only a nipper when he ran away: joined a circus," said Patton. "The other, he stayed on, living behind that pub. But Fred, he often came back to where he was born. I'll tell you who knew Fred, old Solly Baines. He's still alive. Kept kennels outside Southampton, Solly did. You find him—lives off the Lyndhurst road: he'll remember Fred."

After Patton had gone, the Inspector turned to his Sergeant. "If this old gaffer's right, Hoyle's been lying—no mistake about that."

"Aye, I don't doubt Hoyle's been lying," replied the Sergeant, "but we can't pin it on Hoyle. Hoyle's got folks to swear to where he was the whole evening, barring five minutes at a time. And Hoyle can't drive a car: he's never had a car and never driven one—and it wasn't easy driving Saturday night, neither. Hoyle may know something, but 'twasn't Hoyle ran over that body—tho' likely whoever did it reckoned Hoyle'd be blamed."

"That's quite an idea," rejoined the Inspector.

Chapter XVI

I

WHEN DILYS REACHED THE HOSPITAL AND SAW HER father being wheeled away on a stretcher, she begged to be allowed to wait until the doctor had seen him. "You'd much better go home, my dear," said the nurse, "we'll let you know if there's any change…" It was the young houseman, who officially admitted the case, who said: "Let her stay. Dr. Andrew will probably see her for a minute later." The houseman had capitulated after one glance at Dilys's white face and wide, shadowed eyes.

Dr. Andrew was an older man, but he also was moved by the girl's strange, appealing beauty, and aware also of the strained look in her eyes: he knew at once that it was fear which looked out of them.

"Don't worry, my child. Your father will be all right now: it's skilled nursing and treatment he needs. We'll look after him. Had an accident and didn't do anything about it? Well, well, he's old enough to know better, isn't he?"

"Can't I sit with him, just for a little while?" she begged. "I won't be a nuisance, I promise—but I'm sure he'll be better if he knows I'm there. He was so confused and miserable, not really understanding why he was moved."

Inevitably, Dr. Andrew gave way, too—he told himself he was sorry for the child, even while he thought, "My God, I've never seen such eyes in my life."

"Well, you can wait for a bit and perhaps Sister will let you go up for a minute when they've got him settled," said Andrew. "And about getting home: the porter will arrange about transport for you if you ask him. And don't look so frightened: your father's going to be all right."

Dilys never knew how long she sat there, on a chair in a corridor leading to the wards. She hadn't got a watch on—and the mere thought of a watch set her heart pounding, rousing again that sense of horror with the question "Why did he try to make me believe it was earlier than it was when he came home...?" For she was past being reasonable now: the shock of her father's collapse and semi-delirium had induced a conviction from what had begun as a nightmare: she connected her father's state with that body spreadeagled across the road. Dilys had never seen the aftermath of a road accident before, and it had been a much greater shock to her than she had realised. One moment she had been driving in a happy dream, musing on the delights of her stolen evening, on the many charming things which had been said to her, on the success of her careful plans—aware, in a rosy haze of anticipation, of a future in which happiness and security were blended with dancing, pretty frocks...and perhaps a car like the one she was being driven in. All this had been abruptly cut short by the sight of the body in the road, a sight which had haunted her, waking and sleeping, ever since. And it wasn't only the grim sight which had cut across her happiness: there was her father and his strange, unaccountable behaviour; then the visit of the police, and Dilys's first efforts to help her father in a situation which she didn't understand but which filled her with horror and revulsion. The word "accident" was fading out, to be replaced by a more horrible word—"murder." As though all this weren't enough, there was the fact that Michael Reeve might be involved: Michael, whom she had wandered with so light-heartedly, picking primroses in springtime, meadow daisies in hay time, blackberries after harvest, holly at Christmas time—and her father hated Michael, hated the whole Reeve family with all the bitterness of his harsh, unyielding Puritanism.

It was this ever-increasing shadow of fear which obsessed Dilys's mind, so that she was unable to think reasonably or coherently; sitting in the hospital corridor, aware of the queer antiseptic smells which somehow sickened her, Dilys clenched her teeth because she was shivering and tried not to cry because she felt that once she let herself go she would scream.

It was just as the tall Sister came to speak to her that the night porter came up, too.

"Miss Dilys Maine—that you, miss? A gent rang up to say he'd be bringing a car to take you home, and he'd wait outside until you was ready. Name of Brent, he said."

"That's excellent," said Sister firmly. "You look as though you ought to be in bed yourself, my dear. Now we've got your father comfortably settled in a private room. You may come in and see him for just a minute or two, but you mustn't try to talk to him. Don't worry about anything he says, his temperature is up and he's light-headed. It doesn't mean anything and he's not really conscious. After that, you had better go home to bed—you look tired out. Now, remember—no talking."

Dilys went into the small, shadowy room and sat down beside the bed. Her father looked utterly strange, his head bandaged, his eyes sunk in enlarged sockets, a flush on his cheekbones—but he recognised her.

"Dilys?" he asked thickly. "Dilys?"

She took his hand and held it firmly, feeling his hot fingers close round her own. "What time is it?" he asked. "My watch stopped… I don't know the time."

"It's all right, Daddy," she whispered. "Don't worry. It's all right."

"The time," he muttered, "I ought to know. I shall be late…" His voice died away, and a moment later, the Sister touched Dilys's arm and nodded towards the door. As she unclasped her fingers from the hot dry ones, her father said:

"Don't tell them, Dilys. Don't tell them anything."

"I won't tell them, Daddy," she replied, and Sister looked at her reproachfully. A moment later, in the corridor, Sister said: "Now don't get worrying he's doing nicely—and nothing he says means anything. He's just wandering. Now go home and have a good night's sleep. You can ring up in the morning and they'll tell you how he is."

II

When she reached the door of the hospital, Dilys looked round the quadrangle outside and then gave a sudden cry.

"Michael? Why ever are you here?"

Michael Reeve came forward into the bright light at the door. "I heard your father had been brought here, Dilys, and I know you would have come with him, so I drove over to see if I could be any use. Can I take you back home?"

"Oh, thank goodness! Of course you can and I'm terribly

grateful," cried Dilys. "Michael, I'm so worried that I just don't know what I'm doing—I've got to the stage when I can't even think properly."

"You're dead tired," rejoined Reeve, his deep voice very quiet and gentle. "Get in—I'll drive you home to Alice, and she'll put you to bed with a hot drink and tell you 'It'll be all right in the morning,' as my old nurse used to say to me."

He helped her into his old car, and a moment later its tail light turned out of the gateway, leaving the night porter doing a quiet chuckle.

"Name o' Brent, he said," chuckled the latter. "That'll be the bloke who owns the Mermaid—but this one wasn't Brent. This one was young Reeve, and he's stolen a march on the other bloke, and no mistake about it. Providence oughtn't to make young women with faces like that one—asking for trouble, I calls it."

Meantime, Dilys, utterly tired out by her own fears and anxiety about her father, had simply forgotten that the porter had even mentioned Nicholas Brent. The sight of Michael had brought a sense of relief and thoughts of companion-ship which had given her happiness before this nightmare of fear had obsessed her, and she turned to him with a sense of confidence.

"Michael, I'm so frightened. I expect it's silly—but can I tell you about it?"

"You can tell me anything," said Michael, "but wait till I get you home. I'll park in the drive and we can talk there, where it's quiet and safe. This mist's tricky to drive in, and I've got to watch out, and besides, you don't want to shout against this rackety old engine."

It was only a few minutes after Michael had driven out of the hospital gates that the porter saw a car of very different vintage turn into the quadrangle: its silent engine and gleaming bodywork, together with its array of lights—braking lights, winking lights, spotlights—proclaimed it as a modern product of the luxury class. "That's a car worth calling a car, not half: she'd better've waited," thought the porter. "Better in more ways than one, to my way of thinking, with all the stories that's going round." The driver got out and came to the door.

"I've come for Miss Maine—when she's ready to leave, that is. Do you want me to park farther back?"

"That'd be all right, sir, but Miss Maine has left. A gent took her home only a few minutes ago."

Brent stood silent, his face not giving anything away. "I see. Do you know if she got my message? My name's Brent."

"Yes, sir. I gave her the message upstairs, but if you ask me, I'd say she was too worried in her mind to take anything in. Her father was admitted as an emergency case and she's in a real state about him."

"I'm sorry about that—I heard he was seriously ill," said Brent evenly. "Do you know who it was fetched Miss Maine?"

The porter was a man of discretion—as was expedient for his job. "I couldn't say, sir. He wasn't here above a minute, drove in just before the young lady came down."

"Was it an old car—pretty noisy?" asked Brent.

"Well—not in the same class as that one of yours, sir," replied the porter. Brent's hands were in his pockets and the porter looked him straight in the face. "I didn't notice all that, sir, and if I had, well it's not my business to give information, no offence meant."

"Perfectly right," said Brent tersely. "I was only hoping she wouldn't have a breakdown on the road home—some of these hills are tough for old crocks to tackle. Goodnight."

He went back to his car and the porter to his cubbyhole. "If he wants to catch them up, he shouldn't have much difficulty in an outfit like that," thought the latter. "Wild Heron, split new, and the other was a pre-war Ensign. I wonder, now..." But he went back to his evening paper, muttering "Not my business, and a good thing, too."

Nicholas Brent drove out of the hospital gates, edged his car neatly into the traffic stream when he reached the main road and performed all the actions of an experienced driver quite automatically. His mind was in a turmoil, his face— had there been any to see it—was white and grim and set. One word only escaped between his set teeth as he began to accelerate, and the word seemed to fit itself to the soft rhythm of his engine... Murderer, murderer.

It was when he had just crossed Cookbourne Bridge and was turning towards Foxlea that he braked unwillingly in response to a car approaching him which hooted several times in warning, and Brent had to draw right into the bank. The van driver, reducing his speed to a crawl, called out apologies:

"Sorry, sir. I've got a car in tow and I thought you might be turning in behind me. It's a nasty night—I'll wait till you've passed."

As Brent got moving again, he saw that it was Tom Hudson who was at the wheel of the car on the towrope; he stopped abruptly and called: "Have you passed anybody on the road to the mill, Tom?"

"Yes. Reeve—just going up the ridge towards the quarry. I think he'd got Miss Maine beside him."

"Oh, my God! Why didn't you stop him?" cried Brent, and his voice was no longer cool and controlled. As the big Heron shot forwards, Hudson thought he heard Brent call back to him: "The man's a murderer...it's got to stop..."

"Well I'm damned... What does A do now?" asked

Hudson, but the van driver in front of him was shouting back: "I'm getting going again, easy does it over the bridges," and Tom Hudson was towed forward, willy-nilly, towards the traffic of the main road.

III

Michael Reeve's car might have been an old one but it was still capable of putting up a fast performance—if you didn't mind noise. As soon as he accelerated, Dilys realised what he meant when he had told her not to talk until he slowed down or parked. It wasn't so much engine noise as body rattle— every plate and part in the hard-worked, ill-treated coachwork rattling like castanets over worn-out springs and worn tyres. Dilys only said one thing before they reached the bridge:

"Oh Michael, how awful of me! Commander Brent rang up the hospital and said he'd drive over to take me home, and I just forgot all about him and never even left a message."

"Never mind," said Michael. "I expect the porter will explain—he was a decent chap. And last time Brent drove you it wasn't too good, was it?"

Dilys hardly caught the last words, and then they turned over the bridge, roared on for a couple of breathtaking miles on the level, and then began the pull up the ridge which was between them and the Foxlea valley. Michael bent towards her and said, "Only a few minutes and you'll be safe home, Dilys. That's what I've been thinking about all this time—to get you back safely. It's a pretty beastly night and I didn't want you to have any more bother." He laughed a little and added: "It sounds as tho' I'm getting jittered myself, doesn't it—but there've been too many things happening lately... Down we go, all plain sailing now."

A few minutes later he ran the car into the long drive of the Maines' house, pulled up and said: "Tell me what's bothering you. I can't bear to see you looking so unhappy and frightened—you look like a startled ghost."

His voice was perfectly steady, just the cool, friendly voice Dilys had always liked, and he made no attempt to touch her: no arm around her shoulders, no touch of hand on hand, whereby he had sought to comfort her when he had found her crying after her mother had died. He leant back against the window of the car, sitting sideways, well away from her, and said again,

"Tell me—what's the trouble?—or are you imagining things? Is it just that your father's so ill, or something else?"

"It's something else, Michael: something much worse. He was out that night—Saturday. We don't know what he was doing, but when he came in he tried to make me believe it was much earlier than it was; and he'd been fighting—or something like that. He was so ill because he'd had a knock over the head and we didn't know. He ought to have been in bed, but he tried to hide everything. And it may be silly, but I can't help believing it was something to do with the dead man—and the police believe it was. They keep on coming."

"Dilys, I don't know what your father was doing—though I can guess—but I'm certain it wasn't anything to do with the body on the low road. That's nothing to do with him, nor he with it. It's to do with me: somebody's trying to saddle me with murder, but your father's not involved. I swear he isn't. He may dislike me and distrust me because I'm a Reeve and he believes we're all bad, but he'd never have tried to down me by killing a man who was like my brother and then running my car over the body. That's what somebody did, you know. Do you believe for one moment that your father would do a thing like that? You know he's incapable of it."

"Yes. I do know," she said, "because I know him—but the police don't, and they suspect him. I know they do."

"Give them a chance," said Michael. "They haven't had long to get things sorted out, have they? It's only two days since this thing happened, and they had to find out who was on the road that night. Cheer up, Dilys. It's not what you think. Your father wasn't on the low road at all: I'm certain he went scouting round Hoyle's place—and more fool he. Hoyle isn't as bad as folks make out—I know that. And if the police get tough about your father, I'll make Jim Hoyle come across with the truth. So don't go getting in a panic over your father, or telling fibs to the police. That won't help."

"They asked how I got back from the Hunt Ball. I wouldn't tell them, because the time I got back is all muddled up with the time Daddy got back."

"He probably didn't know what time it was when he got back," said Michael. "If he'd had a knock on the head he was probably hopelessly confused about the time and everything else, too; and the police will know they can't do anything about his evidence because he wasn't in a fit state to give evidence. So cheer up, Dilys, and don't go imagining horrors. Now you'd better go in—Alice will look after you."

"Michael, you've been awfully patient with me. I'm terribly grateful. I wanted to tell you—the only reason I've been avoiding you lately is that Daddy was so difficult about things."

"All right. You haven't got to explain. I know," he said. His voice was abrupt and terse, but suddenly he bent forward and kissed Dilys's hand as it rested on the steering wheel. She had stretched it towards him in a vague appealing gesture which he had disregarded, but then, seeing the slender fingers in the faint light from the dashboard panel, he pressed his lips to her wrist almost involuntarily and then drew back quickly.

"Oh, my dear…why must things be as they are…?" he cried. "Just when I thought I was clear of the tangle, out of the mess, I get caught up again in all this foul coil…"

"Michael, what do you mean?"

He recovered himself by an effort. "Never mind now, Dilys. I'll tell you one day—but I've got to earn the right to tell you. Go indoors now, Alice will look after you—and don't go dreaming any more horrors about your father. It will be all right—I swear it will."

IV

After Dilys had let herself in to the dark house, Michael Reeve started his engine again. He was shaking, his vision blurred, his mind refusing to function after that moment when he had nearly told Dilys how passionately he loved her, and he did a thing which he would never have done when he was in a normal state of mind. Instead of patiently reversing his car in the awkward drive, he backed out through the gates onto the road, hardly knowing what he was doing, his foot on the accelerator. Too late he became aware of headlights coming up the narrow road: there was a clang of metal as he struck the approaching car and he jerked forward over the steering wheel as the lights behind him were extinguished when the rear of the old Ensign rammed the front of the other car. His head bemused, his senses spinning, Michael thought. "It's Brent…damn him to hell…"

——————

Almost at the moment that the two cars locked in the impact of bumper and wing, Tom Hudson was at the telephone, ringing the police station at Fordings. Worried to death by what he thought he had heard Brent say, Tom felt he couldn't keep quiet about it.

"Look here," he shouted over the line at Inspector Turner, "I may be making a fuss over nothing, but I've got to do something. Michael Reeve passed me on Foxlea Hill with Dilys Maine in his car; five minutes later Brent pulled up beside me and asked me if I'd seen anybody pass. I told him. Brent said, 'Why the hell didn't you stop him?' and then went blazing on. I think he shouted 'The man's a murderer.' Anyway, if Brent catches Reeve up there'll be murder or I'm a Dutchman—and that girl's there. Do, for the Lord's sake, do something about it." And with that he slammed down the receiver before Turner could ask any questions.

Turner only said dourly: "This is Waring's job. Better tell him and he can sort it out."

Chapter XVII

I

FOR A MOMENT AFTER THE COLLISION, MICHAEL REEVE sat slumped over the wheel, the blood singing in his ears, his eyes still blurred: then, suddenly, he recovered his senses and his head cleared. He jumped out of the car and felt his way towards the rear: it was very dark—the impact had sent his own headlights out as well as those of the car he had hit, but he was in no doubt whatever as to who the driver was. Suddenly a flashlight blazed into his face and Brent's furious voice said:

"You tried it before and you've tried it again, and that's going to be the last time. You thought you could finish me this time—"

"Don't rant!" snapped Michael. "You're talking nonsense and you know it. This time it was an accident, and you know it—you shouldn't come speeding round blind turns on a night like this, or if you do don't bleat when something hits you."

"Hits me! by God, you hit me before, I know that, you dirty murderer—" Brent's voice was shaking and the hand which held the torch was shaking. Suddenly he swung his arm up; the torch hit the car beside him and the light went out, leaving the two men in darkness.

Michael Reeve stood dead still; he was not three paces from Brent, but he couldn't see him in the murk.

"You call me a murderer, Brent—murderer yourself! If you want a showdown, you can have it, here and now. You can't get away—the road's blocked behind you and I'm in front of you, and you can listen, here in the dark. You thought I didn't know about you and Rosemary. I held my tongue: there were plenty of rumours, weren't there, and I wasn't going to pin it on the poor lass that you'd fooled her—you, who pretended to be a woman hater. She might have thrown herself over the cliffs for all I know."

"Don't think you can get away with it, telling lies about the past," said Brent furiously, and Reeve knew from the shrillness of the other's voice that he was nearly out of his mind with rage.

"It isn't lies, and you know it," retorted Michael. "That poor swine you killed told me about Rosemary going over to your place. I knew—and I kept quiet about it. I didn't want the papers to print a smear story about my sister and you— enough had been said against her already, poor wild thing that she was: but when I saw that poor devil in the mortuary, I knew who had downed him—and why. He'd come back to cash in on his dirty knowledge, and you'd finished him and left me to pay."

"You're mad," said Brent thickly. "You're making up a tale which has no evidence to support it."

"So you think. There's evidence, all right. There's Betty Hoyle. She's not dead, you know. She'll have plenty to say when they've got her better, and Hoyle won't stand for this.

He knew about you and Rosemary, but he kept mum, didn't he? You could have ruined him if you told all you knew—snooping around, watching his silly games—and taking a hand when the coast was clear. What did Betty see on Saturday night, Brent? She knew your car, didn't she? So you gave her a lift this evening and chucked her off—and thought you could get away with it."

In the darkness, Michael Reeve could hear Brent panting. He was certain now—Brent wanted to hear just how much he, Michael, knew—and then he'd finish him somehow: break his neck and leave him in the crumpled mess of the two cars. As he listened to the heavy breathing, Michael was certain he could hear another sound: somebody was moving in the darkness, not very far away. "God! It's the police," thought Michael. "They're listening…if I can only madden him into admitting it, they'll hear…and they've guessed most of it already."

Then he realised that Brent was moving towards him in the murk—he couldn't see a thing, but he sensed the other's presence, only a yard away.

"Listen," said Brent, "listen to me a minute. You're fighting for your own life by trying to pin this time on me." ("He's trying to close up, getting me off my guard," thought Michael.) "Don't think I wasn't sorry for you," went on Brent. "You've had a thin deal with that mad family of yours, and then this by-blow came rootling in, threatening to tell some more dirty stories just when you wanted a clean sheet. Oh, I knew—and I played fair. I didn't utter a word to help the police get on your trail. If you'd only left Dilys alone…"

"You can leave Dilys out of this," said Michael furiously. "You were responsible for my sister's death: you wanted to get clean of her and her vixen's tongue—oh, I know—but somebody knew what you'd done, and you had to get rid of them, and get rid of me, too, because I was in your way. Do you think I don't know how you did it?"

"Know, you fool? I'm the one person who couldn't have done it. There's proof of that."

("He won't shoot," thought Michael, "that wouldn't help him. He'll break my neck with one of his Commando tricks…" He side-stepped in the darkness. "If only I can make him mad enough to own it, he's half out of his mind already, or he wouldn't stand yattering here—unless he thinks I've left written proof and he's trying to find out…"—so swiftly thoughts ran through his mind as he stood poised in the murky darkness.)

"Proof," went on Michael. "There's proof enough. No one knows where you were after seven on Saturday evening, do they? You sent the servants out—they know that in Fordings. And Betty Hoyle saw your car behind a hedge on the Greenham Road while she was there with her boyfriend. And you picked Macbane up at 8.15—plenty of time, wasn't there? Don't think I'm guessing. I know."

"Betty Hoyle's a born liar—and she'd say anything to get you out of a mess," said Brent. He was standing still now, and was talking more easily, as though his wits were beginning to work again. "How can you be fool enough to say I left that body in the low road? I drove Macbane over that road when we went to Fordings, and the body wasn't there. Who put it there?"

"You did," said Michael. "You met the poor devil on no-man's-land and killed him there and drove his body to the low road and ran my car over it. You had plenty of time between seven and quarter past eight when you picked up Macbane. And you didn't drive Macbane by the low road at

all: you drove him by the Greenham Road. It was misty—
and he knows no more about our roads than I know about
Timbuctoo. You told him it was the low road he was on and
he took it as fact. They're parallel roads, with the same dips
and rises—how would he have known on such a night?"

There was dead silence, and Reeve went on: "And when
you came to my house to telephone to the police, you dropped
some evidence for them to find, to make certain of hanging
me. Only I found it—after I'd bashed your head for you."

"God!" shouted Brent—and Michael knew that he was
startled out of all caution now. "It *was* you who came at me?"

"Yes. I came at you—I'd every reason to bash your face
in—and then I realised you were up to something that spelt
a noose for me. And it was only tonight I tumbled to how
you'd worked it—by tricking Macbane into thinking you'd
driven him by the low road and so proving the corpse wasn't
there then—and that let you out."

"You tumbled to it," said Brent slowly. "That's the last thing
you're ever going to tumble to. Your time's up."

"And I was right!" shouted Michael.

"Yes. You were right—and that's why you're for it," said
Brent, his voice curiously quiet—and then he sprang.

Michael swung sideways, avoiding the full weight of the
other man's spring, but Brent caught him round the knees,
and they went down together, Michael undermost. Michael
was a big powerful fellow, but his strength was helpless against
Brent, who exerted a stranglehold, his legs and arms gripping
the man beneath him almost as a cobra twines around its victim; then Brent's head butted his jaw, jerking his head back,
slamming into his throat and the prehensile hands came up
to finish the job. It was as a red haze floated across his vision
that Michael became aware that someone else had joined

in the fight: an additional weight came down, crushing the breath out of him, and then Brent himself gave a horrible strangled cry and his gripping hands slackened on Michael's neck. For a second or two a wild fight went on, the sound of men's muscles almost cracking in their all-out endeavour, and then the weight on Michael's body lessened. He caught a great breath of air into his gasping lungs and realised that a light was blazing down on him. A voice cried, "No, by hell you don't... Catch his arm, I've got him down...of all the foul filthy tricks..." and then a final blow from he knew not where knocked Michael into blackness and silence, so that he seemed to go down and down into a bottomless pit.

II

"That's better," said a voice from very far away. "He's a tough, this one: knocked out, that's all."

Michael Reeve made an effort to lift his battered head—and then gave up trying: he felt a cool swab wiping his face, and realised that hot blood was trickling down his neck. "It's all right—a bit of plaster will soon settle that—but it was a near thing," went on the voice. It was Waring's voice and Michael groped for his scattered wits.

"You heard it all?" he gasped out.

"Yes: we heard—and you've got a lot to answer for when you're fit to answer, young Reeve—butting in on our job. You asked for trouble and you came damn near to getting it. That wasn't a knife which cut you: if you can keep your eyes open long enough to see it, you can look."

With an effort, because his head ached intolerably, Michael opened his eyes again: he was still lying on the roadside and the mist swirled round the locked cars in the beam of a torchlight. Waring was kneeling beside him, and in his hand was a jagged piece of thick glass.

"Windscreen glass," said Waring, "all arranged to show how you died in a motor smash."

"Oh, Lord… I rammed his car, didn't I?"

"He rammed yours—more likely. Never mind, we'll argue out the pros and cons later—when you'll be charged with concealing evidence and obstructing the police: but you didn't try to murder Brent with a filthy weapon like this, and he did try to murder you—doubtless intending to improve on the motor smash later."

"Brent—you've got him?"

"We've got his body, laddy. This was razor-sharp and he finished himself with it when he knew the game was up. That's enough for now. We're taking you to the surgery to be strapped up—under police escort."

"O.K.," said Michael vaguely, then he suddenly cried out: "Dilys… Is she all right?"

"Dilys is in bed, being bullied by Alice—I hope," said Waring. "The nuisance those two were to us! All right, I don't expect you to agree, but Dilys is perdition to detection. Keep still—we'll lift you. You've had a packet."

It was when he finally went to bed that Waring said to himself, with a colossal yawn: "I said, 'Here's trouble,' when I first saw her. She may be as good as an angel, but she was the storm centre all right… All the same, he's a lucky dog, that Michael Reeve…and a damned good guesser. He nearly beat me to it."

III

"Well, Michael Reeve just about guessed his way through— which was more than you did—you were properly had," said

Waring, his eyes dancing as he looked at Macbane. "It's true Michael had some private data, which I guessed at in my turn, but he recognised the essential point."

"Let's get it straight," said Macbane. "The main fact is that this wretched chap who was born on the caravan site was killed by Brent, presumably because he tried to blackmail him about his association with Rosemary Reeve."

"That's about it—though there's always going to be a lot of presumption behind this case," said Waring. "Two things are not presumption—they're fact and they suffice. First, Brent diddled you by making you believe he drove you along the low road when he actually drove you along the Greenham Road. It gave him an alibi—proved he could not have left that body in the road because it wasn't there when you drove to Fordings. Once I'd tumbled to that fact, I knew just where I was with Brent. And secondly, if the authorities want first-hand evidence, Brent tried to murder Michael Reeve with a jagged bit of glass. That's enough to satisfy any policeman about Brent's potentialities as a murderer—and the background can be left, thank God. I've no doubt in my own mind that Brent killed Rosemary Reeve and sunk her body out at sea—but we shall never prove it, and it's not going to be raked up."

"Thank the Lord for that," said Ian soberly. "But I'm sure you're right. They said she was a vixen, and she probably gave him hell."

"'No man would wed her, but no man could pass her by,'" quoted Waring. "That made me think a lot. Brent was a hot-blooded man, although he hid it well enough in his 'hermit-crab' phase, as you called it, but Brent didn't want a vixen of a wife to nag at him. He wanted a gentle, compliant, biddable and lovely girl—like Dilys."

Macbane sighed, and Waring retorted: "You've nothing to

sigh about. Your Jennifer will cope with you nicely—which Dilys never could have done."

"Let's get back to first principles," said Ian firmly.

"Or lack of them," said Waring. "I took my stand on two presumptions: that this murder seemed to implicate Michael Reeve, but that Reeve himself wasn't the sort of fool who would have done such a clumsy job; therefore, to my mind, the murderer was someone who had a motive for getting Reeve into trouble, as well as ridding himself of a menace to his own security, and I had quite a selection to choose from. There was Hoyle, Brent, Maine, Hudson, and yourself. It's no use looking superior over the last point, for you were one of the Dilys addicts before Jennifer provided a counter-irritant."

Macbane laughed—he couldn't help it—but Waring went on: "From the moment I saw her, I was convinced that Dilys was a factor in this case, and that Alice Ridley was trying to sidetrack me, and there might have been two reasons: one being that Dilys had seen something when she came back from the ball—and I had to guess my way to who brought her back; the other being that Dilys was in a panic because her father had been out that evening and had got himself involved in the murder."

"In fact, Dilys got you properly muddled up," said Macbane.

"True enough—and there was plenty to get confused about. I spent a lot of time worrying away at the layout, the roads, and the bridle path, because it did seem possible that the murder had taken place either on the Greenham Road, on that desolate tract behind Hoyle's place, or somewhere down in the Foxlea valley; and the bridle path connected up both localities with the low road. Well, there was Hoyle: he had a bad reputation among the countryfolk, and Maine had obviously been trying to make trouble for Hoyle."

"There was the connection again," said Macbane. "Hoyle and Maine—and the bridle path."

"That's it: Hoyle, Maine, and the inevitable Dilys, plus the lie of the land. Now I was prepared to believe that Maine had spent the evening watching Hoyle's place; he might have seen anything and got himself knocked over the head for his pains, but if he'd been a witness to murder, I didn't think he would have been allowed to get home with only a biff over the head. Also, I was quite convinced that if Hoyle had done this job, Hoyle would have got rid of the body over the cliffs, not fooled around planting the body on a road."

"I agree with you there," said Macbane, "but didn't you think Maine himself might have done the job? After all, he was a fanatic, and according to all accounts he was getting odder and odder."

"Admittedly—and I know that the impulse to murder may possess the mind of a fanatic, but I think also that in such a case the impulse exhausts itself in the one deed of violence. The subsequent planning—moving the body and running another man's car over it—seemed to belong to a much cooler and more calculating mentality. You could have done it, had circumstances moved you to murder. Brent could have done it; Hudson could have done it—but I thought not Maine. And so I came back to Brent—could he have done it?"

Waring paused for a moment and then went on: "It seemed pretty improbable—according to the evidence provided by you, but Brent intrigued me. A hermit crab? He looked a hot-blooded vital chap to me: he was in love with Dilys—that was well known—and Reeve was a pretty close runner-up in that direction. Then there was this confused story of Rosemary Reeve: as I saw it, Brent, vital, unmarried, living virtually alone, might well have lost his head over Rosemary Reeve and landed himself in a coil which nothing but violence could cut. That is a situation which has too often resulted in murder. And once a man has taken the law into his own hands, it's possible, if not probable, that he will do it again. Was it possible that it was Brent who was threatened by this wretched racecourse hanger-on? If so, my guess was that the threat was concerned with Rosemary Reeve. Murder was essential for Brent's security, and he planned it so that he could cast suspicion on the man who might cut him out with Dilys."

"It's a logical line of thought," said Macbane slowly, and Waring went on:

"But it wasn't until you said 'I'm a stranger here' that I tumbled to how it was done. Let's leave theories and logic and get down to what we now know are the facts: Brent killed a blackmailer, probably on his own premises—all the servants being out—put the body in his car and drove to the coppice beyond the Rose & Crown, where he concealed his car— which was seen by Maine, as we now know. Brent shouldered the body, took it along the bridle path and put it in Reeve's car (as Reeve later guessed), drove the body to where it was later found, ran the car over it, returned the car to Reeve's, walked back along the bridle path, and picked up his own car and drove to fetch you at Tim Grant's. He then drove you to Fordings, by the Greenham Road, having no difficulty in persuading you it was the low road you drove on. Of course, it was the mist which made the whole mad plan possible. Visibility was so bad that even if he had been observed, he could have counted on doing a bolt unrecognised."

"He took a chance," said Macbane slowly, and Waring nodded.

"He took every sort of chance—but wasn't that characteristic of him? As I saw Brent, he'd the nerve for anything."

IV

"To tidy up the odd bits and pieces," said Waring. "You may like to know that it *was* Reeve who knocked Brent out after the latter had telephoned."

"Good Lord… I've been wondering about that."

"It was a crazy business, but there was a certain grim logic in it," said Waring. "Remember that Reeve was madly in love with Dilys: wouldn't he have noticed that she was no longer at the ball—and that Brent wasn't there, either? And when he had put two and two together, would he have enjoyed the rest of the ball, thinking of Brent driving Dilys home in that superb Wild Heron?"

"No… I mean yes. Reeve would have gone home, too," said Macbane slowly.

"And that's what he did, and arrived in his own house to hear Brent telephoning the police about a body on the road. Remember that Reeve was livid with Brent anyway: he hated him. He suspected (without having any proof) that Brent was connected with Rosemary's disappearance: he knew that Brent was courting Dilys. Was it so very surprising that Reeve lost his head when he found Brent in his own house? He went for him like a lunatic, knocked him out—and knocked the furniture over him, and then realised what he had done—in the light of what he had heard Brent report over the telephone."

"Good Lord! What a situation!" gasped Macbane.

"Yes. The situation sobered Reeve all right. He began to think—and think quickly—especially after he found a blood-stained cap on the floor." Waring shrugged his shoulders. "You can say that if Reeve were a law-abiding man at heart, he would have waited for the police and told them the whole story."

"I don't know," said Macbane slowly. "Being Reeve, he

saw all the possibilities involved and felt that to wait for the police was to ask for arrest."

"That's about it. He ascertained that Brent wasn't dead, and then calmly went and changed his shirt and collar and drove back to the Prince's Hall—and stayed till the end."

"It's crazy!" cried Macbane.

Waring laughed a little. "It's often small things which give a pointer in detection. It occurred to me that Reeve might have done just what he did do—change his shirt and collar and beat it. Reeve, born at Hollydown Manor, would have had more than one boiled shirt in his wardrobe, and would have been used to changing quickly—unlike the farmers, who mostly possess only one shirt and make heavy weather of changing. Of course, Reeve concealed evidence and obstructed the police in one sense, but I don't think proceedings will be taken against him. For one thing, he knew he was suspected, and he believed, rightly or wrongly, that he could get at the truth, clear himself and confound a murderer. He did, too—he saw his way through it eventually and challenged a showdown."

"And Maine?" asked Ian.

"Oh, Maine—he's a very chastened man. He'd heard this story, through his Boys' Club, that Hoyle ran a party of his own on the night of the Hunt Ball—a gambling party. In the bad old days of Michael's unregenerate grandfather it was true—Michael knows that. These days, it's only a matter of a few old codgers tossing dice: but Maine went and crawled around like a storybook detective and got a bash on the head from one of Hoyle's party who knew that Maine was out to make trouble. That'll be argued out in court, and Hoyle will probably lose his licence over it. He told us lies, anyway, saying he couldn't identify the dead man. But Maine came in useful when he recovered his wits, because he attested that he actually saw Brent backing his car off the road soon after seven o'clock that evening. Maine was probably unconscious in a ditch for some time, and when he came to he was completely fuddled. Later, when he heard the story of the dead man he was too confused to think clearly and developed a terrified belief that he must have been involved in the murder. Considering he was suffering from delayed concussion, it's not surprising his mental powers went haywire. And Dilys and Alice panicked accordingly."

"And Betty Hoyle?"

"Betty Hoyle, confound her, could have put the whole thing straight in ten words: Betty and her boyfriend stopped for a petting party on the way to Fordings on Saturday night, and Betty actually saw Brent's car pass—and you in it. Instead of telling the police, she told Brent."

"Good Lord!—I told you she was crazy over Brent."

"—and his motorbike," added Waring. "He gave her a ride on the pillion and chucked her off somehow."

"He must have been mad by that time," said Macbane.

Waring nodded. "Yes. When a man has done the things Brent did, his mind breaks. He was no better than a lunatic at the end, with his obsession about pinning the crime on Reeve, but he planned the thing cunningly in the first case—even to his caution in saying 'I thought it was Reeve's voice'—very convincing that bit, refusing to condemn another man. And the business of letting Dilys see the body, and thus pretending to 'keep her out of it'—very high-minded, it sounded. He knew we should find out eventually that she had been in his car, and there he was sitting pretty, with two witnesses: you for the outgoing, Dilys for the return journey."

"Don't rub it in," said Macbane, and Waring retorted:

"You've got nothing to look melancholy about. You've

got your Jennifer, and she'll suit you much better than that incredibly lovely, muddle-headed Dilys. Michael will have Dilys—and good luck to them. Finally, Dilys's father: Alice is going to go on housekeeping for him, and after all the worry he gave them, I think she's got a lever to keep him 'behaving sensibly,' as she puts it. I like Alice—and I think Maine's luckier than he deserves."

Macbane chuckled. "Alice sounds a character to me," he said.

"You're telling me!" said Waring. "Alice is not only a talented stonewaller, she's a talented detective. She fought me off with one hand while she collected information with the other, and she's got a private information service that leaves the police standing. Do you know that when it was all over she told me she'd realised what must have happened?"

"You mean she guessed?"

"I mean she found out from one of her cronies that a farm labourer who had had a puncture walked along the low road from Bramber Head to the Hollydown turn on Saturday evening between 7.45 and 8.45, and he didn't meet a single car—so Alice knew that Brent had *not* driven you by the low road."

"Well, I'm dashed…" said Ian.

"So was I—and so was Alice. She began to think. And please note that that farm labourer never thought of coming to the police with his information, but he was quite willing to oblige Alice." Waring mused for a moment; then he went on, "All the same, Alice was considerably chastened: she believed in Brent. She wanted Dilys to marry him."

"Dilys was lucky," said Macbane slowly, and Waring nodded.

"Always look on the bright side," he said, and his voice

was kindly enough. "Two rogues dead—Brent and his victim were both of a pattern, for all their differences in fortune and opportunity. And two decent fellows set on the right path—you and Michael Reeve."

"And two good girls with husbands to look after them," said Macbane.

"Make it three," said Waring. "Don't leave out Alice."

"You mean…?"

"Oh, she'll marry Maine. I haven't a doubt of it. She knows she's got him under her thumb now—so Maine is settled, too. Dilys is delighted. She said she often hoped it'd happen."

"Dilys…" said Ian softly, and Waring laughed a little, not unkindly.

"I know. I felt just the same: she's so incredibly lovely she leaves a chap breathless. But you know I think she'll make a very good farmer's wife, so it didn't turn out so badly." He got up and stretched out his hand to Ian Macbane. "Goodbye—and good luck to you and your Jennifer. If ever she needs to deflate you, she can just remind you that you're not always so observant as you like to think you are. It's good for all young wives to be able to say 'Even Homer nodded' to their husbands occasionally."

"I deserved that," replied Ian.

FINIS

If you've enjoyed *Two-Way Murder*,
you won't want to miss

THE CHIANTI FLASK

by Marie Belloc Lowndes,

the most recent BRITISH LIBRARY CRIME CLASSIC
published by Poisoned Pen Press,
an imprint of Sourcebooks.

poisonedpenpress.com